REVENGE

A BRUCE AND SMITH THRILLER BOOK 2

RANDALL KRZAK

A Bruce & Smith Thriller: Book 2

Randall Krzak

Copyright © 2021 Randall Krzak

ISBN- 978-0-9789441-1-7

❀ Created with Vellum

To Sylvia, my true flower of Scotland,
And to our son Craig, of whom we're very proud.
There's no doubt I have the best family in the world.
Thank you for loving me.
I love you.

ACKNOWLEDGMENTS

Cover Design By: DarnGoodCovers.com

Revenge would not be a reality without those who helped me along my journey, including: Tai Baker, T.J. Beach, Richard Bishop, Gordon Brooks, TJ Brooks, Bobbie R. Byrd, Teresa Carey, Oliver F. Chase, Jeannie Delahunt, Felix Bruno De La Mata, Mark Iles, Michele Kapugi, Michael Kent, Everett E. Kergosien, Sylvia Krzak, C.B. Laurence, James McLeod, Alpha to Omega Review Group, Craig Palmer, Lynn Z. Puhle, Vivienne Sang, Jeff Walby, and the Writer's Café-Mocha Team.

1

J avier's Condo
     Arlington, Virginia

"Duty, Honor, Country. Those three hallowed words reverently dictate what you ought to be, what you can be, what you will be." General Douglas MacArthur, during his farewell speech at West Point Military Academy, 12 May 1962

Colonel Javier Smith woke to the strains of "Born in the U.S.A." echoing in the room. He rolled over and grabbed his phone. "Yeah?"

"Are you up yet?" AJ Bruce spoke in a sultry voice. "It's five a.m. You wanted me to make sure you're ready for your big day." She chuckled.

"You're pretty cheerful this morning." Javier glanced at the clock as it ticked over to a new hour. *Yep—five a.m.* "How much coffee did you drink?"

"Just started my second cup." She slurped her coffee. "Sorry, I can't make it today—something's come up I need to deal with. See you tonight?"

"You betcha." *She's probably saving the world again.* Javier broke the connection and shook the cobwebs from his head. He propelled his six-foot-four-inch body from the bed and dashed into the bathroom for a shave and a quick shower. After drying himself, he stood in front of the mirror and gave himself a once-over. *Still in decent shape.* He patted his washboard abs. *Not bad for a forty-five-year-old soon-to-be-retired colonel.* He ran a hand through his black hair, streaks of gray now beginning to show. *No need to hide the gray—AJ likes it.*

He returned to the bedroom to dress. Before he finished, he glanced at the ribbon rack on his uniform. *First and last time to wear all of them at once.*

Javier ran a finger along the top decorations. A dozen other ribbons followed. *Each one brings back memories but earning the Combat Infantryman Badge and the Senior Parachutist Badge means more than all the others.*

After dressing, he glanced in the mirror a final time and adjusted his uniform. Satisfied, he strode into the kitchen and poured a cup of coffee. *I'm glad AJ bought me this Braun BrewSense—makes life easy not waiting for my morning brew, and there's enough to fill a travel mug or two.*

After draining his cup, Javier filled a travel mug, picked up a shoulder bag, and stepped into the corridor of his condo. His foot-steps echoed in the empty stairwell as he hustled down three flights to the garage. He hopped into his vehicle—a black Hummer H3. Although the SUV was a few years old, he maintained it in excellent condition, which led to multiple trophies for competing in off-road driving competitions.

Javier sipped on his second coffee as he drove through the busy streets of Arlington, Virginia, lined with blocks of juxtaposed condos, joining other early commuters heading to work. *Wonder what life will be like after today?*

Ten minutes later, he found a rare empty parking spot near the mall entrance to the Pentagon. After climbing out of his Hummer, he adjusted his uniform and walked with dignity and purpose inside the building. Once he cleared security, he strolled through the corridors, nodding to a few officers he recognized before arriving at his office located within the Special Operations Division on the E-Ring.

A plain white envelope with his name typed on the front in bold letters lay on the center of his otherwise empty desk. He removed the cover from his head, placed it on the credenza, and sat in his black executive-style chair. Curious, he opened the envelope.

Inside, a single sheet of paper on Chief of Staff of the Army letterhead:

COLONEL SMITH,

Your presence is required in my office at 12:45. You are hereby ordered to attend a meeting afterward in the JCS Conference Room. Please be in full uniform.

Gordon B. Brown
General, U.S. Army

AT LEAST HE'S *not giving me the full Chief of Staff of the Army official treatment.* Javier dropped the note on the desk. "I told them no send-off. I prefer to remain in the shadows. Why doesn't anyone listen?" He shook his head and chuckled. "I wonder who's behind this? Can't be AJ, as she doesn't have any sway with the Pentagon, so it must be one of the Snakes."

AT THE DESIGNATED TIME, Javier presented himself at General Brown's office. He snapped to attention and saluted.

"Relax, Colonel. You're acting like a new soldier." Brown chortled.

"Given your normal tendency to ignore military etiquette, no need for it on your final day with us."

Javier relaxed. "Sorry, General. Not every day I get invited to Chief of Staff territory." He smiled. *In fact, first time ever, but who's counting?*

"Take a seat." Brown moved around his desk and took the chair opposite Javier. "I wanted to have a brief discussion before the ceremony. What are your plans for the future?" He shook his head. "With your leadership abilities and field experience, we would have loved to pin a star on you."

"You hit on the primary reason I'm retiring, General." Javier gazed into the general's face. "I'm a field rat, through and through. Sticking me behind a desk in the Pentagon is like a prison sentence. If I had accepted a star, I assumed my field days with Special Ops would be behind me."

Brown nodded. "Fair enough. Since you're leaving us, what will you do? Perhaps write a book or two about your exploits? Even the unclassified missions would make interesting reading."

"I'm still young enough to do something else. I thought about writing, but I ditched the idea. I'd rather remain active, so I'm planning to start a security business. With my love of foreign environs, I plan to seek out international clients."

Brown glanced at his watch. "Understood. Once you establish your company, send me word. Perhaps I can steer some work your way, although I'll have to check on revolving door regulations for former government officials receiving contracts. I'm sure we might find a few loopholes."

"Thank you, General."

Brown glanced at the wall clock. "Time to go. Can't have the guest of honor late for his last task before he walks out the door."

Moments later, they entered the Joint Chiefs of Staff conference room. Although its unofficial name was the gold room because of the color of the carpeting and drapes, Javier knew those working with the Joint Chiefs referred to it as the tank.

When Brown and Javier stepped into the room, everyone came to attention. Brown leaned toward Javier. "Follow me." He led the way around the rectangular, polished table to two chairs at the far end. Behind the chairs, an array of flags represented the U.S. and the various military components.

After standing at the end of the table, Brown motioned for everyone to relax. "This is a bittersweet day for many of us. While we're here to pay our respects to a courageous officer, we're also losing one of our finest—the recipient of the Distinguished Service Cross and the Silver Star, just to mention a few. These two are for extraordinary heroism in combat with enemy forces. Personally, I think he should have been awarded the Medal of Honor instead of the Distinguished Service Cross, but politics got in the way. He also bled for our country, receiving the Purple Heart with oak leaf cluster."

He turned to Javier. "Colonel Smith, the citizens of our great nation will never know how they could sleep at night because of your many successful missions."

Brown glanced around the room. "On such an occasion, I would normally read the biography of a retiree. As much as I'd like to, I think I'd break a few secrecy laws. Besides, we'd be here forever."

Everyone chuckled.

"So, instead of my normal remarks, all I can do is wish you all the best, wherever your journeys take you." Brown came to attention and saluted.

Javier returned the salute. "Thank you, General."

Brown picked up a framed certificate of military service. "This isn't much, but it's typical of the military to hand out pieces of paper. I trust you will find a place for this."

"Yes, sir. I have just the spot—next to the framed words of General MacArthur in my den." Javier took the proffered certificate and glanced at the words before placing it back on the table.

Brown picked up a flag folded into a triangle. "Please accept this flag on behalf of a grateful nation. Last week, it flew over Special Operations Headquarters and yesterday here at the Pentagon. Somewhere, there's a certificate verifying this."

More chuckles came from those in attendance.

"Thank you, sir." Javier took the flag, clenching his teeth to keep his emotions in check. "I'll get this into a presentation box and put it on my desk."

"I know you requested no speeches about your career, nor did you want to make one. We'll respect your wishes."

The doors to the conference room opened, and four men wearing U.S. Army dress blue uniforms including swords rolled a cart in, stopping next to Javier. On top, a massive cake with yellow and black frosting. The inscription read: *Bon Voyage to the Head Snake.* Next to the cake, a bowl of punch.

The men stepped back in unison and saluted with military precision.

Javier returned their salute. "The Snakes! I might have known you'd show up."

"Someone had to ignore your requests. We couldn't let your retirement come and go without a farewell." Viper glanced around. "Where's AJ?"

Javier's smile disappeared. "She couldn't make it. Something to do with another terrorist threat." He shrugged. "Never mind, she'll join us later to celebrate."

"Colonel, why don't we wrap things up and dig into the cake and punch? This is where I should bow out, so I have plausible deniability, but I know from a reliable source the punch contains an extra kick." Brown pulled a small bottle of whiskey from a bag beneath the table and poured a generous amount into the bowl. "Don't tell anyone, or they'll can me."

"Sounds great, General. I'll keep quiet, and thank you, sir."

As the room erupted with applause, everyone formed a line to shake Javier's hand.

Viper cut the cake with a bayonet while Mamba dished out the punch.

The attendees scattered around the room into small clusters once General Brown departed. Before long, the Snakes returned to Javier's side.

Viper held a wrapped package in his hand. "A small gesture of our appreciation, Cobra. Whatever your plans are, know we'll follow you anywhere if you'll have us. After all, we've survived conflicts in places most people have never heard about." He chuckled. "And some they're familiar with, such as our last one in Colombia." He handed the parcel to Javier.

"Thanks, guys. We've had several exciting missions, haven't we? Who knows what the future might bring?" Javier unwrapped the package and burst into laughter. Inside, framed collages: vipers, mambas, rattlers, and adders.

"Fantastic! I'd rather put photos of real snakes on my wall to admire than snapshots of your ugly mugs."

The men laughed and clapped Javier on the shoulder.

"Well, old-timer, we need to get back to work. Before we go, we have one final duty to perform." Viper picked up the certificate and flag while Adder grabbed the framed photos.

"What's that?"

"Escort you out of the building."

Viper led the way out of the conference room. With two Snakes on either side, they marched shoulder-to-shoulder along the corridor, their precision footsteps echoing. Officers and enlisted personnel lined the hallway, snapping to attention and saluting as Javier passed.

Once outside under the portico, he shook hands with his friends. "See you this evening for the celebration?"

"Wouldn't miss it." The Snakes nodded an unofficial farewell to their leader before they saluted and returned inside.

Blinking back tears, Javier turned around and gazed at the Pentagon for a final time. He returned a salute from two non-commissioned officers as they passed on their way into America's symbol of military might before he headed to the parking lot. *The end of a journey—what does the future hold for me now?*

A MAN in the rear of a black van parked near the mall entrance lowered his camera and grinned. *Soon, Coronel, you will receive a fitting punishment for what you did to my brethren. I will carve more scars on your face until you beg for death.* He gestured for the driver to start the engine. *But you shall never receive mercy nor a dignified ending.*

2

Virtue Feed & Grain
Old Town, Alexandria, Virginia

AJ BRUCE FLICKED HER HEAD, tossing her brown hair to the side before pulling it all back with both hands, wrapping it off her neck in a knot and releasing it. *Where is he?* She frowned as she glanced at her watch. *Should have been here an hour ago.* She shook her head. *He knows I'm the impatient type.* AJ pulled her hair over a shoulder, absentmindedly raking the snarls out. She waved at a passing waiter.

"Yes, ma'am. Can I get you another coffee or something with less caffeine and more alcohol?"

"Another coffee for now. Oh, and a muffin—any kind. I'll switch my drink when the others arrive."

"Very good."

While she waited, AJ read the details about the restaurant on the back of the menu: *The historic brick building housing Virtue Feed & Grain was once a feed house in the 1800s. Playing on the original use of the building as a warehouse—*

"Here you are, ma'am. Another Americano, extra coffee, no sugar."

She sipped the hot brew. "Perfect. Thanks."

"Did you order one for me?" The bass voice seemed to resonate from the floorboards.

AJ jumped to her feet and hugged Javier. "About time. I thought you'd be here an hour ago. Where are the Snakes?"

"Slithering around." Javier's eyes twinkled. "They thought I should join you first. They'll make an appearance when they're ready."

"Always the clowns, aren't they?" She returned to her chair.

He sat next to her. "Yeah. But, when necessary, they're as dangerous as anyone who puts on a uniform."

"Excuse me, sir. Do you mind if I take a picture of you and your beautiful wife? It's for a course at the community college. I want to be a freelance photographer." A short man with an ill-fitting black toupee stood near the table with a camera in his hand. He leered at AJ before pointing to a couple sitting at the bar. "They're helping me —I just took their photo."

"Uh ... Yeah. But she's not my—"

AJ kicked Javier under the table as she frowned at him.

"What I mean is ... sure, you can take our photo." He leaned closer to AJ and put his arm around her. "How's this?"

The photographer aimed a professional camera with an attached flash at them. "Perfect. Now smile!"

Javier jerked back at the intense flash, almost falling out of his chair.

"Sorry, sir. If you give me your email address, I'll send the photo to you."

"An email address? Hmm." Javier pulled a pen from inside his sports coat, scribbled on a clean paper napkin, and handed it to the photographer. "How much?"

"No charge. I overheard a conversation at a nearby table about you retiring from the military today, so I wanted to do this for you.

Thank you for your service." He turned and strode to another table, glancing back at them.

"How strange." AJ watched the man as he worked his way toward the exit. "Did you really give him your email address?"

"No way." Javier rolled his eyes. "Are you crazy? Do you honestly think I'd give a total stranger my email address? I gave him yours."

"What?" AJ laughed. "Just checking. What did you really give him?"

"I'm always suspicious of strangers. I gave him an address I created a few weeks ago just for this type of scenario. Until I can check out any unknown person wanting to make contact, they won't get my regular address."

AJ nodded. "Makes sense—I do the same. So, where are the Snakes?"

"Look behind you."

Four men dressed in dark suits and starched white shirts approached. Each wore a tie in vivid colors, draped over a shoulder. They could have been produced from the same mold: tall, short hair, broad-shouldered, trim waists.

"Excuse me. We're looking for a handsome couple." Viper smirked. "Do you know where we might find them?"

AJ stood and smiled before she hugged him. "'Bout time you showed up. I'm hungry."

"You're beautiful, AJ." Viper pointed at Javier. "Why are you with him?"

She laughed. "Because he's a colonel—or was."

"Ouch. That hurts." A rueful look crossed Javier's face.

A waiter appeared and pulled out chairs for the men. After they were seated, he handed out menus. "Would anyone like wine? We have an excellent selection." He offered a wine list to Javier.

"I think we'll start with beer—Three Notch'd Minute Man." Javier scanned the choices. "Perhaps we'll order wine later."

The waiter nodded and scurried away.

"Hey, guys. I can't keep referring to you by the names of snakes."

AJ pointed at Javier. "Even though he thinks he's a cobra, I still call him Javier."

Everyone chuckled.

The waiter reappeared with their drinks as the laughter simmered. "Are you ready to order?"

"Yes." Javier glanced around the table. In response to the nods, he ordered for everyone. "We'll start with the Virtue chips and dips." He gestured toward the Snakes. "Bring plenty—these guys are always hungry."

"Yes, sir. Anything else?"

"Another round of beers. For our main course, we'll have the slow-roasted prime rib—heavy on the meat—go easy on the vegetables."

"Right away, sir."

THE MAN TUCKED his camera into a shoulder carrying case and left the restaurant. Glancing around, he spotted his ride across the street. He took pains not to appear rushed as he strode to a gray, windowless van and jumped through the rear doors.

"Did you get it?" A man turned from the passenger seat as he scratched his scraggly beard.

"Yes. A clear close-up of their faces."

"Excellent. Make copies and give them to our men. I don't want any mistakes." The man tapped the driver on the shoulder. "Let's go."

TWO WAITERS APPEARED at the table. One held a tray with fresh drinks, while the other struggled with a platter loaded with bowls of tortilla chips, *queso gringo*, mango guacamole, chili con carne, and salsa *roja*.

As everyone dug into the food, AJ bent down, pulled a package from under her chair, and handed it to Javier. "Since I couldn't attend your ceremony at the Pentagon, I brought you something to remember me by."

"Aw, shucks. You didn't have to do that. Besides, I'll never forget you." Javier unwrapped the present and burst into laughter. "Did you guys put her up to this?"

"Who, us?" Viper swiped a hand through his blond hair, a look of astonishment on his face. "Why, I never." He tried to keep a straight face but started laughing when Javier showed them the gift.

"With this photo of a taipan, my wall of shame will be complete— five framed photos of snakes!" Javier shook his head.

"Better add a sixth one, Cobra." Viper grinned. "Don't forget to put one of yourself on the wall."

When the laughter died away, AJ took a sip of her beer and raised a brow at the Snakes. "I'm still waiting. Tell me about yourselves—I mean the real you when you're not impersonating snakes."

"Since I'm sorta the unofficial leader, at least when Cobra isn't with us, I'll go first." Viper leaned toward AJ. "I'm Charles Gable from a small town in northern Michigan. Please call me Charlie. We're all majors, but I outrank the others." He turned to the other Snakes and grinned.

Adder pretended to shove a finger down his throat as if he was going to vomit.

Rattler and Mamba shifted their eyes toward the ceiling.

"Hey, Charlie. Pleased to meet the real you." AJ chuckled.

Adder rubbed the side of his crooked nose and laughed. "His seniority over us is about a month, so it's no big deal. I'm Dougie Dabney and hail from Boston, although I haven't lived there for years, which is why my accent has faded. Please don't call me Douglas— only my mother does."

Everyone chuckled and calls of "Douglas" echoed around the table in falsetto voices.

"Just don't leave him alone with food." Charlie winked. "He'll eat anything, given the chance."

AJ turned to the twins. "So, what're your real names? I know you all from our recent mission together but only by your callsigns."

Rattler jumped to attention, followed by Mamba. They glanced at each other before speaking at the same time. "We're the Walker brothers from San Francisco."

Mamba pointed at himself. "I'm Raymond, although I prefer Ray." He gestured at Rattler. "This is my younger brother, Oren."

"You're older by a minute because I let you go first. It was too cold —didn't want to leave Momma."

Their voices increased in volume as each of the Snakes vied for AJ's attention when the waiters reappeared. Soon, the six friends became quiet as they dug into their prime rib, sunchoke-potato mash, and grilled broccolini.

When the last morsel disappeared, Javier stood and gazed around the table. "Thanks to all of you for giving me the kind of retirement I asked for. Nothing extravagant, just a pleasant evening with friends."

"Hey, don't get sentimental on us, or I'll take AJ away from you." Charlie grinned.

"Go ahead and try—she'll whip you in no time." Javier put his hand on AJ's shoulder as he returned to his seat. "Over the next few days, I'm gonna do a lot of thinking about my future. AJ already knows—I'm planning to open an international investigative agency. Are you guys up for a new challenge? You'd have to give up your commissions or switch to the reserves. Of course, getting approval for a transfer could take months. Or you could join us later when you finish your commitments."

"Someone has to keep you out of trouble." Dougie waved a hand. "I have enough time in next month to retire, so I'll join you."

Charlie pursed his lips. "Sounds like a good transition to civvy street. Besides, every mission with you has been an adventure. Why not another one or two? Let me ponder the options, and I'll let you know ASAP."

The Walker brothers nodded in agreement.

Javier raised his glass. "To friends and the establishment of The Brusch Agency." He chugged the remains of his beer.

The others raised their glasses and repeated Javier's toast.

"In case anyone's wondering, Brusch is an amalgamation of Bruce." Javier pointed toward AJ. "And Busch, my real last name."

"Always thought you were more than a Smith when I first met you." AJ batted her eyes at him.

"What can I say? I'm just an ordinary guy doing what seems right."

Groans erupted around the table.

Over the next two hours, beer and laughter continued to flow.

After the glasses were finally drained, Javier and the Snakes shared handshakes and man hugs.

AJ gave each of the Snakes a hug and a kiss on the cheek.

With promises to give serious consideration to Javier's offer of joining the agency, the Snakes departed.

At last, Javier and AJ were alone.

"Guess I better pay the bill." Javier stood, leaned over, and kissed AJ's forehead. "Thank you."

"You're welcome." AJ rose and squeezed Javier's arm. "Don't suppose you can escort me home? Just to the door—I have an early start tomorrow."

Javier dropped the black leather bill holder on the counter as they walked past. "Keep the change."

Outside, they turned left and strolled arm-in-arm the four blocks to AJ's condo. They held each other and kissed before she pushed him back. "Down, boy. I'm an old-fashioned girl."

"Yeah, I know. I'm an old-fashioned guy, but I think our meanings are different."

She leaned toward him, allowing her lips to brush his. "Good night, Javier. I'll see you tomorrow evening."

"Night. I'll wait until you're inside before I leave. No telling what scumbags might be lurking around."

AJ laughed as she stuck her key in the door. "My hero!" She entered the building, turned back, and blew him a kiss.

Twenty minutes later, a taxi dropped Javier at home. He nodded to a couple coming out of the building. The man held the door for Javier.

"Many thanks. Enjoy the evening." Javier strode across the foyer and entered the elevator. He pulled his keys out as he walked along the hallway to his apartment.

And stopped.

Alarm bells rang as Javier inspected the door, open a fraction. The hair on his arms stood up as a current of electricity shot down his spine. *Lock picked—no sign of forced entry. Someone's here or been here.* He patted his shoulder—no weapon. *Damn! I left it in the safe.*

He eased the door open.

Darkness.

After flicking on the light, his jaw dropped.

Everything on the walls now rested on the floor. Frames were torn apart, and glass covers were broken. Cushions were sliced open, contents spewed forth.

Out of the corner of an eye, Javier caught a glimpse of someone moving in the shadows. He lunged and crashed into the remnants of his coffee table.

The shadow dashed out the door.

By the time Javier climbed to his feet and rushed into the corridor, it was empty.

3

J avier's Condo
    Arlington, Virginia

JAVIER WALKED BACK into his condo, shut the door, and threw the deadbolt. He surveyed the damage in the living/dining room, shaking his head. An inspection of the kitchen and the master bedroom showed the same devastation—items ripped from walls, soft furnishings cut open, drawers dumped, tables in pieces. *TV and stereo still here. Nothing else of much value in the place. Looking for something in particular? But what?*

He rushed into the guest bedroom. *Everything seemed normal. Must have scared him off before he finished.* Javier shifted a framed photo of the Pentagon on the wall near the bed and looked behind it. Good. *Safe's untouched.*

He entered the kitchen and clenched his fists at the sight of the fridge, its door open, and the contents scattered across the floor. Javier waded through food, smashed containers, and broken bottles.

In a corner, the remains of his coffee machine cluttered the floor. Using the toe of his shoe, he poked through the detritus and found a bottle of beer intact. Beneath a pile of sliced pastrami, he located an opener. He popped the cap and drained the warm brew before yanking his phone from a pocket and dialing 9-1-1.

"Connect me to the police—there's been a break-in."

Moments later, a gruff voice came on the line. "Police. What's the problem?"

"Someone broke into my condo and trashed the place."

"Anyone injured?"

"No." Javier gave his name and address.

"We'll dispatch someone right away."

"Okay, thanks." Javier cut the connection and sat on the lone cushion not slashed by the intruder. *Should I call AJ? Naw—she's got an early day. I'll tell her later.*

He took photos with his phone while waiting for the police to arrive. Once he finished, he put water in the electric kettle and searched for an unbroken cup and a jar of instant coffee. *I'd prefer another beer, but better wait.*

Twenty minutes after Javier finished his coffee, the doorbell rang. He peered through the peephole—three uniformed officers, one wearing sergeant stripes. He opened the door.

The sergeant glanced around as he stepped inside. "Whoa! What a mess!"

One of his subordinates followed him, the other remaining in the corridor.

The sergeant pulled a camera from his pocket and began taking photos. "You pissed someone off. Any ideas?"

Javier shook his head. "No. Have there been other break-ins in this area? Aren't you supposed to find the person who did this?" *As if I would trust this guy to do anything.*

The sergeant chuckled. "We'll be lucky. Was anything of value taken?"

"Nothing of monetary value here—just personal possessions." *But if I find out who did this, I'll strangle him before dropping him in the Potomac.*

"To be honest, most of these crimes go unsolved. We'll make some notes and enter them into the system. Leave things as they are. A crime scene investigator will be here in an hour or so to take more photos and dust for prints." The sergeant gestured at Javier's hands. "Better see to those cuts, too."

Yeah, don't call me, I'll call you. Javier nodded and showed the officers to the door. After they left, he grabbed another beer from the kitchen floor and picked up a dining chair. Javier stepped over the mess and moved into the hallway. He straddled the seat and opened his drink as he waited for the arrival of the crime scene investigator.

TWO HOURS LATER, a civilian carrying two black bags stepped off the elevator and approached Javier. He set down his bags and pointed to a lanyard. "CSI. Had a break-in?"

"Yeah." Javier yawned. "How long will it take? I want to clean up some of the mess before calling it a night."

"Won't take long. I'll get photographs of anything out of place and dust all the hard surfaces for prints." The man rubbed his receding hairline. "Can't promise anything, but I'll do my best."

Javier gestured toward the open door. "It's all yours. I'll stay here unless you want me inside."

The CSI shook his head. "I'll call if I need you."

JAVIER WOKE WITH A START. He glanced into the face of the CSI man.

"Sorry to disturb you, sir. I'm all done. I picked up a few prints, and we'll run them through the system to see if they match anyone. We'll let you know."

Javier stood and shook hands. "How long will it take?"

The man laughed. "How long is a piece of string? There's always a backlog, but eventually, these will be checked out."

"Okay." Javier watched the man retrieve his bags and disappear into the elevator. He re-entered his apartment, locked the door, and headed to a closet, where he found a roll of plastic trash bags, a broom, and dustpan.

Two hours later, he collapsed onto the ripped mattress in the master bedroom and dozed.

WHEN HE AWOKE, sunshine filtered through the blinds. Javier climbed out of bed, went into the guest bedroom, and pushed aside the Pentagon photo. *Glad the perp didn't find the wall safe.* He worked the combination and pulled out his laptop. Heading back to the kitchen, he made another cup of coffee, picked up a barstool, and sat at the island. As he sipped, he booted the computer and began typing.

To: Viper, Adder, Rattler, Mamba
From: Cobra
Condo trashed by unknown perp while we partied last night. Nothing taken. A few cuts after I fell over the remains of the glass coffee table chasing a shadow, but nothing to worry about. Everyone up for a beer later? I need to make some plans and want to bounce them off you.

AFTER HITTING SEND, he closed the laptop and returned it to the safe. He pulled out a loaded SIG Sauer P226 pistol and two extra magazines, shoved them into a backpack, and headed to the garage.

Javier climbed into his Hummer and weaved through the streets of Arlington and Annandale. Before long, he crossed I-495 and continued to his destination in Fairfax: Division VII Headquarters of the Virginia State Police.

Once inside, he asked for directions to the office of the division commander.

A man with short, gray hair sitting behind a desk covered with multiple folders glanced up. "Got an appointment?"

Javier shook his head.

"No one sees the commander without one."

"I spoke with him an hour ago. He told me to drop by."

"Hmph." The man glared at Javier. "He didn't say anyone would be visiting."

I doubt he needs your permission. "Please let him know Colonel Smith is here."

The officer picked up a phone and spoke in a quiet voice. As his face reddened, the grip on the receiver turned his knuckles white. Once he hung up, he lumbered to his feet. "Follow me."

They went down a corridor and stopped at the third door on the right. "Captain Zorkin is waiting for you."

Javier knocked on the door and entered after hearing, "Come in."

A silver-haired man wearing a state police uniform rose from the desk and came around, hand extended. "My God! Look at you—been a long time."

Javier shook hands. "Hey, Brian. It would've been a bit quicker except for the guy manning the desk. He'll wrench his jaw chewing bubblegum the way he was. Does a good job of running interference, but seemed upset he didn't know I was coming."

Brian laughed. "You mean, Lefty? I wanted to let him go because he doesn't do much except some filing and answering the phone, but he needs another fifteen months before he can retire with a full pension. Don't want to rob him of what he deserves. After taking two bullets to save the life of his partner, it's the least I can do." A sheepish grin crossed Brian's face. "I think I forgot to tell him I was expecting you. Guess I owe him an apology." He gestured toward two chairs. "Have a seat and fill me in on what you've been up to."

"Since I retired from the military and no longer have a job, I'm starting an investigative agency. We're gonna concentrate on foreign cases whenever possible. One of the things I'll need is a concealed-carry permit."

"Didn't you have one when you were stationed in North Carolina? If it hasn't expired, Virginia will recognize it."

Javier pursed his lips. "Since most of my time at Fort Bragg was in training for my next assignment, I never got one. Besides, who was going to bother a bunch of Delta Force guys heading off the base?"

"Someone out of their mind, I guess." Brian chuckled. "I can vouch for you and get things rolling. Before you leave, I'll print out the application and have you sign it. Shouldn't take more than three or four days for approval to come from Richmond. Still favoring a SIG Sauer?"

"Yeah. In fact, it's locked in the weapons box welded into the back of my Hummer. Didn't know if you'd want any info from it."

"We'll need the serial number but won't need your SIG for anything."

"Sounds good. I'm going to apply for my private investigator license and anything else I'm required to do to set things in motion."

"I'll give you a hand. What're you going to call your outfit?"

"The Brusch Agency. A play on my last name and a woman I know."

Brian raised a brow and grinned. "A one-night stand, or is it serious?"

"Could be something more, one day." Javier smiled. "For now, we're taking things slow and easy. She's a keeper if I can catch her."

"Wish you all the best." Brian glanced at the clock. "Is there anything else I can do for you right now? I have to meet with the Fairfax County Board of Supervisors. Always a pain, but from time to time, it works in our favor."

Javier stood. "I'm good, Brian. Many thanks for your help."

"Not to worry. Let me get the form for you."

∾

WHEN JAVIER ENTERED VIRTUE FEED & Grain at four p.m., he found the Snakes sipping beers at their usual table. Tucked under his arm, the laptop he had retrieved from his condo.

As he sat, someone shoved a glass at him. "Better hurry up, Javier. You're a beer down, and it's your round."

He placed his laptop on the table, took a sip of his drink, and smacked his lips. "Just what I needed after last night." He provided details of the break-in.

"Wait a minute. Did you get a glimpse of the perp?" Dougie drained his beer. "Who'd you piss off?"

Javier laughed. "That's what the police sergeant asked." He shook his head. "No. At least nothing useful. His build seemed familiar, but I don't know why. I can't place him. Perhaps it'll come back to me." He raised his hands, displaying shallow cuts on both palms.

"Whoa! Looks like you met a meat grinder!" Dougie winced. "Painful?"

"Not too bad—all were surface cuts when I fell on the remains of the shattered glass coffee table." Javier took another sip of his beer. "Anyway, I've started the ball rolling to set up my agency. A friend of mine will help me cut through the red tape."

"Wouldn't be AJ, by any chance?" Charlie nudged Javier's shoulder. "I'm sure she'd help."

"Didn't ask her—she has enough on her plate, so I contacted an old buddy. We played football together at West Point. Now he's a captain in the Virginia State Police."

Charlie leaned back in his chair. "Oh, friends in high places!"

"Well, I got enough friends in low places." Javier maintained a straight face as he leveled a stern look at each of the Snakes.

Everyone laughed.

"On a more serious note, remember that photographer from last night? He sent an email with attachments to the address I gave him." Javier opened his laptop and booted. When it was ready, he pulled up the email:

· · ·

ENJOY YOUR REMAINING days on this earth. Check out the attachments and meet your new friends.

"THERE ARE six photos of beheadings—five men and a woman." Javier ground his teeth. "I'm gonna need your help—AJ's, too. I want someone I can trust watching my back. We need to find out who's behind this and turn the tables before they try to follow through with their threat."

4

Virtue Feed & Grain
Old Town, Alexandria, Virginia

AFTER THE SNAKES DEPARTED, Javier ambled to the newspaper rack next to the entrance. He sifted through the national and regional papers until he located the *Alexandria Times*.

Back at the table, he flicked through the pages until he reached the classified ads. He placed a thumb under each ad as he scanned them. Engrossed in his research, Javier didn't sense anyone approaching as he took a pen from his pocket and circled a promising ad. *This one would work.*

"Hey, big boy." AJ handed him a beer and took a seat. "I've never known you to be so unaware of your surroundings—anyone could have snuck up on you. Is reading that hard?" She laughed. "You've just retired, and already you're losing a step."

Javier sipped his drink. "Sorry. I've been busy since I last saw you." He explained about the break-in. "They even smashed the coffee maker you bought me."

"I'll get you another machine—neither of us can be without our morning coffee." A half-smile creased AJ's face. "Perhaps the cops will get lucky, and the fingerprints they found might lead them to someone."

"They seemed to think it was a random event. I can't see it connected to any of my missions in the military since they were all overseas." Javier shrugged. "No matter. I think it's time to move." He reached across the table and took AJ's hand. "Since you live in Old Town and the Virtue is our favorite place, I can't justify remaining in Arlington."

"Where would you locate your agency?"

He grabbed the paper, slid it over, and tapped the highlighted ad. "Right here. The building is already zoned for mixed use, so I could live there, too."

AJ raised her brows. "Have you set up a viewing?"

He shook his head. "Not yet. I just found the ad." Javier pulled his cell phone from a hip pocket and placed a call. After completing his conversation, he broke the connection and smiled. "We can see the property in an hour. Enough time for another beer and a quick walk. The property's only fifteen minutes from here."

AN HOUR LATER, Javier and AJ stood in front of a three-story brick building. Four concrete steps led to two doors, one dark brown, the other a light oak. Brass signs with black lettering indicated the names of the businesses.

"Hello, are you Mr. and Mrs. Smith?"

AJ glanced at Javier, a bemused expression spread across her face before they turned toward the voice.

A petite woman with shoulder-length blonde hair smiled as she approached and extended her hand. "Hi. I'm Lulu. Are you ready to check out this fantastic property? This one's a winner, that's for sure."

AJ and Javier shook Lulu's hand in turn.

He turned and scanned the nearby buildings. "How long has it been on the market? This appears to be a respectable neighborhood."

"The senior partner of the law firm who owned the building and lived on the top floor passed away. The junior partners had been after him to sell for a couple of years and move to larger premises in D.C. With his death, they've put it up for sale. Did the ad mention all furnishings are included?"

"Yes. Did you find out if there are any problems with establishing an investigative agency in this area?" Javier gazed at the building. "I'd hate to buy the building and then find out I couldn't work from here."

"I checked with my boss, who confirmed your agency wouldn't create a commercial code violation." Lulu turned on a radiant smile and gestured. "Shall we go inside?"

AJ and Javier locked arms and joined her at the top of the four steps.

Lulu faced the street and spread her arms wide. "This is one of the premier streets in Alexandria and a great business location. There are excellent public parking facilities for clients, easy access to public transportation, and a short trip to local airports."

"We're familiar with the area. I—we live in Old Town." AJ squeezed Javier's arm. "Don't we, hon?" She smirked.

"Uh. Yeah." Javier's face reddened. "I don't think I told Lulu when I spoke with her."

"No problem, Mr. and Mrs. Smith." Lulu beamed. "I'm happy to hear you're already sold on the area. My job is nearly done as this place sells itself." She pulled a key ring from an oversized handbag. "Let's go into what should be a perfect place for you."

They stepped into the foyer, a plush, red carpet covering the floor. Above, high ceilings with original ornate trimming spoke of a time in the past. Lulu guided them to the left.

"This building was constructed in 1872 and still retains many original features, including the hardwood floors. The ceilings are all eleven feet high. All of the colors on the walls are typical of what was used when it was first built." She stomped her foot on the polished heart of pine. "Still solid. This room was used as the reception area for clients and would work well for your business, too."

Javier glanced around the room and nodded. "Yes, it would."

"Shall we continue? There's so much to show you."

FORTY MINUTES LATER, Javier, AJ, and Lulu returned to the reception area and sat in brown leather chairs arranged in a semi-circle in front of the desk.

Lulu reached into her bag and removed a folder. She handed it to Javier and glanced at the wall clock. "Gosh! I've taken a lot of your time. I hope I didn't bore you—I just love these historic buildings and sometimes get carried away. The folder contains more information about the property, and my contact details should you have any additional questions or decide to make an offer."

"We'll be in touch—there's lots for us to discuss." Javier offered his hand. "We have two other properties to look at, but we'll let you know either way."

Lulu's perpetual smile faltered. "Oh. I thought, ... well, it doesn't matter what I thought." The radiance returned. "This is a fabulous buy for the money and won't be on the market for long. I look forward to hearing from you."

AJ nodded. "We'll contact you as soon as possible."

"Oh, okay. Have a nice day."

After Lulu left, AJ and Javier strolled arm-in-arm back to the Virtue for dinner. Once a greeter escorted them to a table and took their drink order, Javier leaned back in his chair and grinned.

AJ raised an eyebrow. "What's the grin for?"

"Just thinking about how fast we're moving. Did you notice how crestfallen Lulu was when I mentioned we were looking at other properties?"

She chuckled. "Yes, I caught it. She'll earn a large commission when a sale goes through. I think she assumed you'd jump at the chance. By the way, where are the other properties? And … when did we get married?"

Javier shook his head. "Aren't any. I just didn't want her to think we were desperate. She assumed we were married—didn't see a reason to correct her." He winked. "After all, we've pretended before."

"Yeah, during our mission in Panama. Oh well, no harm done. I think the building is a perfect location with plenty of space to hold the agency."

"Agreed. We'll let Lulu simmer overnight. I'll call her tomorrow and put in an offer."

"Sounds good to me, hubby." AJ laughed and drained the last of her beer. "I forwarded the email you sent me with the beheading attachments to MacKenzie and Makayla. They'll work their magic and trace where the email originated, and any details associated with the account. Any new emails from the wacko photographer?"

"Nothing yet. What do you think the photos mean?"

AJ shook her head. "I'm not sure. Someone obviously has you in their sights. I think it's a stretch to say the beheadings represent you, the Snakes, and me, but it's a possibility not to be overlooked. More likely, someone's trying to scare you. The bigger questions are who and why? How many people have you pissed off?"

"Probably a few thousand." He chuckled. "Well, I'm not intimidated—I'm angry. Once we know who's behind this, I'll pay them a visit. The Snakes already agreed to back me up." *Need to spend more time digging through the cobwebs. Who did I piss off? Where and when?*

"I will, too." AJ took the folder containing their bill. "My treat. Let's go back to my place for a nightcap. I don't have an early morning."

"Sounds promising."

"Don't set your expectations too high."

"I can always hope."

A MAN SITTING in the passenger seat of a gray, windowless van focused his lens on Javier and AJ, snapping several photos. He grinned as he fingered his toupee. *Soon we will know everything about you.* He placed his camera in a bag by his feet and pulled out a picture of six headless bodies and a Sharpie. He crossed out the first two bodies. *You will meet your maker soon. Inshallah.*

5

F ixer-Upper Property
Outside Culpepper, Virginia

ALBERTO CABRERA, also known as Abdul Rahman, sat at the stained Formica kitchen table. He sorted the driver's licenses, social security cards, and credit cards into neat stacks near two small boxes on the chipped tabletop and glanced at the waiting men.

"In order to carry out Allah's wishes, we must be prepared to blend into our environment. You were chosen because of your courage in our last battle and unswerving loyalty to Allah. Furthermore, your light skin coloring will allow you to blend in. We—I honor you with this opportunity to strike fear among the infidels in their capital. You must not fail."

"Abdul—sorry. Alberto, when will we attack?" Gamal laced his fingers together and twiddled his thumbs.

Alberto picked up the first set of papers and slid them toward Gamal. "You will now be called Bennie Johnson. As our photographer, you'll be responsible for tracking our target and learning everything you can about him." *This man deserves to die for what he did to me.* He rubbed the three-inch scar on the left side of his neck. *He should die a slow and painful death—just like Michael, may Allah bless him. We need to find the rest of his men and sacrifice them in Allah's honor.*

"Find out what he does, where he goes, and who he meets with. Do the same with the woman who was with him when I took this picture. I'll give you the camera I used." Alberto ground his teeth. "When I was destroying infidel dogs in ISIS, I learned preparation is critical to success. We won't set a date—yet. Track their contacts—we need to find the four men who supported the leader in Mexico."

Bennie ran a hand through his long, black hair as he checked each document. "These are perfect. What about a phone and cash?"

"Patience." Alberto picked up the second set of papers and passed them to a bald man with dark, piercing eyes. "Zafar, you'll use the name Justin Thompson. As our combat expert, you'll be responsible for killing our targets should the opportunity present itself. May Allah guide your bullets."

"Thank you, Alberto." Justin grinned. "I will not let you down. Inshallah."

Alberto tilted his head. "I know, which is why Allah selected you." He pushed the final set of documents toward a man missing the pinkie and ring finger on his left hand. "Maheer, as the infidels would say, 'I've saved the best for last.' Your new name is Walter. You must prepare explosive devices capable of causing this man great pain before he meets his God."

"You do me great honor." Walter rubbed the stumps where his fingers no longer existed. "It will give me pleasure to spill his blood."

Alberto reached into one of the boxes and pulled out three cell phones. The new names were taped across the keypads. "Each phone contains three numbers—for the rest of us, so we can keep in contact." He reached into the second box. "Cash—two thousand dollars for each of you." He gestured toward a wooden crate resting near a closet door. "Pistols and ammunition are there."

The three accomplices grinned as they took the proffered items.

"Will we keep using this house? It's far from Washington, so I'll be doing a lot of driving." Bennie pursed his lips. "Traffic on I-66 can be heavy and slow-moving, especially when people go to or from work, which will hamper my ability to react quickly should the need arise."

Alberto scanned the room. Faded wallpaper hung in strips, almost reaching the floor. Holes showed where electrical switches were once installed. Most of the doors on the kitchen cupboards were missing or hanging askew. "I bought this house because it needs a lot of work, so the neighbors won't question workmen coming and going. However, we'll also rent a place closer."

"What about transportation? Most Americans own at least one vehicle." Justin's eyes gleamed. "I would like a pickup truck."

"They are arranged and will be delivered this evening by the man who provided the documents." Alberto laughed. "He has no idea who we really are—I told him we were cousins setting up a new drug distribution network."

"But Alberto, he has our photos." Justin frowned. "What if he reports us to the authorities?"

Alberto shook his head. "Once we receive everything he's supposed to deliver, you can arrange an accident for him. One he won't recover from."

AFTER COMPLETING his morning *Fajr* prayers, Alberto turned on the radio. When the announcer finished the news update, Alberto smiled. He pulled chopped dates and yogurt from the fridge, added a dollop of honey, and stirred the concoction with a slotted spoon.

Loading up a clean utensil, he closed his eyes in anticipation of his breakfast. Alberto grimaced when his phone rang. He checked the caller ID and accepted the call. "As-salaam-alaikum. Well done, Justin. I heard on the radio our fixer ran into a problem. Are you sure it was the right man?"

"Wa-alaikum-salaam, Alberto. Yes. The license plate on the vehicle matched what you gave me. I nudged his car into the bridge abutment at seventy-five miles per hour. His vehicle spun around twice, hitting the concrete wall each time, before flipping over. With dents on the front, back, and both sides, no one should be able to see where I pushed him."

"Agreed. In any event, the announcer on the radio said there was only one person in the car, and he died at the scene."

"Anyone who stands in Allah's way will earn the same fate, Alberto. What is next for me?"

"Just a moment." Alberto took a small spoonful of his breakfast and chewed as he thought. "Go to one of the shopping malls. Find out what people your age are wearing in this area and buy some of the same things so you will blend into the crowds. We must wait for Bennie's information before we plan our attack."

WALTER PUSHED a shopping cart through the aisles of the home improvement store. Ticking items off a mental list, he purchased gloves, metal pipe and caps, nails, and a stack of plywood sheets and decking boards. He finished with a stop in the tool section, selecting hammers, pliers, a hacksaw, an electric saw, and a folding Workmate bench.

As he headed toward the check-outs, he stopped in an aisle he hadn't visited. *Better grab some paint and brushes, too. Glad I convinced Alberto to keep the property near Culpepper. Perfect for making my toys.* He glanced at his left hand. *No mistakes this time—can't lose any more fingers.*

After securing everything in the windowless, gray van provided by Alberto's fixer, Walter drove across the street to a competitor's store. Once again, he filled a shopping cart with his necessities: ball bearings, a grinder, a drill, a pipe threader, and four rolls of duct tape. He finished his shopping expedition at a farm supply store, picking up two twenty-five-pound bags of fertilizer. As with his first two stops, he paid for everything with cash.

Back on the highway, he drove within the speed limit, arriving at their temporary shelter in an hour. After hauling everything inside, he parked the van in the lean-to garage. *Tomorrow, I'll pick up the fireworks and an additional cell phone.*

ARMED with several cameras and a cooler full of cheese sandwiches and soft drinks, Bennie spent the day camped outside the property where Javier lived. He routinely took photos of pedestrians entering the building and vehicles using the underground garage.

Bennie switched his location every hour, sometimes using his blue Chevrolet Camaro, and other times on foot, acting like a tourist. *No sign of him. Where is he?*

Toward the end of the day, he lost his patience and entered the lobby carrying a package. He stopped at a desk where an elderly security guard sat. "Excuse me. Do you know where I might find a ...." Bennie glanced at the parcel. "Colonel Javier Smith? He needs to sign for this insured package."

The guard chuckled. "You missed him. He left an hour ago. Said he'd be back in a day or two. You'll have to come back because only Mr. Smith can sign for it."

Bennie shook his head. "Thanks. It can wait. I'll return this way in a couple of days."

After leaving the building, he returned to his car. Before departing, he placed a call. "Missed him—not sure where he went. A guard said he'd be back in a couple of days."

The echo of Alberto slamming a fist on the table reverberated through the phone. "Find him, Bennie. I don't care what you must do but find him. He must be punished!"

6

Denny's Restaurant
Alexandria, Virginia

JAVIER SMOTHERED a yawn as the waitress placed a steaming cup of black coffee in front of him. "Thank you."

"Are you ready to order?"

He took a final glance at the menu. "I'll have the Grand Slam Slugger and a large orange juice." *Not that I need it, but, hey, I'm retired!* He patted his stomach. *I better watch my intake though.* He shook his head. *Naw—later.*

The waitress nodded. "Coming up." She hit a few keys on her tablet before walking away.

Javier pulled a folder from his backpack and began reading. He took a sip of his coffee, spilling some on a photo. "Damn! How clumsy can I get?" He grabbed a napkin and wiped away the offending puddle.

A passing waitress carrying a coffee pot stopped at Javier's table. "Need a refill, hon?"

"Sure." He pushed his half-empty cup toward the waitress.

"Here ya go." She picked up the soiled napkin and departed, her hips swaying.

Can't wait for breakfast. I'm hungry. Javier picked up the still-damp photo, moved it to the edge of the table, and sifted through the remaining ones.

"Waaah!"

A child with red hair and a face covered with freckles leaned over the seat in front of him.

Javier smiled at him and wiggled his fingers.

The child cried again as his mother pulled him back into his seat. "Leave the man alone, honey. Our food will be here soon."

Yeah, kid. I could cry, too. When's my food arriving?

"Sorry for the wait, sir."

The original waitress set a white ceramic skillet filled with pancakes, bacon, sausage, hash browns, and eggs in front of him.

Javier inhaled the aroma. "Smells good."

The waitress smiled. "Enjoy. Be right back with your juice."

Javier loaded his fork and resumed reading. He barely noticed the appearance of his juice as he worked his way through breakfast. Once he finished, he pushed the plate aside and pulled out his phone.

After several rings, a cheerful voice answered. "Good morning!"

"Lulu? Javier Smith here."

"Oh, Mr. Smith. I was hoping you would call. I don't like to pester clients, but I'm anxious to find out if you made a decision."

I bet—big commission on the line. "I have. This one will be perfect if we can reach an agreement."

"Oh, yes, sir! One of the partners hinted there might be room for negotiation of the one point five million asking price."

"Excellent. Please start the ball rolling with an offer of one point one million. Tell them I'm offering cash." *Maybe I can settle for a couple of hundred thousand above that. Would wipe out half of my inheritance, but worth it.*

"I'll talk to them right away. If they accept, I'll write up the formal offer—I'll let you know."

Javier flagged down a waitress and requested a cup of coffee to go and his bill. He left Denny's and climbed into his Hummer as his phone rang. He glanced at the number. *An Alexandria area code, but I don't recognize the number.* "Hello?"

"Mr. Smith, it's me—Lulu. I spoke with one of the partners. They countered with one point three million. Is it doable for you?"

Javier scratched his chin and grinned. "If we can close the sale as soon as possible, subject to satisfactory inspection, I agree."

"Yeesss!"

He pulled the phone away from his ear until Lulu finished her celebration and became quiet. "Lulu, still there?"

"Oh, Mr. Smith! You've made my day. This is my first sale!"

Thought so. "Let's get the paperwork moving."

"What about Mrs. Smith? I'll need her personal details so you can both sign."

"Uh. Well. Ya see, we're not married." *Perhaps one day.* "She's just a friend—a very good friend. Can you still have the deed put in both of our names?"

Lulu laughed. "No worries, Mr. Smith. I'll take care of things and will be back to you soon."

"Thanks, Lulu."

Javier leaned back and tapped a drum roll on the steering wheel. *Things are coming together.* He started the Hummer's engine when his phone rang again. Without looking, he answered. "Something happen, Lulu?"

A male voice chuckled. "Not sure who Lulu is, Javier, but last time I checked, my name was still Brian."

Both men laughed.

"Sorry, Brian. Just had a call from a realtor. My offer on a property in Alexandria was accepted."

"Must be a day for good news. I wanted to let you know Richmond approved your concealed-carry permit. You can pick it up any time. Also, you're fast-tracked for your private investigator license—a few things for you to take care of, but they waived most of your training because of your military experience."

"Fantastic news, Brian! Today's a day for celebrating. I'm meeting AJ at the Virtue tonight for dinner. Care to join us?"

"I'd love to, Javier, but I'll need a rain check. Tonight's the Lion's Club meeting, and I'm giving a speech."

"Have fun. We'll get together another time."

JAVIER ENTERED THE VIRTUE FEED & Grain, his laptop tucked under an arm, and headed to the bar. After ordering a beer and chicken wings, he weaved through the tables, selecting an empty one against the far wall.

Taking a sip of his Three Notch'd Minute Man beer, he booted his computer. After checking his email and finding nothing of interest, he opened a new Word document, tapping an index finger against his lips before he began composing. *What do I need? Better cover every contingency.*

Javier glanced up as Luke approached.

The general manager placed Javier's wings on the table and sat across from him. "The bartender said you wanted to speak with me?"

He nodded. "Yeah. I need a favor, Luke. Things are falling into place to get my investigative agency up and running, but I need somewhere to conduct interviews with potential employees. Would it be possible to reserve a space here? I really don't have anywhere else to go until the contract on my new property is closed."

"Sure. The smallest place is the stage area upstairs. It's bigger than what you need, but it'll give you some privacy. When do you want it?"

"I'm getting an ad together now. How about next Wednesday and Thursday, say from two to eight p.m.?"

Luke grinned. "Not a problem. Perhaps we'll pick up some new business from your prospective employees."

"That'll be one of the tests." Javier laughed. "Everyone stopping after their interview for a drink or food will get bonus points."

Luke stood. "You'll be some boss. He—"

"Hello, boys." AJ hung her bag over the back of the chair. "What're you two cooking up?" She grabbed a wing from Javier's plate.

"I'll let him fill you in. Want a beer?"

AJ nodded. "The usual."

"Comin' up."

She turned to Javier and gestured at his open laptop as she sat. "Whatcha workin' on?"

He filled her in on the news about the property. "I'm working on an ad to put in the papers and online." He turned his computer around. "What do you think?"

"Let me see."

INTERESTED IN NEW and exciting job prospects with opportunities to travel domestically and abroad? Want to broaden your mind? Look no further— get in on the ground floor of a new business coming to Alexandria—The Brusch Agency. Must have a strong work ethic and be self-motivated. Previous experience highly desired but not mandatory. Job-specific training will be provided, where relevant, to successful applicants. Excellent pay and benefits. Details available upon application. Positions include:

Executive Assistant
Logistics Specialist
Computer/Software Expert
Research Analysts (2)
Private Investigators or applicable Military Specialties (6)
Accountant (part-time)

AJ NODDED. "You're missing an important position."

"What?"

"A short-order cook who knows how to make proper coffee."

Javier chuckled. "The executive assistant can keep the coffee coming, and I already spoke with Luke about food—they'll deliver."

"Where do I sign up?" AJ reached across the table and took Javier's hand.

"Job getting to you?"

AJ nodded. "I knew being sidelined behind a desk would stress me out, but I never realized how bad it could be. Endless meetings with no objective, stacks of paperwork, and no opportunity to keep my skills sharp. I dunno how long I'll be able to keep this up."

Javier squeezed her hand. "There's always a spot for you at The Brusch Agency." He chuckled. "Besides, your knowledge of tradecraft will be essential to the organization."

"I think being an equal partner would be more fitting." She pursed her lips. "What would my title be?" She raised her brows. "Not that it would matter."

"How about chief bottle washer?" Javier snapped his fingers. "Ah! Recreation specialist." He wiggled his eyebrows.

"That's inspiring." A hint of a smile creased AJ's face.

"I'm sure we can come up with a fitting title." Javier drained the last of his beer and took one of the two remaining wings, pushing the plate toward AJ. "Want anything else?"

AJ snatched the wing and chewed. She shook her head. "You're cooking tonight, remember? I'm all set for the ribeye steak, baked potato, and salad you promised."

"Shall we go?"

Both stood. After stopping by the bar to pay their bill, they headed out the door, arm-in-arm.

Bennie kept his camera focused on the entrance. *Great idea to check with the restaurant and tell them I was looking for Javier because his photos are ready. Hopefully, he'll show up.*

He grinned when his patience was rewarded, and he took more snaps. He muttered in Arabic, "As Allah wills." After his targets turned the corner, he picked up his phone and hit the speed dial. "Alberto. I found them!"

7

CIA Directorate of Operations
Langley, Virginia

AJ WEAVED through heavy traffic on the Capital Beltway, missing bumpers by inches. She leaned on the horn and cursed slower motorists before slamming a hand on the steering wheel of her gunmetal gray Honda Pilot. "Dammit, I'm late again. Do you think this is a parking lot? Move your ass!"

After blowing her horn at a Volvo crossing in front of her, she spotted her exit and sped along the breakdown lane, flying down the ramp. She flew through a red light and whipped her vehicle toward the security checkpoint at the CIA facility in Langley, skidding to a halt at the end of a line of cars waiting for access.

"C'mon, c'mon!" When her turn came, she flashed her badge toward the sensor and shot past the barricade before the arm fully lifted. She hurried along a line of parked cars, swerving into the first empty spot. Grabbing an executive parking pass from the console, she flung the placard on the dash, jumped out of her car, and raced inside through the pillars lining both sides of the lobby beyond the CIA seal.

Once through the turnstile, AJ rushed to the elevator, the heels of her black leather shoes clicking on the tiled floor. Two minutes later, she waltzed into her section and stopped for a black coffee at the community pot.

"About time, boss lady." MacKenzie Campbell twirled the end of a blonde plait as she leaned against the door to AJ's office. "I'm sure you said you would be coming in early—much earlier than this."

"Yeah, well ... things happen." She smiled as she stared into oblivion, remembering the previous evening with Javier.

"Heello! Earth to AJ." MacKenzie nudged AJ forward into the office before edging onto a chair.

AJ sat behind her desk and sipped her coffee. She grimaced. "Who made the coffee—I've had better dishwater." She lifted the drink to her lips and stopped. "In fact, it's terrible."

When MacKenzie laughed, it reached her blue eyes. "Claudia, the newest member of the team from the office next door. I heard she doesn't drink tea or coffee—only Coke—but wanted to help out."

"Definitely needs some training." AJ pushed the mug away. "So, anything new on the alert board for Latin America or projected to be heading our way? I have a meeting with the other heads of the counter-terrorism divisions, and they'll expect an update."

"Since you dealt with the drug cartel, FARC, and Islamic State triumvirate, things are still quiet in our area of responsibility. Even Mexico is bending to our requests for more information, whereas before they were reluctant partners."

AJ flicked her long, brown hair over her shoulder. "What's Makayla up to?"

"We might be identical twins, but she works out in the gym more than I do." MacKenzie laughed. "She's probably teaching some rookie the latest Krav Maga moves she learned."

"I pity the poor person. From time to time, I work out with Makayla, and it's no picnic. She means business and never lets up."

"That's why she's one of our best and why I don't train with her.

She always kicks my butt, and I've got the bruises to prove it. If only you'd allow us into the field, we could show what we can do."

AJ shook her head. "Ain't gonna happen. I told both of you before —your strength is in your research abilities. I don't think you're cut out for an overseas assignment yet. Perhaps one day."

MacKenzie rolled her eyes as her mouth opened and closed.

"When your sister decides to make an entrance, I need to speak with both of you. Something's come up which might pique your interest." AJ glanced at the wall clock. "I better get ready for the meeting."

MacKenzie stood. "Catch ya later, and I'll bring my errant sister."

AJ STROLLED into the conference room and sat at the oblong table in front of the Latin America placard. She placed her coffee mug down, glanced around the room, and nodded at two people she knew. *I'm not the last one for once. Wonder what's keeping everyone?*

The chief of the counter-terrorism center entered, followed by two section heads, who slid into their chairs. Eyes roaming around the room, the chief sat. "Begin."

Uh-oh. No pleasantries today. Wonder what's up his ass?

Each of the section leaders gave their updates.

The chief studied the ceiling. "Doesn't anyone have anything concrete to mention today? I can't believe the entire world is quiet." He pointed at AJ. "Latin America—what do you have?"

AJ swallowed. "Well, Chief. Like everyone else, our AOR is quiet at the moment. There's limited chatter but nothing to suggest any imminent threat. I—"

The chief slammed a hand on the table. "Dammit! I'm meeting with the director this afternoon. I can't go in and say we don't know what's going on."

AJ stared at the wall behind her boss. *Moron. Even when we give you the intel, you don't understand anything.* "I was going to say we are continuing to work with our 'Five Eyes' partners. There are rumors of

Hezbollah trying to expand their networks in South America, but nothing concrete so far. What we are seeing is an increase in cyber-crime. Some of it is related to drug cartels, but there's also an element that could be linked to external terrorist groups. Efforts are still underway to further investigate these links."

"Excellent." The chief grinned. "Something I can take with me. Keep on it." He stood and walked out.

AJ shook her head. *He's worse than the section chief I replaced. Is it worth my sanity to keep attending countless meetings that don't achieve anything?* She picked up her mug and suffered another sip before heading back to her office.

AJ GLANCED up from her computer screen when she heard a knock on her open door. She waved for the twins to enter.

As usual, they dressed alike—tan slacks, short-sleeve green tops, and braided hair. They plopped into the chairs in front of AJ's desk.

"So, what's up, boss?"

AJ shook her head. *I wish I could tell them apart. Can't go by their badges—they're always swapping.* "Good morning. Unless you'd like to be addressed as Thing One and Thing Two, please confirm your badges identify you properly."

Makayla and MacKenzie turned to each other, shocked expressions on their faces. "Us? Of course, our badges are correct."

"I guess I'll have to trust you." AJ opened a folder. "I haven't had a chance to update you, but last week I spoke with a friend in Operations. They have some openings coming up in basic field training."

Makayla and MacKenzie grinned.

"Unfortunately, your reputations preceded you. No one doubts you're both brilliant analysts—your IQ scores are off the charts. However, my friend thinks your over-exuberant personalities won't work in an environment where you can't draw attention to yourselves."

The twins looked at each other before speaking in unison, "But we can tone it down when needed."

"Field operatives must become part of their environment and not be noticed. Somehow, I don't see you fitting into this role." AJ raised a hand to ward off any further objections. "I'm sure the only time you two are introverted is when you're asleep."

Everyone laughed.

"So, what do you suggest?" Her badge identified her as MacKenzie, who often took the lead in speaking when the twins were together. "At first, working for the CIA was a thrill, but too many people are always telling us what to do. We don't require constant supervision."

AJ nodded. "I know this, which is why I keep my requests for updates from you to a minimum. However, many of your colleagues feel threatened by your brilliance and try to find something wrong with your work. After all, I don't think any of our other employees graduated from an Ivy League school at the age of nineteen."

Makayla raised a hand. "What can we do? This is our nature. We've been working here since graduating from Princeton. Yet, you're the only boss we've had who allows us to stretch ourselves and take on more assignments."

"I understand. Which is why I spoke with Human Resources today."

"What about?" MacKenzie's eyes seemed to widen with alarm. "Are we in trouble again? We said we wouldn't create any more disturbances in the cafeteria."

"No, you're not in trouble. I've been trying to find a way to tap into your genius without you being stifled by bureaucracy and might have come up with a solution."

"Cool! Tell us." MacKenzie and Makayla leaned forward.

"Hold on—you may not like it." AJ glanced from one twin to the other. "As you're aware, my friend Javier—"

"Yeah, more like a lover than a casual friend, if you ask me." Makayla struggled to hold her laughter. "Is that what the cool kids call their lovers these days?"

MacKenzie and Makayla turned to each other and fluttered their lashes. "Friend."

"Never mind." AJ tilted her head. "As I was saying, Javier's moving forward with his investigative agency. He happened to mention last night he needed at least two experienced research analysts who could work with minimal supervision."

"But we have jobs." MacKenzie frowned. "We might be good, but we're not magicians."

"Here's the deal. He's willing to take you both on a part-time basis. HR informed me it's possible for you to continue working here part-time if you decide to give the private sector a try. Javier also mentioned you would be required to go through the field training he'll be setting up."

'Woohoo!" The twins performed a celebratory dance while seated, arms above their heads as if they were cheerleaders.

"When do we start?" Makayla rubbed her hands together.

"As soon as Javier has everything up and running." *I hope he knows what he's in for. They'll drive him nuts.*

"Count me in." Makayla glanced at MacKenzie.

MacKenzie raised a brow. "Heck, yeah. If Javier hires us, will you be coming along? You keep telling us how much you detest being behind that desk. I remember you said there was a job for you, too."

"If you mouth off about that to anyone, I'll deny it." AJ grinned. "You better get back to work. I want to finish up and head out early for a change." *Need to do some thinking about my future, too.*

HER DAY COMPLETED, AJ secured her computer, spun the combination lock on her safe, and headed out of her office. Once in her car, she turned on the radio and began humming to a familiar classic rock tune.

She pulled into the rush-hour traffic and began the crawl home, her fingers tapping on the wheel to the sound of the music. When she reached her exit, she signaled and shot along the ramp.

The traffic light flicked to yellow.

AJ gunned her engine.

The piercing rip of an airhorn roaring at full blast filled the air.

AJ turned in the direction of the thunderous duo blasts of an air horn. Her eyes grew wide as an eighteen-wheeler sped through the intersection toward her. She spun the wheel and gunned the engine.

Baaang!

8

Virtue Feed & Grain
Old Town, Alexandra, Virginia

JUST BEFORE TWO P.M., Javier entered the area designated as the Stage Table, carrying his laptop under his left arm and a tall glass in his right hand. He sat at one end of the table—a solid wood structure large enough for sixteen guests. A pitcher of ice water and several glasses rested on a tray in front of him.

He yawned. *Long night rescanning the earlier applications, checking out their references, and reading the background checks.* While waiting for the computer to boot, he sipped his Diet Coke. *Plenty of experienced applicants. Should be enough to get The Brusch Agency up and running.*

He logged into his email—five more applications—all showing experience. *Now we're talking!* Javier scanned the latest submissions and grinned. *Pity they didn't respond earlier. Will keep this group on the back burner for now, but when we expand, I'll know where to turn.* He reread the first line of an email from the bank:

.   .   .

Based on your excellent credit report and the nature of your new business, we are prepared to loan you up to two hundred fifty thousand dollars.

HE CLOSED HIS EYES. *Yes! Things are falling into place.*

"Excuse me?"

Javier glanced up.

A clean-shaven man with a short slender build and dark red hair stood at the end of the table. "I-I'm a bit early. I'm Elton. Elton Taylor. I applied for the executive assistant job."

Javier motioned to the chair on his right. "Take a seat, Elton. Let me pull up your application and do a quick review." He read through the document. "Huh. Uh-huh."

"Excuse me, sir. May I have a glass of water?"

"Help yourself. And do us both a favor."

"What's that, sir?"

"Relax. Your application looks fine." Javier smiled. "So, why are you interested in working for The Brusch Agency?"

"Since I finished my degree at Northern Virginia Community College two years ago, I've been working as a receptionist and the manager's assistant at a senior citizens' home. It's okay, but ...."

Javier nodded for him to continue.

"I prefer something more exciting, and when I saw this position advertised online, I thought it was perfect. I live with my parents two blocks away, so I can be here whenever I'm needed. I'm a hard worker, too." A glimmer of a smile creased Elton's face.

Javier blinked at the mention of Elton's parents. "Do you realize there might be late nights and weekend work, not to mention you'd have to sign a nondisclosure form? That'd mean no discussion about any cases with your parents."

Elton's head bobbed. "Yes, sir. My parents are in good health so being away from them won't be a problem. I'm pretty tight-lipped about what I do, too."

"There are seven other applicants for this job."

Elton glanced at the table as his shoulders slumped in apparent rejection.

Javier raised a hand. "However, you're the only one with any related experience. You'd still need some training, but that's not a stumbling block. The job is yours—on one condition."

Elton locked eyes with Javier. "Yes, sir?"

"Well, there're two conditions." He tapped a finger against his lips. "The first is, stop calling me sir. And would it be okay for me to call you ET?"

"Yes, sir! I mean .... What should I call you?"

"My parents named me Javier, so that'll work." He stretched out a hand. "Welcome to The Brusch Agency. What are your plans for the rest of the day?"

ET grinned. "I was too nervous to eat, so I'm going to get a burger downstairs. Afterward, I'll share the news with my parents, if that's okay. Oh, I better give notice to my current boss, too. He'll be surprised."

"I tell you what. I'll pay for your meal. After you eat, if you want to get on the clock right away, come back up. You can use my laptop to take notes during the rest of the interviews."

"I'll be right back!" ET jumped to his feet and began rushing away. He stopped and turned back. "Thank you, sir, ah, Javier."

Over the next five hours, Javier interviewed twelve applicants, offering jobs to an IT specialist, a logistics expert, and four private investigators while ET took notes. With a short break before the final two interviews of the evening, Javier stood and paced before calling AJ.

He disconnected the call after the sixth ring. *Where is she? I thought she'd sit in on the interviews. Hope everything's okay. Perhaps work got in the way.*

Before he returned to his seat, a shadow blocked the light. Javier glanced over his shoulder.

A giant African American approached, a hand outstretched. "You must be Javier. I'm Thomas John Parker. My friends call me TJ."

Javier's hand disappeared in the handshake. He looked up into the man's face. "What are you, seven feet tall?"

An intense stare emanated from TJ's dark eyes. He spoke in a deep, resonant voice. "Not quite. Six foot nine."

"Take a seat." Javier gestured toward a chair and returned to his. "What was your military occupational specialty?"

"Ninety-seven echo."

Javier tapped his chin. *Fits—his mere presence would intimidate anyone.* "Interrogator, right?"

TJ nodded.

"Ever fire a gun at someone?"

TJ tilted his head and focused on Javier. "A stupid question. If you read my application, you know I served in Iraq and Afghanistan. Self-protection was paramount."

"Just wanted to hear your response." Javier grinned. "I'm planning to use two teams of investigators. One will be handling overseas assignments, and it's possible there might be some combat-oriented activities."

TJ smirked. "Sounds like where I belong—especially if there's danger—I thrive on it. What's the pay?"

"There'll be a one-year probationary period. During that time, you'll earn seventy-five thousand, plus overtime, expenses, and bonuses."

"Don't seem like much."

Javier gestured at ET.

"The average salary for a private investigator in Alexandria is sixty-two thousand, plus you would be responsible for your own overhead costs." ET glanced up from the screen. "The agency will provide medical insurance, which will also cover any requirements overseas, Metro or parking reimbursement, and a 401K package."

TJ flexed his biceps. "What about a gym membership?"

Javier shook his head. "No. Exercise and training equipment will be located on the basement level of our facility and be at your disposal."

"Count me in." TJ half-rose and offered a hand to Javier.

He stuck his hand into the vice and tried not to wince as TJ mangled it. Javier stood. "Welcome aboard. We'll be in touch in a few days with the contract."

TJ waved a hand and departed.

As soon as TJ disappeared from sight, Javier flexed his crushed fingers. "Hope the last guy doesn't have a grip like his. We better make sure our gym is fully equipped."

ET nodded and pointed toward the far end of the table. "Your visitor."

Javier turned and spotted a tall, well-toned woman with blonde hair and blue eyes. "Can I help you?"

The woman stepped forward. "I made an appointment— Samantha Bennett. Call me Sam."

Javier glanced at ET, who shrugged.

"Well, Sam, why didn't you put your full name on the application?" Javier gestured at an empty chair as he returned to his seat. "Please sit."

She smiled. "If I'd done that, would you have given me an interview?"

"Sure, why not? I don't care about anyone's gender or sexual preferences. What's important to me is whether a person can hold their own in a tough situation."

Sam gazed into Javier's eyes. "I believe you. Serving in a combat role in Afghanistan shows what I can do when cornered."

"Agreed. Although there's a bit of subterfuge with your abbreviated name, the job is yours if you want it—assuming your references and background check work out."

"I accept."

After shaking hands with Javier and ET, Sam left.

"That's the last interview." ET glanced at the screen. "I can't believe you filled all of the investigator positions in one day."

"I like to think I'm a pretty good judge of people and set up today's appointments with those I felt would make the grade based on the info in their applications. That's why I didn't ask a lot of questions during the interviews, as my mind was already made up. The jobs were theirs to lose." He chuckled. "Sam thought she was clever, but I had already uncovered her full name."

"Why did you pretend you didn't know?"

"I wanted to see how she would react. Same with TJ's interview. Thanks to the Army Chief of Staff, I had access to their service records, to include performance reports. The information contained in their applications was a perfect match. I also spoke with their former commanding officers. The short face-to-face interviews with Sam and TJ allowed me an opportunity to find out if they would be compatible with me."

"Wow! You were definitely prepared." ET gestured toward the laptop. "There are still some open research analyst positions. When should I set up those interviews?"

"I already have some people lined up—just waiting to hear if they're interested. If they are, no need to meet with anyone else." Javier stood. "Why don't you call it a night? We'll meet here again tomorrow at ten a.m. with the new logistics specialist and the IT guy —might as well get some furniture and equipment ordered."

"Sure thing."

JAVIER THUMBED HIS CELLPHONE CLOSED. *Where is she? I'm getting worried.* He leaned back in his chair and closed his eyes.

A chair scraped on the floor. "Every time I come in here, I always find you. Do you live here or something?"

Javier's eyes popped open. "What happened?" He pointed at the red welt across AJ's forehead. "I've been trying to reach you for hours."

She gently touched the area and winced. "You won't believe it. I was on my way here when an eighteen-wheeler came through the intersection straight at me. I slammed on the brakes, smacking my head against the windshield."

"There's more to it, or you would have been here earlier."

AJ grinned. "Can't fool you. It just missed my bumper as it roared past and crashed head-on into another vehicle, killing the car's driver and injuring the truck driver. I called 9-1-1 and waited for the ambulance and police to arrive because I was a witness. One of the paramedics checked me over—he wanted my phone number, too, so he could follow up." Her eyes twinkled. "Afterward, the police grilled me as if I had caused the accident."

Javier chuckled. "Yeah, your beauty would have mesmerized the driver, and he forgot what he was doing." He leaned across the table and squeezed her hand. "I'm glad you're okay." Their eyes locked, and he held her gaze. *Things are starting to add up and don't look good. Why are we in someone's sights, and who are they?*

"What do you think?" AJ waved a hand in Javier's face. "Hello... Where are you? You didn't hear a word I said."

"Uh. I was thinking."

"Is that what caused the smoke?" AJ laughed. "I spoke with MacKenzie and Makayla, and both jumped at the chance to work for you—us."

"What do you mean, us?"

AJ tilted her head, a smile reaching toward her eyes. "I'm still keeping my options open, but I'm leaning toward a career change, too."

"Fantastic! I filled the other positions today, so we're ready to rock and roll!" *I better give Cesar his first assignment—keep a discrete eye on AJ—she'll create hell if she finds out. I know she can look after herself, but it'll keep my nerves in check.*

9

F ixer-Upper Property
Outside Culpepper, Virginia

ALBERTO WHACKED Bennie across the face. "*Estúpido!* I didn't tell you
to follow them. You're not trained in surveillance. What if they
spotted you?" He glared at Bennie and stomped to his seat. "The
guard would have found it suspicious when you said you wanted to
deliver the package in person. He could also have heard you when
you shouted, 'Alberto, I found them!'"

Bennie's head dropped to his chest as he gazed at the floor. He
rubbed his face and gasped. "I-I did what I thought was right. You
wanted me to find them."

Alberto squeezed his hand into a fist. "Perhaps. But why didn't
you pay some kid on the street to find out where they went instead of
doing it yourself? I know why—you're estúpido." He shook his head.
"I gave you enough money to hire someone." *Perhaps I made a mistake
pulling him from the collapsed building and bringing him with me.*

"I didn't think."

"You got that right. In the future, just do what I tell you and nothing else. Remember, Allah is judging us." He gestured at the table. A small parcel wrapped in brown paper and tied with string sat in the center. "Keep taking photos of the targets from a distance. There's more cash in the package—use it to hire two or three locals who know how to follow people. No more amateur stunts."

"Yes, Alberto." Bennie reached for the parcel.

"Start moving your equipment to our new property. The address is written on the bottom of the package. Don't return here—Walter will be the only one still using this location."

Bennie nodded as he picked up the parcel. "I won't let you down, Alberto."

"I know you won't." *Or you'll meet Allah sooner than you expect.* He shook his head again. *Allah, I pray for deliverance from idiots.*

Two hours later, Alberto pulled into the driveway of their new rental property in Centreville. He stared at a mature maple tree in front of the red brick and gray vinyl-sided house. *In another life, perhaps I could have lived here.* He shook his head, got out of the car, and went inside.

Justin sat in a recliner in the family room, wearing torn jeans and a black shirt emblazoned with Nationals on the front and number thirty-one on the back. He turned down the volume of the TV. Although he kept his eyes on the European soccer match being shown, he climbed out of the chair and stood.

Alberto glared at him. "What happened in Langley? The driver you hired missed the target."

Justin shrugged. "I had my sniper scope on the intersection the entire time. The woman slammed on her brakes before the truck hit her. The driver drove past but couldn't stop in time—killing someone in another car."

"I know—I saw it on the news. What happened to the driver?"

"An ambulance took him to a nearby hospital, and I followed. He was in bad shape with a head wound. They also suspected he might have a concussion. I pretended to be a relative and begged to join him. At first, they said no."

"And?" Alberto frowned.

"Once they stitched him up in the emergency room, they allowed me to see him. With no one watching, I injected him with ten grams of pentobarbital. Alarms went off, and two nurses rushed into the room. They told me to wait outside, so I left."

"Won't they find the injection point?"

Justin shook his head. "No, I don't think so. I pushed the needle between two stitches on his face. There was enough drug to kill. Since he went into cardiac arrest, they'll assume he died because of the accident. Besides, he might have had a real heart attack—I don't think my injection would have worked so fast."

"Doesn't matter what caused his death. Well done." Alberto glanced at Justin's clothing. "What are you wearing? You look like a bum."

Justin crossed his arms. "You told me to find out what people in the area wore. I went to one of the shopping malls and watched decadent Americans wasting their money on trivial things and fast food. They love their sports teams, especially the Washington Nationals, so I bought one of their shirts." He glanced at his jeans. "This is the fashion. We used to patch clothes with holes, but here they buy them brand new, complete with damage."

"Did you get a shirt for me?"

"Yes, but with a different number—thirteen."

Alberto grinned. "My favorite." He sat on a leather sofa and motioned for Justin to return to the recliner. "Bennie will be arriving later. I told him we would no longer use the house in Culpepper—except for Walter. If the authorities capture him, they won't be able to link us to him."

"Won't he talk?"

"No. Unless the Americans send him to Guantanamo Bay, where they use enhanced interrogation techniques, he'll never give us up."

"Okay. I moved most of my equipment into a nearby storage unit.

I found a range where I can practice, but it only allows for distances up to five hundred yards."

"Will that be enough?"

Justin rubbed his chin. "I'd like twice the distance, but it'll do for now. I'll keep looking for something better."

WALTER BACKED the van as close to the rear door of the house as possible. After glancing around to see if anyone was watching, he opened the rear doors and unloaded two portable workbenches and several vises.

When he finished unwrapping his purchases, he stopped in the kitchen for a glass of cold water. *Better head to Save N Store.* He grabbed the key for the secure storage unit from a shelf near the door, hopped in the van, and started out of the driveway.

Walter stopped and stared at the house. He returned inside and headed to the living room. *I'll open the curtains—make it seem like someone's up. Otherwise, the nosy neighbors might stop by again to see if everything is okay.*

He returned to the vehicle and drove in a practiced manner, obeying all speed limits and traffic signs until he entered the storage facility.

Inside his medium-sized unit, he closed the roll-up door and turned on a flashlight. He checked the labels on the myriad containers and crates until he located what he wanted. *Wonder when the lights will be turned on? Would be easier than using a flashlight.*

Once he loaded the acetone, hydrogen peroxide, and sulphuric acid into the van, he wrapped each of the six bottles in foam padding and secured them in an upright position with elastic luggage straps. Satisfied, he began the journey home, stopping at a Burger King along the way.

Two hours later, Walter headed to the basement where he had set up his laboratory. *The Americans are their own worst enemy. Everything*

I need to make my bombs was easy to obtain. The hard part is not blowing myself up. May Allah guide my hands.

He used an oval metal animal-feeding trough to mix his ingredients. He took his time, not wanting to repeat the disaster of his first training session in making triacetone triperoxide when he lost two fingers on his left hand.

Finished, Walter moved to one of the portable workbenches, where a section of metal pipe rested between two vises. He marked equal lengths with exact precision and used a hacksaw to make the outer shells of his bombs. He smiled. *My favorite weapons—which will bring death to the infidels. Allahu Akbar!*

ALBERTO SAT on a bench near the Manassas National Battlefield Park. Closed because of darkness, he had the area to himself.

The flickering lights of an oncoming vehicle caught his attention.

Still no one.

A black Cadillac stopped in front of him. The trunk popped open.

Alberto stood and walked to the back of the car. He yanked out two gym bags and closed the lid.

After the car departed, he walked to his own vehicle, depositing the bags on the back seat. He checked the contents and smiled.

Plenty of cash to continue our war of revenge. In Allah's name, we shall triumph.

10

V irtue Feed & Grain
Old Town, Alexandria, Virginia

DRESSED in a blue sport shirt and tan chinos, his hair still damp from a shower, Javier sat at a corner table, waiting for three new employees, Elton, Sindee, and Bruno, to arrive. He opened his laptop and grinned as he reread the short email:

To: Mr. Javier Smith
From: Virginia State Corporation Commission
Congratulations! The establishment of The Brusch Agency as a Virginia Limited Liability Company is hereby approved and duly recorded in all relevant databases. Good luck!

. . .

JAVIER SIPPED ON AN ORANGE JUICE, the remains of his breakfast on a nearby plate. After checking for additional emails, he turned his laptop off.

"Good morning, sir!" Elton stood at attention near the table.

"Hey, ET. Stop with the formality. I told you before to call me Javier or boss but stop with the sir. That retired when I did. And don't call me Mister Smith." Javier gestured to an empty chair. "Take a seat."

"Yes, sir—I mean, okay, Javier." Elton grinned as he sat. "I'm so excited—this is my first stable job—with a professional."

Javier chuckled. "I hope I don't disappoint you. We both put our pants on the same way." He gestured at the menu, still on the table. "Want something to eat while we wait for the others?"

"No, thanks. I had a big bowl of Cornflakes this morning."

Of course, you did. I'm surprised it wasn't Wheaties. "Okay." He waved to a passing waitress and asked for a coffee.

She glanced at Elton, who nodded.

Javier reached down by a table leg and retrieved his backpack. He pulled out an envelope and pushed it toward Elton. "This contains your keys for our new property, along with the security alarm codes. There are also two copies of your contract. Check it over, and if you're satisfied, sign and date both of them. You keep one, and I'll take the other." Javier yanked two more envelopes from his bag. "These are for Sindee and Bruno. Take care of things for me."

Elton nodded. "Sure thing, boss."

Sindee and Bruno followed the waitress, who carried a loaded tray. After she deposited four cups, a pot of coffee, and a plate of donuts on the table, she departed.

"Everyone's made it." Javier grinned. "Let's eat and drink up. It's about a fifteen-minute walk to the office."

Conversation at the table trickled to a minimum as everyone became serious about claiming their share of the coffee and pastries.

Once everyone finished their snack, Javier waved for the tab.

A waiter rushed over, holding a black bill holder. "Anything else, sir?"

Javier shook his head. "Not today—time for us to head to work." He peeked inside the folder before pulling out his wallet. Slipping the funds and a substantial tip into the folder, he handed it back to the waiter and stood. "See you again—soon."

Once on the street, Javier pointed and set off at a rapid clip, the others trailing behind.

"Hey, boss." Elton stopped and sucked in air. "Where's the fire?"

Javier chuckled. "No fire—just need to work off the calories."

"Well, can we do it at a slower pace?"

Javier waited for the others to catch up. "It's good to push yourself when walking, especially in today's temperate weather, while enjoying the sunshine. When we arrive, I'll give you a tour of the building. ET's office is set since he'll be the face of our business, at least for any walk-ins. Sindee, you and Bruno will have your choice of offices."

When they approached the new home of The Brusch Agency, Elton glanced at the facade of the three-story brick building before scampering up the steps. He stopped in front of the light oak door and grinned as he pointed to the sign. "We're official!"

The others joined Elton, who, with great ceremony, pulled a key out of his pocket and released the lock. After pushing the door aside, he bowed. "Lead the way, boss."

Javier chuckled and stepped inside. A faint odor of fresh paint and varnish permeated the air. "Let's open some windows. Don't need anyone getting high from the fumes."

Sindee rushed to the nearest window. After struggling with the lock, she pushed the window open and took a deep breath. "Paint fumes always go for my chest." She coughed.

"I'll get the next ones." Bruno smiled as he opened two more windows without expending any effort.

Elton headed through an archway into an office on the left. "This is mine, I assume?"

Javier nodded. "Yes. No one gets past you without authorization." He joined Elton inside, with Sindee and Bruno following.

"All employees of the agency have unfettered access to this floor and the one above, as well as the basement." He glanced at his new employees. "The top floor will be my home. It's off-limits to everyone—employees and clients. Guests should be cleared in advance."

"No one?" Bruno frowned. "What if we have an emergency?"

"There'll always be exceptions, but that is my guiding rule. Everyone working here can come and go as they please. There's a small gym in the basement, along with showers. We'll use the kitchen at the back of this floor for our break room, and anyone who wants to try their hand at cooking can do so." Javier glanced at each of them. "One stipulation—no obnoxious odors."

Sindee glanced at Bruno. "Take heed."

"Who, me?" Bruno's face reddened.

The team laughed.

"Ready for the tour?"

AFTER THEY FINISHED THEIR WALK-THROUGH, they returned to the reception area.

Javier sat in a chair and motioned to the others to grab seats on the sofas facing one another near the large windows. "First things first. As you spotted on the tour, we're short of furniture and supplies. What we have came with the sale. Put your thinking caps on and make a list for your respective areas of responsibility. Don't scrimp on what you need, but the bank isn't bottomless."

Everyone laughed.

"The security system should be installed in the next day or so. Watch for anyone hanging around paying too much attention to the building."

"Got it, boss." Bruno popped one fist into the other.

"I'm heading upstairs for a bit. I dropped a load of my personal stuff off this morning before going to the restaurant but want to get it stored in a closet. The movers are supposed to deliver my furniture and the rest of my belongings tomorrow."

Elton raised his hand. "How long do you want us to hang around today?"

"As long as it takes to square away your area, ET." He handed a Sam's Club card to him. "I want you and Sindee to take a trip and pick up whatever we need. If they don't have it, figure out who does, and we'll get things arranged. Don't forget to sign the back of the card." He turned to Bruno. "I'm sure you'll have an idea of what you'll require in the IT arena." He held out a black American Express card and a small Post-It note. "Use this. The pin number is on the paper."

"We're on it, boss," Elton, Sindee, and Bruno chimed.

Javier shook his head. "I'll be upstairs." He pointed to the phone on Elton's desk. "Just hit one, and the phone will ring in my apartment."

AFTER CLIMBING up the stairs to his new home, Javier walked from room to room. With a master bedroom, two guest bedrooms, a living room, an eat-in kitchen, and a bathroom, the top-floor accommodation was perfect. *I'll use the smallest bedroom as a private office, so I don't have to traipse downstairs during the night.*

Javier sat on the sole piece of furniture. The chair creaked under his weight. As he stood to adjust the cushion, his phone rang. "Hello?"

"Hey, Javier. Zorkin here. The first group of background checks came back from the FBI. Everything's fine."

Javier grinned. "Excellent. So, nothing showed up to cause any concern?"

"Not a thing."

"Perfect. The first three are working downstairs now. When Cesar joins us, I want him to keep an eye on AJ without her finding out. I know she can look after herself, but I'll feel better."

"Anything in particular you're worried about?"

"No, but something is sending shivers up my arms when I think about her—especially after that incident with the truck."

"Understood. Listen, I gotta run. I'll be back to you as soon as the other background checks come in."

"Thanks again, Brian." Javier broke the connection and headed downstairs.

A MAN WEARING sunglasses sat in a black Ford F150 across the street from The Brusch Agency. He shuffled through the photos taken earlier when Javier and his employees arrived. *Excellent. Decent facial shots of each one. Need to find out where they live—perhaps some pressure to force one of them to let us inside. But which one is the weakest link?*

He started the engine and pulled into the sparse traffic, a grin spreading across his face. "Allah will judge you, and your blood will fill the streets."

11

T he Brusch Agency
       Old Town, Alexandria, Virginia

THE HARD SOLES of Javier's boots connected with each step as he thundered down the two flights of stairs to the ground floor. The reverberation of his footsteps marked his passing. Even the plush stair carpeting couldn't deaden the sound.

When he stepped into the reception area, Elton, Sindee, and Bruno stood in a semi-circle, their mouths agape.

He glanced from their shocked faces to behind him. Seeing no cause for alarm, he turned back and widened his arms. "What gives?"

"Sounded like the place was caving in, boss." A cheeky smile creased Bruno's face. "I didn't know whether to run or hide."

Elton and Sindee both nodded, tight lips attempting to block their grins.

"Can't help it if I'm a bit heavy on my feet—comes from being a ground pounder." Javier studied each employee and smiled. "You guys should look in the mirror." He laughed. "If I didn't know any better, I would think this a modeling agency." Javier put his hands on his hips. "I mean, check yourselves out." He pointed at Elton. "I didn't notice during the interviews, but what do I see today? Someone tall, rake thin with pronounced cheekbones, and dark red hair scraped back off his porcelain skin."

"I wanted to become a model, but my mother was against it." Elton pursed his lips. "She said to find a real job."

"Well, she might be right. I'm not sure how much male models make, but I heard it's less than women earn." Javier gestured at Sindee. "And look at you—a gorgeous blonde, poker-straight hair, doe-eyed and bee-stung lips. Do I detect a hint of Eastern European bone structure?"

"Yes, my grandmother was from Poland." Sindee flashed a glamourous smile. "I tried modeling, but one photographer was a perv—wanted me to strip and lie on a couch so he could shove his camera between my legs. That was enough for me—I went back to college."

Javier turned to Bruno. "What about you? I'm sure with your height, deep-set eyes, dark Bedouin curly hair, and a long-distance runner's physique, modeling would be something you might enjoy."

Bruno shook his head. "No, thanks!"

Everyone laughed.

"It would take some theatrical makeup for the three of you to blend into a crowd and participate in a stake-out. Good thing you'll be in the office—at least most of the time."

"Hello!" AJ strolled into the room. "Javier, I thought you were setting up an investigative agency." She smothered a grin with a hand. "Looks more like a talent agency."

"How did you get in? The front door is locked." Javier turned and glared at his new executive assistant.

Elton gulped. "Y-Yes it was."

"You forgot you gave me access." AJ dangled a set of keys. "I parked behind the building and came in through the back door."

Javier pursed his lips. "Sorry, ET. I should have known better."

"No worries, boss."

"So, what brings you here? Shouldn't you be saving the free world or something?"

AJ laughed. "Since you retired, perhaps some of your brain cells did the same. Did you forget you invited me over for a confab? MacKenzie will reach me if something urgent breaks."

Javier shut his eyes. He shook his head and grimaced. "Sorry, I forgot." He turned to his new team. "Wrap up what you need to and take the rest of the day off. Be here early tomorrow, and we'll move things forward." He offered an arm to AJ. "Shall we head upstairs?"

"As long as you behave yourself. Otherwise, ..."

"Promises, promises."

Elton, Sindee, and Bruno snickered as Javier and AJ departed.

JAVIER AND AJ climbed the stairs and entered the third-floor eat-in kitchen. "Coffee?"

"Of course." AJ pulled out a stool at the island. "How are things going?"

Javier poured coffee from the pot he brewed earlier. He placed a cup in front of AJ and sat in a chair next to her. "So far, so good. ET, Sindee, and Bruno are getting settled. I gave them corporate credit cards so they can order what they need for their respective areas. I'm hoping we'll be up and running within a week."

"Moving fast." AJ took a sip of her black coffee. "Did you give any more thought about my suggestion of a backup field team?"

"Yep. I think it's a fantastic idea. Never can tell when a situation might arise where an all-female field team might be needed. However, I don't have the funds right now to create one."

"I've been giving it some more thought." AJ raised a hand. "Hear me out before you discount my suggestion. You've already chosen two women to handle minor cases. Why not expand their training so they could be deployed in more dangerous situations to support the others?"

Javier nodded. "I want everyone working here to cross-train into other areas so we can be a lean and efficient force." He tapped a finger on his lips. "But I like groups of four. Where will I find the others?"

"Duh!" AJ pretended to pout. "Depending upon the situation and my availability, I could be part of the team. What about Sindee? I read her file—she's been doing some martial arts training and belongs to a shooting club."

"Would the CIA let you come and go at short notice, or are you still considering a career change?"

AJ laughed. "Still pondering. If I make the jump, I want to land in a suitable position."

"I'm sure it can be arranged." Javier nodded. "It's one thing to shoot at targets but something else when the targets can return fire. I'll set up a confidence course. First, we'll find out what Sindee and the others can do and set a baseline for training."

"That's all I ask." AJ leaned closer. "Anything else planned for today?"

Javier gave a soft laugh. "What did you have in mind?"

AFTER CLOSING UP THEIR AREAS, Elton, Sindee, and Bruno headed out of the building. Elton locked the door and joined the others on the sidewalk.

"See you guys tomorrow." Sindee gestured to her right. "My apartment is just down the street. Time to check on my cats and do a few laps in the pool."

"Have a great night." Elton and Bruno headed in the opposite direction.

Flicking her long hair, Sindee shouldered her blue and white backpack and dashed between moving vehicles to the other side of the street. She hummed "Strangers in the Night" by Frank Sinatra as she headed home.

Twenty minutes later, she turned left into a three-story apartment complex. As she unlocked an entrance door, a man appeared.

"Hold the door, please!"

Sindee propped the door open with her foot and turned.

The man held two shopping bags in each hand from the nearby grocery store. "Thanks. I'm Bennie. Just moved in today and needed some food and cleaning supplies. Have you lived here long?"

She pointed to the store's logo on the bags. "I shop there, too. It's so convenient." She smiled. "Welcome to the building, Bennie. I'm Sindee. Been here about two years. Which floor are you on?"

"Second. How about you?"

"Top floor in the corner away from the parking garage." She gestured toward his bags. "Can I give you a hand?"

Bennie shook his head. "Thanks, but I'm at the opposite end. Perhaps I'll see you around?"

"Sounds good. See ya. Maybe we can get together some time."

"I'd like that."

ONCE SINDEE ENTERED THE ELEVATOR, Bennie wiped the smile off his face. He left the building and crossed to a bronze late-model SUV. Tossing the bags in the back, he climbed in beside Justin, the driver. "I found out where she lives."

"Excellent. We'll come back this evening and grab her. Can we get in?"

"Yes, I checked—through the parking garage. There aren't any barriers."

Justin nodded. "Perfect. Let's find a place to eat."

"How about a bowling alley? They usually have decent food, and we can bowl and watch sports on their big screen while we wait."

"Excellent idea."

Five hours later, the bronze SUV returned to the apartment complex and headed into the multi-story parking garage. Justin backed into an empty slot closest to the third-floor walkway to the apartments.

They climbed from the vehicle and stepped out of the garage.

"Wait a minute—forgot my bag."

Justin pursed his lips. "Which way?"

Bennie returned to the vehicle, retrieved his backpack from the rear seat, and rejoined his accomplice. He pointed. "This way—at the far end."

They crabbed along the corridor. On the left, a safety railing to keep people from falling. On the right, doors identified each apartment. Curtains were closed, but shadows cast by internal lights filtered outside.

As they approached the end of the walkway, Bennie turned and put a finger to his lips. "Keep watch." He pulled a set of lock picks out of his back pocket. "Shouldn't take long—these locks are simple to bypass."

Justin gave a thumbs-up.

Bennie knelt by the door and worked his magic. The door swung inward, and he slinked inside, a cat rushing outside.

A woman sat on a sofa, her back to the door. Headphones covered her ears as she pecked away at the keypad on her phone.

Bennie crept forward, pulling an extendable baton from his bag.

Thwack!

The headphones popped off as the woman's body tilted to the side.

Bennie took zip ties from one pocket and secured her hands. From another pocket on the side of his backpack, he pulled out a roll of duct tape. After he stretched a piece across her mouth, Bennie picked her up in a fireman's carry and dashed out of the apartment.

Justin covered their escape, his gun aimed at an approaching figure, lowering it when he recognized his partner. "That her?"

"Yeah, let's get out of here before someone spots us!"

They shoved the woman into the back seat.

Justin gunned the engine, tires squealing as they headed toward the parking garage's exit.

Little did Justin and Bennie know, but when they pushed their captive into the SUV, a necklace with the script *Heidi* fell onto the ground.

12

T
he Brusch Agency
Old Town, Alexandria, Virginia

ELTON YAWNED as he studied the early morning sky. Shades of red, yellow, and orange fought for dominance as dawn arrived. He turned and unlocked The Brusch Agency's front door and stepped inside. As he entered the reception area, a noise startled him.

Clink.

He picked up a heavy-duty stapler from his desk and followed the sound, stopping outside Javier's office. Elton eased the door open.

"Good morning, ET." Javier pointed at the stapler. "Hunting?"

Elton's face reddened. "I—I heard a noise and came to investigate."

Javier put his coffee cup on the saucer, creating yet another clink. "I think you need some firearms training. You won't stop many people with your weapon of choice." He slid a hand across his face, attempting to smother a grin. "I'll set something up."

"Yeah—well, when you put it like that, I agree." Elton sat in a chair opposite Javier's desk, keeping the stapler in his lap. "What's the plan for today?"

"I received a text last night from an old friend—Mitch Delmonico. He's with the Drug Enforcement Agency and will be stopping by later today. Show him right in when he arrives."

"Will do." Elton glanced at the triangle shape of an American flag inside a display case on the credenza. "The supplies I ordered will be delivered later today. We need to buy a few furnishings for your office, too. Way too spartan."

"Guess I'm a frugal type of guy." Javier waved a hand, encompassing the room. "Do what you think is best to spruce up your area and my office. We need to project professionalism and competence while also providing a welcoming environment."

Elton grinned. "You can count on me." He stood and strode down the corridor to reception.

The doorbell rang. He rushed to the main entrance and glanced through the peephole.

Two workmen dressed in the uniform of a local supplier stood outside. Each man leaned against a laden hand truck.

Elton popped the door open.

"Delivery for Elton Taylor."

He nodded and leaned against the door. "Right on time. Can I see your paperwork?"

"Just a sec." A heavyset workman pulled a clipboard from the top of his hand truck and handed it to Elton.

He scanned the invoice. "Seems in order." He gestured to the reception area. "Just unload everything, and I'll sort things out later."

"Gotcha. We have another load to bring in."

When the men finished, the heavyset man handed Elton the clipboard. "Double check the invoice and sign on the dotted line."

He scanned the document and scribbled at the bottom of the page. "Many thanks."

The man removed a copy and handed it to Elton. "You're welcome."

As the men departed and Elton began to shut the door, someone shouted in a thick New York accent.

"Hold the door!" A short, swarthy man with black wavy hair, wearing jeans and a sports coat, dashed up the stairs.

"Thanks. I'm Mitch. Javier is expecting me."

Elton nodded. "Right this way. Would you like a coffee?"

Mitch shook his head. "No thanks. Had my limit for the day."

After Mitch entered Javier's office, Elton returned to reception to unpack the delivery.

JAVIER STOOD and offered a hand to his long-time friend. After shaking, they sat in front of Javier's desk. "So, what can I do for the DEA?"

Mitch laughed. "That's what I've always liked about you—no beating around the bush."

"When I was in the military, I used to call it efficiency. Now, time is money." Javier chuckled.

"Couple of things. First, I want to congratulate you on your retirement."

Javier nodded. "Many thanks. When are you pulling the plug?"

"Me? Not for a few more years. My oldest son is a freshman at Georgetown, and the other will join him next year. After they graduate, Bella wants to head back to Lombardy where she grew up."

"Sounds like a plan."

"Figure I'd buy a cab and schlep people around—at least when we're not checking out the vineyards." He shook his head. "Not sure yet. Bella wants to open a deli."

"Why not both?"

"I thought the same, but she wants to do something together." Mitched sighed. "Plenty of time to make our minds up. The primary reason for dropping in was to dangle some work in front of you."

Javier leaned forward. "Whad'ya got?"

"A British colleague of mine needs some help. Intel revealed a drug smuggler is using Bermuda as a base to ship his product into Florida."

"Why aren't you taking care of it?"

Mitch frowned. "We're overstretched in the area, and this guy's volume is too small for us to take an interest in—at least right now. This would be an off-the-books assignment, which would give you an easy win while at the same time, I'll improve relations with the British."

"What do you need from us?"

"Surveillance of the smuggler's routine, contacts ... that sort of thing. Nothing too difficult."

"What's the risk assessment?"

Mitch pursed his lips. "I understand it's low—at least the druggie isn't known to be prone to violence. He doesn't have a big group—six at the most."

Javier pursed his lips as he stared at the ceiling. "Okay. How many operatives do you think we'll need?"

Mitch pulled an envelope out of his coat pocket. "I think three or four max to handle this. All the details are here, including Cedric's contact info."

"Cedric?"

"The name of my British counterpart."

Who to use? Perhaps a couple of the Snakes can take some leave. Take two of my new team. Should be enough. Or just one Snake and three newbies—good way to give them some experience. "Count us in."

"Fantastic!" Mitch glanced at his watch. "I better run—have a meeting in an hour at headquarters. If any questions arise, give me a shout."

The men stood and shook hands.

Javier showed Mitch back to reception.

A distraught Sindee sat in a chair, chest heaving, eyes wide.

"What's the matter, Sindee?" Javier rushed over.

"S—Sorry, I'm late. L—Last night. A problem at my apartment building." She took a deep breath. "I've been with the police all morning."

"Go to my office—I'll be right there."

"Okay." Sindee hurried along the corridor.

Javier turned to Mitch. "Thanks again for stopping by and offering the work. We'll get moving on this ASAP."

"Do you need my help first?" He pointed toward Javier's office. "She seems distraught."

"Naw. Got it covered, but thanks."

Mitch nodded and headed out the main door.

JAVIER RETURNED to his office and sat behind his desk. He picked up his cup, took a swig of lukewarm coffee, and grimaced. He set the cup down. "Fill me in."

A more composed Sindee nodded. "Last night, someone broke into my neighbor's apartment. Early this morning, one of her cats was scratching at my door. When I opened it, the cat meowed and wandered in. I went to my neighbor's door—her name is Heidi— Heidi Ross. The door wasn't shut, which is how the cat escaped—she never lets them out."

"What did you do?"

"I called to her, but no response. Thinking she might be in the bathroom and didn't hear me, I nudged the front door open wider, stepped inside, and called again. A glass was knocked over on the coffee table, with red wine spilled on the carpet. Heidi's phone was on the floor—she never went anywhere without it." Sindee shuddered.

"Relax—you're doing fine. No sign of her?"

She shook her head. "I looked in each room. Her apartment is a mirror image of mine, so I know the layout. She wasn't home, so I checked with reception in case she had run down there and didn't shut her door. They hadn't seen her either. The manager dialed 9-1-1 and reported a possible kidnapping."

"Perhaps, your neighbor was out of paper towels to clean up the mess and went to the grocery store."

"Could be, but it's not far away. Anyway, a police car showed up with two officers. I showed them to Heidi's apartment. One of the cops called her name—still no response. They checked in each room then focused on the spilled wine."

"Hmm."

"There was some blood, too. They called for backup and a forensics team." Sindee gasped, pulled a card and her phone from her bag.

"Remember something?"

"Yes! What if I was the target?"

"Why would you think that?"

"Other tenants always teased Heidi and me. They said if they didn't know us, they would think we were sisters. Same height, body shape, hair color." Sindee frowned. "Could it be a case of mistaken identity?"

Is she right? Is it a case of mistaken identity, or did someone think they could use her to get to us? Maybe a prank? Or is the person who sent the photo of six beheadings somehow involved?

Javier grabbed his coat and stood. "Let's go."

"Where?"

"Police station." *Don't know what's up, but we better find out—before someone gets hurt. If Sindee was the intended victim, we'll need to arrange a safe house and a surprise.*

13

H ideout
Centreville, Virginia

HEIDI STIRRED from a fetal position on a cold concrete floor. She raised her head and eased an eye open. Dim light emanated from a solitary fixture on the ceiling at the bottom of a set of stairs. Faint footsteps came from above.

She struggled to a kneeling position. Heidi touched her face, and a whimper escaped from her swollen lips. Dried blood crusted her upper lip.

"Help." Heidi gasped. "Please. Someone. Help .... Me."

She collapsed.

HEIDI AWOKE TO DARKNESS. Something scurried across the floor. A blanket was draped over her. She felt around—still clothed. *Thank*

God! She touched the back of her head and felt a goose egg. She winced before passing out again.

AFTER SHE REGAINED CONSCIOUSNESS, the same dim light cast eerie shadows around the room. Someone had placed a bottle of water and a sandwich wrapped in plastic next to her, along with a rolled rug.

Pushing herself onto her knees, she drank half of the lukewarm water. She wet her fingers and dabbed around her nose and mouth to rinse off the dried blood. Voices in the distance—strange, yet familiar.

Heidi pulled the sandwich from the bag and sniffed. "Ugh—I hate peanut butter."

Her stomach growled in response.

She nibbled the edge of the bread to minimize eating the filling, turning the sandwich as she progressed. When she finished, Heide drained the remainder of the water, unrolled the rug, and stretched out, covering herself with the blanket.

Tears trickled down her face. *Where am I? What are they going to do to me?*

THE DOOR at the top of the stairs banged open. A second light popped on, illuminating Heidi's prison. Footsteps rushed down the steps.

"Get up!" Someone wearing a clown mask kicked Heidi in the ribs.

She groaned, grabbing her side. "Stop! Please stop! Why are you doing this to me?"

"I want information about your boss—you will tell me everything, or you'll be sorry."

Heidi struggled to a sitting position and stared at the man, her eyes blinking with confusion. "My boss is married—has three kids. I—"

The man backhanded her. "Don't play games with me. Your boss is single."

"But ...." Heidi rubbed her face where the man's long fingernails scratched her skin. "I babysit for Mr. and Mrs. Brown every weekend when they go dancing."

"Liar!" The man reared back, ready to throw another punch at her. "His name is Smith."

"Have—have you confused me with someone else? I'm a cashier at Giant. Matt Brown is my boss and has been since I started work four years ago." She shook her head. "I don't know anyone named Smith."

Without a word, the man turned and raced up the stairs, shutting the main light off before slamming and locking the door, plunging the basement into darkness.

Heidi's head dropped onto her hands. Tears streamed, wetting her stained shirt. *Where am I? What's going on?*

ALBERTO SAT at the kitchen table in the Centreville house. He twiddled his thumbs while he waited for Bennie to return from the basement. He turned when a door slammed.

Bennie lunged into the room and grabbed an empty chair. He pounded a fist on the table before shoving the seat back and banging his head on the table.

Alberto chuckled. "Well? Did the woman talk, or does she need to be persuaded?"

Bennie glanced at him. "I think she's lying. She's definitely the woman who came out of Smith's building. I followed her straight to her apartment."

"Did she recognize you when you grabbed her from the apartment or dragged her downstairs?"

"No. I'm sure she didn't. I knocked her out before we took her. When I went downstairs, I wore a mask." He tossed the mask on the table.

Alberto shook his head. *A clown mask—typical. These men are clowns.* "Perhaps, I should speak with her."

"A great idea." Bennie grinned. "You should be able to extract what you want from her. Perhaps threaten her with rape? She's a brazen infidel who should learn her place."

"If I cannot get what I need, we will dispose of her. What you do with her at that time is none of my concern." Alberto stood and went to the fridge. He pulled out two bottles of water and a bar of Hershey's chocolate, shoved them in his pockets, and headed to the stairs.

"Do you want to borrow my mask?"

Alberto tilted his head. "I thought you would use a scary mask, not one to delight children. Better to show my face and threaten her if she doesn't speak." He opened the door and flicked on the extra light.

Bennie followed.

Alberto raised a hand. "Remain here. I shall handle this myself." He turned and shuffled down the stairs.

HEIDI DOZED after Clown Mask disappeared. The bright light disturbed her. *Now, what? More scare tactics?* She knelt, facing the stairs.

When Alberto reached the basement floor, he glanced around. Spotting several chairs, he picked up two and approached Heidi. He stopped in front of her and placed one of the chairs near her. "Please, sit. It must be uncomfortable on the floor."

After she sat, Alberto did the same. He reached into his pockets. "Are you thirsty? Perhaps hungry?"

When she nodded, he twisted the cap and offered the open bottle. "Drink."

Heidi grabbed the bottle and took a deep swallow, water splashing down the side of her face and onto her clothes. She stopped when over half the water was gone.

"Chocolate? We don't have much food right now, but there is a

Hershey bar or two. If you answer my questions, I will send someone to Burger King."

She tore into the smooth milk chocolate. Heidi ate part of the bar before using the wrapper to cover the rest and dropped it on the blanket.

"Excellent. Are you ready to answer my questions?" Alberto smiled.

Heidi nodded. "I think so. But I told the clown about my boss. He called me a liar and threatened to rape me." *He didn't, but this guy doesn't know the truth.*

"Tell me what you told my colleague."

As Heidi reiterated her earlier conversation, Alberto watched for any telltale signs of lying: change of voice, the direction of her eyes, and unusual gesticulation.

When she finished, Alberto tapped a finger on his lips. "I'm not sure everything you said is the truth."

Heidi hung her head. *How did he know?* "I gave a little white lie when I said how long I had worked at the store. I only began there six months ago. But, I've known my boss for four years and have been babysitting for him during that time. Everything else is accurate."

Alberto stood. "I see."

Before Heidi could react, Alberto shot forward, slamming a fist into her chest.

The chair rocked back, and she tumbled to the floor. A whimper escaped her lips.

"Your lies will be your undoing. You will remain here until you convince me otherwise."

Heidi rubbed her chest. She took a deep breath and grunted. *Can't let him know how much that hurt—he'll keep doing it until he kills me.*

"You will stay in the dark. No more water or food." He walked up the stairs and flicked the lights off. After shutting the door, he locked it.

Heidi lay on the carpet in the dark. She heard the footsteps fade.

I'll rest and see if I can find something to use—anything that might work as a weapon. It works on detective shows, so why not for me?

ALBERTO RETURNED to the kitchen where Bennie still sat, Justin next to him, typing on a laptop.

With a sigh, Alberto sat in his chair. "Justin, find an abandoned gravel pit or something similar. The girl doesn't know anything." He turned to Bennie. "You grabbed the wrong girl. How could you screw this up?" *They can't do anything right. How did I offend Allah to end up with these incompetent subordinates?*

Bennie shook his head. "But Alberto. Look here." He yanked his phone from a pocket and thumbed through several photos. "Here." He tapped the screen. "This is the girl I followed. I took her photo before she crossed the street."

"Hmm. The woman downstairs does look the same. Perhaps a sister?"

"Maybe, Alberto." Bennie shrugged. "What should we do now?"

Alberto turned to Justin. "Find anything?"

"Yes. About an hour away—an old gravel pit. From what I read, the company removed what they wanted, let rainwater fill in the excavation area, and stocked it with fish. Now, the area is a local hangout for fishermen and couples."

Alberto rubbed the scar along his chin, the result of his previous encounter with Javier. *Could we use her to draw out the one we want?* He shook his head. *Too dangerous—she might find a way to warn them.* "Do it. Take her when it is almost dark. In case someone spots you, Bennie, you will pretend to be her lover, and Justin will be her brother. When you find a good place, take care of her."

Bennie nodded. "Don't worry, Alberto. We will ensure she doesn't leave the area—alive."

Justin grinned. "Any problem with having some fun with her first?"

"You can threaten her with rape, but don't defile her." Bennie pursed his lips. "If she's the wrong girl, a swift end is what she needs —nothing else."

"As long as you finish the job, I don't care what you do." Alberto stood. "I'll be in the living room—there's a baseball game I want to watch. Something to do with tigers and Indians."

AFTER THE SUN SET, Bennie and Justin headed to the basement. Both wore clown masks. One of them flicked on the dim light, and they thundered down the stairs.

Heidi bolted upright, keeping the chair between her and the two men. "Stay away from me!"

"Relax, Princess." Justin stepped closer, a cloth in his hand. "We're going to take a little ride."

Heidi rushed to a corner of the room, pressing her back against the wall. "Don't come any closer, or I'll—"

"You'll what?" Bennie pointed at the ceiling. "Sound-suppression tiles. While someone upstairs might hear you, no one outside this building will." He grinned. "You belong to us."

Heidi jerked away as Bennie tried to grab her hand. She swung a fist, catching him on the side of his mouth. "Bastard!" She stepped forward, thrusting a knee between his legs.

He collapsed to the floor, hands cupped over his injured groin.

Before Heidi realized where the other clown was, Justin grabbed her in a bear hug. He worked the cloth into Heidi's mouth before pinning her against the wall.

"Help me, Bennie!" Justin grabbed one of Heidi's hands and wrenched it behind her back. "Quit playing with yourself and tie her up."

"But she kneed me. It hurts like hell!"

"Just help me." Justin grabbed Heidi's hair and slammed her forehead into the wall.

She dropped to the floor.

THE ROCKING of a vehicle brought Heidi out of her stupor. She moaned as she struggled against her bonds, eventually yanking a hand free from the loosely-tied rope. *Where are they taking me?* She glanced around and spotted the glow-in-the-dark, T-shaped release tab installed in the trunks of newer vehicles. *Need to wait for a chance to escape—going too fast right now.*

The car slowed and turned to the right, continuing along a rut-filled road.

Heidi bounced a few times against the trunk's roof. "Ow!"

A few minutes later, the vehicle stopped. Two doors slammed.

Footsteps drew near.

Heidi tensed as she grasped the release tab.

The trunk opened. Hands reached inside and yanked her out, dumping her onto the ground.

Both men laughed.

One waved a gun. "Get up, Princess. Time to go." Justin gestured toward a thicket. "We're gonna have some fun."

Heidi pretended to stumble, keeping her hands together as if they were still tied, as she followed a narrow path along the edge of a lake. When one of them grabbed her, she lashed out with a foot, catching the man in the kneecap.

"Get out of the way, Bennie! She's gonna escape!"

Heidi ran through the thick trees. "Help! Rape!"

A shot echoed across the water. "Come back, bitch!"

Another shot.

Heidi screamed and lurched forward.

Justin stood over her, the pistol aimed at her head. "You're mine."

14

T he Brusch Agency
Old Town, Alexandria, Virginia

JAVIER WANDERED into the conference room carrying an iPad, followed by AJ. Seven of the twelve brown leather chairs surrounding the rectangular oak table were occupied.

After taking his seat at the head of the table with AJ to his right, he glanced around the room. "Once the money starts rolling in, we might need a bigger place."

Everyone chuckled.

"Anyone see TJ?" Javier raised a hand high in the air to mimic TJ's height.

"Right beside you, boss." TJ spoke in his normal soft but deep voice.

Javier turned and glanced upward. "How about climbing down from those heights and joining us?"

"Sure thing." TJ took an empty seat.

"Okay, now that everyone's here, a couple of announcements." He gestured toward AJ.

"Sindee, I spoke with one of my contacts in the Alexandria police." A slight frown creased AJ's forehead. "No sign of your neighbor yet, but they've put out the word to their confidential informants. A check of available CCTV cameras didn't provide any leads so far, although one device did capture a late-model SUV leaving the parking garage around midnight. The vehicle was yellow or bronze. Are you aware of anyone in the building with a vehicle like this?"

Sindee shook her head.

"No plates on the SUV, so this appears to be a planned incident. When I hear more, I'll pass it along."

"Many thanks, AJ. Let's hope they find Heidi soon." *Alive.* Javier glanced from Sindee to AJ. "While everyone's getting settled in, I want to establish some routine. Every Monday and Friday, we'll meet here for about an hour. At Monday meetings we'll discuss any new business and events from the weekend, while on Fridays, we'll catch up on what's happened during the week. Any questions?"

"Yes." Sam glanced at the others before directing her attention toward Javier. "What if something urgent comes up?"

Javier nodded. "Good point. Of course, if something warrants the attention of the entire team, we'll drop everything and discuss it. I think we can all agree, the fewer routine meetings, the better we'll all function."

He opened the iPad and read for a few moments. "Okay, team. We have our first overseas client, compliments of the DEA."

"Who gets the assignment?" Wilder "Wild" Harris swept his hands through his thick, brown hair.

"There'll be four. The team lead will be one of the Snakes, but I don't know which one yet—depends on who can break away from their normal duties and use some of their accumulated leave." Javier gazed at the eager faces. "Sam, Wild, and TJ—you're up. Cesar, I'll talk to you later—I have something separate for you."

"All right!" Sam and Wild high-fived.

TJ pursed his lips and focused an intense stare on Javier. "So, what's the job? I assume the mission is drug-related, but where?"

Javier grinned. "Have any of you been to Bermuda?"

They all shook their heads.

"Your contact will be Doctor Cedric Yates. He's aware of an American drug smuggler using the island as a transit point to push his product into Florida. Dr. Yates would prefer the U.S. deal with him. Not enough volume to interest DEA since they're stretched to the breaking point, so they contacted us.

"The team leader will be here tonight." Javier turned to Sindee. "Set up flights, hotels, and two rentals for three days from now. Plan everything for a ten-day vacation—things will be adjusted based on what the team uncovers."

Sindee nodded. "What about visas? Can we get them in time?"

Javier shook his head. "I checked last night. Not needed for visits of less than six months."

"I've arranged a specialist training program for you. Not long— two days at a private facility near the Farm." AJ glanced at Sam, Wild, and TJ. "You'll get a day of personal security and a day on the pistol and rifle ranges." AJ chuckled. "Rest up—you'll need it as the instructors will try to grind you down and won't let up during your training."

"Any other questions?" Javier surveyed his team. When no one spoke up, he nodded. "Okay. Back to work."

Moments later, Javier and AJ settled themselves in Javier's office. Each held a cup of black coffee. After blowing on his steaming drink, he grinned. "Hard to believe a dream is coming together."

"Yeah. I'm glad Phil decided to retire and join you. Although I'll miss him in the office, he'll be a great asset."

"Anyone else I can steal?" Javier chuckled.

"Now that you mention it—no." AJ's eyes glinted with excitement. "Well, there might be someone available soon."

"Who? Have you made up your mind yet, or are you enjoying being desk-bound at the CIA?"

"Don't push it—if it's meant to be, you'll be the first to know." She drank some of her coffee, wincing at the strong flavor. "Who made the coffee?"

"ET. Why?"

"Taste it."

Javier took a sip, almost dropping his cup. "Remind me never to let a tea drinker make the coffee. I enjoy my coffee, but this is thick enough to repair potholes."

"Agreed. I think he needs some on-the-job training."

"Care to show him?"

"Sure. Before I go, I have an update on that trucker who tried to run me over. According to my police contact, he's still in the hospital —it seems he suffered a concussion when his head smacked against the windshield. They're keeping him for a few more days."

"Still think it was a random accident?"

"I'm not sure. No driver's license or insurance documents. Nothing to indicate who owns the vehicle. Everything's a mystery." AJ glanced at her watch and stood. "I better go. Need to provide an update at today's counter-terrorism meeting with the director. Later on, I'll send Sindee a list of companies she can contact to arrange comms gear, weapons, and anything else you might need."

Javier rose and brushed his lips across her cheek. "Have an enjoyable day. You coming over this evening?"

"You bet."

After AJ departed, Javier returned to his desk and picked up the handset on the newly installed phone system. He punched a button labeled Cesar. "Can you come in for a minute?"

"Be right there."

Moments later, a squat, muscular man with close-cropped black hair entered. He spoke English with a Puerto Rican accent. "What's up?"

"I need you to do me a favor, but it'll be difficult."

Cesar laughed. "That's why you hired me, right?"

"Good point. The job has two objectives. First, I want you to see what you can uncover about the accident AJ had. The police haven't identified the trucker yet. See what you can find out."

Cesar nodded. "One of my buddies might be able to assist—he's a police detective who owes me. What's the second objective?"

"I'm having another strange feeling—one like someone's watching us. Remember I mentioned the photo I received with six headless bodies? Something about that snap I can't shake." Javier pursed his lips. "I'm not sure why, but I wonder if the woman is supposed to represent AJ? Who did we piss off?"

"You only had the one mission together, right?"

Javier nodded. "Yeah. As far as I know, all but one of our opponents were killed. But the body of an Argentinian named Alberto was never found." *Is he behind AJ's accident and the kidnapping of Sindee's neighbor?* He shook his head. *Too much of a coincidence.*

"What do you want me to do?"

"Keep an eye on AJ. Don't let her catch you. She'll make both our lives miserable." *And kick my butt, too.*

Cesar stood. "On it, boss. I'll give you an update as soon as possible."

"Thanks, Cesar. I knew I could count on you."

ABOUT FIFTY YARDS from the front of the building, two men dressed in T-shirts with the logo of local sports teams and blue jeans leaned against a wall partially hidden by overhanging branches of an oak tree.

As Cesar left the building, they hopped in an older model gray Toyota Corolla. They pulled away from the curb, following Cesar.

The passenger used his cellphone to snap a photo as they passed. He checked the quality. "Good enough." He turned to the driver. "Let's head back. Perhaps we'll spot someone else."

15

Disused Gravel Pit
Outside Independent Hill, Virginia

HEIDI ROLLED ONTO HER BACK, chest heaving. She turned her head and raised her hands, a fruitless gesture to defend herself from a fired round. Tears trickled down her face as she squeezed her eyes shut.

Justin leaned closer, his pistol aimed at Heidi's stomach. "You deserve to be gutshot, bitch. I want you to suffer!"

"Wait!" Bennie grabbed Justin's arm. "What are you doing? Alberto—"

"Shut up." Justin glared at Bennie as he pulled away. "What's the matter with you? We were told to take care of her. Besides, I want her to suffer. A gutshot will cause more pain and take longer to kill her."

Bennie shook his head. "I understand. But it's my fault we took the wrong girl. It shouldn't end this way." He stepped forward.

"Why do you care?" Justin shook his head. "She's an infidel."

Heidi's eyes flicked from one kidnapper to the other as they debated what to do with her. *Will I get another chance to escape?* She glanced to her left—the lake was nearby. *Perhaps a way out? I'm not an Olympic swimmer, but I'm desperate to get away from them. The adrenaline should give me the burst I need.*

"It makes no difference—we can't start killing everyone."

Justin focused on Heidi's face, his finger tightening on the trigger.

Heidi stared at him. *Although I'm scared out of my mind, I won't show any fear.* She grabbed a handful of sand and flung it at her executioner.

"Aah!" Justin jerked his arm as the sand struck his face.

Blam!

In a reflex action, he pulled the trigger, missing the side of Heidi's head by no more than an inch.

"No!" Bennie shoved Justin to the ground and fell on top of him, fists flailing.

Heidi scooted across the sand, rushing into the cold water. With a brisk pace, she swam away from the shore, her now-soaked clothing causing her to struggle.

Shouts behind her caused Heidi to slow and take a quick look.

Both men were now on their feet but still struggled for control of the pistol.

Heidi's adrenaline kicked in as she resumed swimming, veering toward an older couple sitting on a beach and a man fishing on his own on the other side of the small lake. She made short work of the distance, her long arms and legs biting into the water, straining muscles to escape and propelling her along.

"Help!" Heidi cruised into shallow water in front of the fisherman.

The man dropped his rod and rushed across a stony area into the water. "Give me your hand."

Heidi extended a hand as she stumbled on a submerged rock.

"Are you alright? Let me help you." He grabbed her arms and guided her to shore.

"T-Two men tried to kill me." She pointed across the lake.

"Where?" The fisherman turned to the couple. "Hey Larry, Jenny! This woman needs your help."

The woman yanked a blanket from a beach chair, rushed forward, and draped it over Heidi's shoulders.

"What happened?" The fisherman led her to his empty chair as Larry approached.

"I—I was kidnapped." She pointed to the far side of the lake. "Two men—t-they were going to kill me." Heidi held a hand on her forehead as she scanned the area from where she escaped. "I don't see them—I hope they left."

The woman pulled a phone from her bag. "I'll call 9-1-1."

"No! Do you mind if I call a friend instead?"

The couple glanced at each other. After the man nodded, the woman gave Heidi the phone.

Before entering a number, Heidi glanced around. "Where are we?"

"An abandoned gravel pit near Independent Hill." The man reached into his bag and pulled out a pistol and his Virginia State Police identification. "Don't worry—we'll protect you."

A glimmer of a smile creased Heidi's face. Her hands shook as she punched in the numbers. She took several deep breaths to calm her thumping heart. *They could have killed me!* A tear trickled down her face.

Moments later, a female answered. "Hello?"

"Sindee! Thank God! It's Heidi." She pulled the phone away from her ear at the ensuing shriek.

"Where are you?"

Heidi repeated the location.

"Are you safe? I'll tell Javier, and we'll be on our way."

"Yes, I'm okay for now. You won't believe it—I'm using the phone of an off-duty state trooper and his girlfriend."

"Sit tight, Heidi—we'll be on our way."

The state trooper waved a hand to get Heidi's attention. "Tell them to meet us at the Independent Hill State Police office."

Heidi relayed the information.

"Hang on, Heidi—it'll take us about an hour to reach you."

"Okay." Heidi broke the connection and handed the phone back.

"I think you'd be safer in our area office." The officer finished putting his belongings in his backpack. "Of course, we'll need a statement from you while we wait for your friends." He stuck out his hand. "Guess we better introduce ourselves. I'm Sergeant Larry Supernaut." He gestured toward the petite blonde. "This is my girlfriend, Jenny."

"Pleased to meet both of you. Thank you for saving my life."

"We better go." Larry grabbed the lawn chairs.

Heidi nodded and smiled as they collected the couple's belongings and headed up the slope to their vehicle.

SINDEE RAPPED on Javier's door and rushed inside. "Sorry to interrupt anything you're doing, but this is important."

Javier pulled his feet from the slide-out shelf and set down the folder he was reading. "What's up?"

"Heidi—she just called me. She wants us to meet her."

"Where?" Javier jumped to his feet, slid on his shoulder rig, and donned his sports coat.

"She's safe. She got away from her kidnappers. An off-duty state trooper is taking her to the state police station in Independent Hill. She wants us to meet her there."

Javier nodded. "Let's go."

They dashed out the back door of the building and climbed into Javier's Hummer. With a squeal of his tires, Javier pulled into traffic and headed west.

Gunning the engine and blowing the horn, Javier weaved through traffic, sailing through several traffic lights as they turned red.

"Javier! Slow down." Sindee held onto the panic strap. "I told you Heidi's safe. A state trooper and his girlfriend are taking her to the police post. They'll begin questioning her while they wait for us to arrive."

He nodded and slowed down. "Sorry, Sindee. Got a bit carried away." Javier grinned. "Reminds me of the calvary rushing to the rescue."

Sindee laughed. "From which movie?"

"Pick one. But you're right—no need to rush. The state police need to handle this—we'll offer protection after they finish with her." Javier glanced at Sindee. "She can't stay at her apartment—the kidnappers might return and take her out."

Sindee nodded. "She could stay with me, but I'm not sure that'd work since I live next door." *And would we both still be in danger?*

"I have a better idea. There's a spare bedroom in our building for any of the team's use. Heidi can stay as long as she wants. You should come, too. There's an empty room in my quarters. If the kidnappers come back to your complex, they might find you."

"I'm sure she'll take you up on the offer. I guess I should, too—at least until I can find somewhere else to live."

∼

LARRY CLIMBED behind the wheel of his late-model silver BMW and started the engine. Jenny sat next to him, with Heidi in the back.

"Won't take long to get to the station." He pulled out of the beauty spot and onto a two-lane paved road. "Mind telling me what happened on the other side of the lake?"

Heidi glanced out the window, peering at the thick woods as they sped along. "I was kidnapped from my apartment in Alexandria but don't know where they took me. There were two men. Both wore clown masks except for out at the lake." Her body shook. "They wanted me dead, didn't they?"

"Appears so. Do you think you could work with a sketch artist?"

"Yes—anything to catch those bastards."

∼

ABOUT AN HOUR LATER, Javier pulled into the parking lot of the Virginia State Police Bureau of Field Operations area office in Independent Hill. He parked in a visitor slot, and they dashed inside the single-story brick building.

Javier and Sindee stepped to a counter and identified themselves.

The officer noted their names on his computer and gestured to a waiting area. "See the woman with the sunglasses? She wants to speak with you."

Javier and Sindee strode over to the petite woman.

She stood as they approached, hand outstretched. "You must be Heidi's friends."

"Yes." Sindee glanced at Javier. "We got here as soon as we could."

"My boyfriend is with her now in one of the interrogation rooms. He said as soon as they finish, Heidi will be brought to you."

"Thanks."

She pointed at a shelf. "There's coffee if you want some. But I'll warn you—tastes like it was made yesterday."

Javier shook his head. "I'll pass."

"Okay. I'm heading home. I hope everything goes okay."

SINDEE REMAINED in her chair after the woman left and flipped through the pages of an old magazine she pulled from a pile on a scuffed table.

Javier paced the waiting area and glanced at a wall clock. *What's taking so long? We've been here an hour. She's a victim, not a criminal.* He returned to a seat next to Sindee.

At last, a side door opened. Heidi rushed out, accompanied by a tall, muscular man with short blond hair.

He held an envelope as he approached Javier. "Sir, I'm Sergeant Supernaut. My girlfriend and I brought Heidi here. She appears to be in good health, considering the trauma of her kidnapping. She gave a good description of both men." He handed the thin package to Javier. "Normally, I wouldn't do this, but Captain Zorkin requested I give you a copy of the incident report, including sketches of the men. We'll do our best to identify them and bring them in."

"Thank you, Sergeant."

"You're welcome to take her home whenever you're ready." He pulled Javier aside. "I'd recommend a medical exam, too. Who knows if she's been raped? If so, the hospital might find a viable specimen if they didn't wear a condom. It needs to be done within seventy-two hours of an assault."

Javier frowned. "Good idea. Thanks."

JAVIER, Sindee, and Heidi left the building and hopped in the Hummer. As soon as there was a clear space in the traffic, Javier merged with oncoming vehicles, and they headed toward Alexandria. *How do I mention a rape test kit?*

"Mr. Smith?"

Javier glanced in the rear-view mirror and grinned. "Please call me Javier. Mr. Smith is too formal and makes me feel old."

Heidi chuckled. "I-I withheld some information from the police. I told them there were two men. I lied. There was a third one. He came into the basement without a mask. His face was ugly—covered with scars as if he'd been cut and burned. Some of his face was covered by a scraggly, black beard. I think his name is Alberto. The two who kidnapped me and took me to the lake—one of them referred to another person—I think they called him Alberto, too. Could it be the same person? Oh! I heard one of them call me an infidel."

"Thanks for letting us know." Javier beat a tune on the steering wheel. *A Muslim connection? Something to consider.* "You might be on to something." He snapped his fingers. "Why didn't you mention the third man?"

"I knew from Sindee you own an investigative agency. I never mentioned she was my neighbor. Since they wanted information about you and your employees, I thought you'd like to know."

"Thanks, Heidi." *Here goes.* "Would it be possible one or more of them raped you?"

She shook her head. "No. My clothes weren't disturbed. They never threatened to rape me."

Thank God. "It still wouldn't be a bad idea to get checked out. We could stop at the hospital on the way."

Sindee grasped Heidi's hand. "I think it's better to have one done just in case something happened, and your mind is blocking out any trauma."

"I-I guess you're right."

AFTER LEAVING the hospital three hours later, they continued their journey to The Brusch Agency. Javier parked in his normal spot behind the building. Once they entered, he locked the exterior door.

"Sindee, please take Heidi around and show her where everything is. Introduce her to anyone still here. Also, take her to the spare bedroom."

"Roger, boss." Sindee smiled as she motioned for Heidi to follow.

Javier stepped into his office and sat behind the desk. He twiddled his thumbs as he stared at the ceiling. "Hmm. Wonder if this Alberto is the same one who got away in Mexico? If so, I can understand him being pissed at me." He pursed his lips as he grabbed the phone. "No one threatens my friends and me without paying a penalty. We'll check into this guy some more. If he's behind the threats and Heidi's kidnapping, he'll pay a high price.

"Perhaps with his life."

16

The Brusch Agency
Old Town, Alexandria, Virginia

JAVIER PECKED AWAY on his keyboard. He frowned as he reached for coffee. Taking a swig, he grimaced. *Too cold to drink. Wonder if there's any left in one of the pots?*

He stood and walked toward the door.

Someone knocked.

Javier twisted the knob and yanked the door open.

Elton stood with a hand in mid-air, ready to knock again. "Javier, someone in reception wants to speak with you."

His mind still on his typing, Javier handed his cup to Elton. "Did you happen to get a name? While you're at it, could you check for some hot coffee, too? This is well past its best."

"The man said to tell you his name is Viper."

Javier laughed. "I've been waiting for him to show up. His real name's Charles Gable, and he'll be leading the team heading to Bermuda. He goes by Charlie."

Elton took Javier's cup and nodded. "I'll bring him in and get you some fresh coffee."

"Thanks. Better bring some for Charlie, too. Could you also let Sindee know I want to speak with her when I finish with Charlie?"

Moments later, Elton escorted Charlie into Javier's office. He handed Javier a new mug of coffee and departed.

Javier pointed to a chair. "Take a load off, Charlie. So, you drew the short straw?"

Charlie chuckled. "I had the most accumulated leave of the four of us, so I'm your man. When my commander asked what I planned to do on my leave, I couldn't lie to him. After I explained, he said not to worry as he knows you. But he did order me to stay out of trouble."

"Glad you volunteered. I don't want you putting your career on the line, so think things through before you react. As you know, this'll be the team's first deployment together, so having a seasoned individual leading them will help to cover any rookie mistakes."

"I remember you bailing me out a few times. Now it's my turn to pass my knowledge on to others."

Javier rolled his eyes. "Just mission-related stuff. I'm sure they'll figure out how to party on their own time."

"Spoilsport." Charlie drained his cup. "So, where's my team? Time's a-wasting if we're to depart in three days."

"Relax. They're going through a personal security crash course— one day of driving and another of weapons training. All being well, they'll return tomorrow evening."

"In that case, I'm going to head to Virtue Feed & Grain for something to eat. Want me to pick something up for you?"

"Naw. I'm good. AJ's picking up Chinese for tonight."

Charlie nodded. "Tell her I said hello. Catch up with you later." He stood, shook hands, and headed out of Javier's office, closing the door behind him.

Javier stared at the ceiling, one hand resting on the computer's keyboard. *Things are moving along, but I need to keep a log. Wonder if I should have ET do this?*

Sindee knocked twice, entered Javier's office, and took a seat. She waited in silence while he continued to poke away at his keyboard.

Javier finished typing and glanced at Sindee. "Everything ready for Bermuda?"

She nodded. "All set."

"Excellent." He rubbed his jaw. "I wanted to speak with you about your apartment. Since Heidi's kidnappers were asking about our agency, it might not be safe for you to return there. No sense tempting fate."

"Agreed. I already thought about that." Sindee grinned. "In fact, Heidi and I plan to find a place together to keep our costs down. Since we're already friends and spend a lot of time in each other's company, we figure this is the next step."

"Okay. But until you find a place, I'm glad you decided to stay in one of the spare rooms here. Cesar can take you home to pick up whatever you need. Once you and Heidi find a new location, we'll hire a company to move both of you."

"Aw, thanks, boss." Sindee smiled.

"Always method in my madness."

"Such as?"

"Happy employees tend to be more productive." *Won't tell her about the security apparatus we'll install to keep them safe.* "Keep me posted."

"Will do." Sindee stood and headed back to her own office.

Sam, Wild, and TJ hoisted their beer bottles before taking a sip. A waiter slid a bowl of hot, salty popcorn next to them, winding his way through the tables and dropping off additional servings.

Wild took a long swig of his beer. "Man, I needed that. What a day! Those driving instructors are crazy!"

Sam grabbed a handful of popcorn and tossed a couple of kernels into her mouth. She laughed. "I know what you mean. When I went to the first test, I stopped as requested by the pair of armed guards at the checkpoint. One came up to the window and tapped on the glass with his AK-47. He spoke in the worst Spanish I've ever heard. He wanted my identification. I ended up shoving it through the window vent. After he glanced at it, he gave it back through the vent and waved us through."

"So, what happened?"

"After we drove away, the instructor said I came up with a great way to provide what the guard wanted without rolling the window down." Sam grinned. "I didn't have the heart to tell him I did that because the main window wouldn't come down."

Everyone laughed and drained their bottles as a waiter set replacements on the table.

"That's nothing." Wild chewed some popcorn before washing it down. "My instructor asked me why I sped toward a vehicle trying to back onto the road. A guy stood with his hand in the air for me to stop. I was going to when another man stepped out with an AK-47. Since I was too close to back up, I gunned it. The instructor finally agreed with my decision, although he said I should be more cautious." He turned to TJ. "Anything exciting?"

"Not really. My instructor got mad when I swore. We came across a roadblock I couldn't bust through—two vehicles blocked the way, with a third one behind. When I began to reverse, the engine cut out. I hollered, 'Shit!' and started to climb out of the car when the instructor said the exercise was over. He admonished me for swearing because he didn't think the situation warranted it. Although he had a grin plastered across his face, he suggested I learn to keep my cool at all times. He had disabled the vehicle with an engine kill switch to see how I would respond."

"Well, we survived our day of driving." Sam stood. "I'm looking forward to the weapons stuff tomorrow." She gestured toward the sign for the restrooms. "Be right back."

When Sam returned, they drained their glasses. "Pizza?" Sam pointed to the Pizza Hut sign down the street.

"Sure, but I want one to myself." TJ rubbed his stomach. "What I don't eat now I'll have later or for breakfast."

"Works for me." Wild yawned. "After we eat, I'm heading back to the hotel to crash. Be another busy day tomorrow."

~

As JAVIER CLOSED his office door, footsteps echoed along the corridor. He turned and spotted Cesar.

"Hey, Jefe, got a minute?"

"Sure, Cesar." Javier unlocked his door. "C'mon in." He slid into one of the chairs in front of his desk and pointed to another. "Grab a seat."

Cesar nodded. "Wanted to update you on what I found out about AJ's accident. I met with an old police buddy. They discovered some fingerprints this morning and are running them through IAFIS."

"What if they don't belong to anyone in the system?"

"They'll ask the FBI to check with Interpol."

"I get the feeling the fingerprints won't match anyone in the U.S." Javier pursed his lips. "But who knows?"

"My contact also said they were able to lift the VIN from the vehicle—at least most of it. Although someone had tried to obliterate the number, the police used a chemical etching process to recover the numbers, but the last digit was too damaged to confirm."

Javier nodded. "Their work will make it easier to narrow down the correct vehicle and hopefully find the owner. Keep me posted."

"Will do, Jefe." Cesar glanced at his watch. "I better get going. AJ will be heading for her run soon, and I want to be in position in case anyone follows her."

Both men stood, and Javier stretched out his hand. "Just remember not to let her see you. She'll raise holy hell with me if she finds out."

Cesar grinned. "No worries, Jefe. I'll be in my own workout gear, so if she does spot me, I can write it off as a coincidence."

AFTER TYING HIS LACES, Cesar began warming up while waiting for AJ to appear along the Belle Haven to Old Town trail. When he finished, he ducked into a thicket where he could still monitor the route. He plugged in his earbuds and waited.

Before long, Cesar's head bobbed to the music massaging his ears.

Snap!

He turned.

Nothing.

As he resumed monitoring the trail, Cesar sensed something to his right. He reached into his fanny pack, grabbed his SIG Sauer P226, and began pulling it out—

Whack!

17

D isused Gravel Pit
Outside Independent Hill, Virginia

JUSTIN FORCED his legs into Bennie's stomach and shoved, toppling his colleague onto the sand. Chest heaving, Justin glanced around for his pistol. "Hey! Where did the woman go?"

Bennie rubbed his stomach and scanned the area. "I don't see her." He turned and glared at Justin. "It's your fault. You shouldn't have tried to kill her—she didn't do anything."

"What's the matter, gone soft for the infidels?" Justin shook his head. "Perhaps you've been in this decadent country too long. You're forgetting your allegiance to Allah." He bent and retrieved the weapon from where the sand partially covered the barrel and shoved it in his belt.

"No. I'm realistic. It's one thing to carry out Alberto's quest for revenge against those who attacked us in Mexico, but we can't take on everyone in America." He heaved a sigh. "Leaving too many bodies around increases our risk of being caught and expands the number of our enemies."

"You might have a point—just. How will we explain to Alberto what happened?" Justin rubbed his jaw where a bruise had formed.

"Why tell him the truth? He'll kill us." Bennie started up the slope toward their vehicle. "C'mon. We better head back."

"Coming." Justin pursed his lips as he took another look around before following Bennie.

THE DOOR SLAMMED behind Bennie and Justin as they entered the kitchen. Justin went to the fridge and yanked out a jug of orange juice while Bennie pulled glasses from a cupboard.

As they poured the juice and sat, Alberto walked in. "Well? Did you take care of things?"

"Piece of cake, as the Americans would say." Justin glanced at Bennie. "After we sent her to her god, we weighted her body, took it to the middle of the lake, and pushed it in."

Alberto glanced from Justin's face to Bennie's. "Where did you find a boat?"

"Uh. There was one on the beach." Justin grinned. "No one was around, so we borrowed it."

"I see." Alberto drummed his fingers on the table as he stared at the ceiling. "That's one loose end tied up." He tossed a small piece of paper on the table. "The man we hired to kill the CIA woman was released from the hospital." He twisted his lips into a frown. "The man failed to complete his contract yet expects his payment—he sent me a text earlier, along with where he wants to collect the money."

"He wants to be paid yet didn't do the job—are all Americans so greedy?" Bennie laughed. "Where do we find him?"

"American greed and arrogance. He's probably too embarrassed to admit failure—or perhaps, he's working for the woman or some of her friends." Alberto gestured at the paper. "This is where he lives. He's expecting payment in two days. He wants the money in small bills and placed in a backpack. Take care of him tonight—but make it slow and painful—and final. Failure cannot be tolerated."

Bennie and Justin glanced at each other and nodded.

Justin poured another glass of juice. "Anything else?"

"Leave me." Alberto waved them away. "I must think."

LEFT TO HIS THOUGHTS, Alberto wandered into the living room, sat in a brown leather recliner, and adjusted the chair's position until he was comfortable. *I think this immoral country is corrupting Bennie and Justin.* He shook his head. *Once we've exacted revenge, we'll return to the Middle East, where we can continue our jihad against the Israelis and those rushing to be their friends.* A frown creased his forehead. *Wish I could visit Mamá in Buenos Aires again, but she refuses to speak with me since I pledged allegiance to Islamic State.*

He fished his phone from his shirt pocket and dialed.

A male voice answered, "Hello?"

"No names. Do you recognize my voice?"

Silence. "Uh, yes."

"Good. How is your work progressing?"

"By the end of the week, I will have twelve packages ready for your use."

Alberto chuckled. "Excellent. Can you make two smaller ones that can be attached to the bottom of a vehicle?"

"As you wish. Do you want activation by a sensor or remote control?"

"Hmm." He tapped his index finger against his lips. *I want to witness their deaths.* "Remote control."

"Okay, I'll put a prototype together as soon as I can and find a place to test it. If it works, I'll make two operational devices for you."

"Keep me posted." Alberto broke the connection and grinned. *At least one of my team remains loyal to Allah.* He put the phone back in his pocket and closed his eyes.

Two hours later, Alberto woke with a start. The room had

dimmed as the sun headed toward the horizon. *What disturbed me?* He climbed out of his chair and walked from room to room, checking all windows remained locked.

After he finished examining every external door and window, he stepped into the utility room. *There!*

Somehow, a squirrel had become trapped in a gap at the top of a vent.

Screeech!

Its claws scraped along the aluminum casing, the sharp noise sending shivers down Alberto's spine. He smiled and reached up to open the vent.

After chittering as if the squirrel was chastising Alberto, it rushed out the slot, its bushy tail ruffling in the air.

"Go, little one. No one will hurt you here." Alberto secured the vent and strolled to the kitchen. After grabbing a glass and filling it with milk from the fridge, he sat at the table.

Should we pick off our targets one by one, or should there be a directed assault on their property? He pursed his lips. *Might be safer taking one out at a time. I must decide soon—if we go with an attack on the building, we'll require more men.* He stood, headed into the living room, and picked up the TV remote. *As long as the coronel and his woman are killed, what does it matter? We shall honor Allah either way.*

BENNIE AND JUSTIN finished the meal they picked up at a drive-through restaurant. After tossing the remains on the floor of the vehicle, they cruised around the streets of Fairfax as dusk descended.

"Take your time, Bennie." Justin glanced at a row of townhouses. "We'll wait until later to take care of the trucker. The last time you drove past his home, the lights were still out."

Bennie continued along a two-lane, tree-lined street and pulled into a gas station at a small neighborhood shopping center. "Need to fill up."

"Don't take all night. The fewer people who see us, the better."

Bennie topped the tank and dashed to the cashier's window to pay. Returning to the vehicle, he climbed in and started the engine. He glanced at Justin. "Where to?"

"Keep driving around the area, but don't go past the target's house again. We'll wait another hour or so before we check."

After an hour had passed, Bennie turned onto the target's street once again.

This time, lights illuminated various rooms.

"Good, he's in." Justin pointed along the street. "Stop by those trees. We'll go pay our friend a visit."

They parked, got out of the vehicle, and walked back to the house, with Justin carrying a briefcase.

Bennie rang the doorbell while Justin scanned the neighborhood.

A porch light popped on, and the door cracked open. "Whaddya want?"

Justin turned and gazed at the tall, thin man. He wore jeans and a blue and red checked shirt. Perched on his head was a dirty baseball hat. "Excuse me, but are you Tobias Smithson?"

"Might be." He studied the two tanned men. "Why?"

"We're from the insurance company. We brought you a check for your recent accident."

The man grinned. "Why didn't you say so? Yeah, I'm Tobias, but everybody calls me Smitty. C'mon inside." He stepped back, holding the door for Bennie and Justin to enter.

"Want a beer? I was just sitting down to catch the ball game. Can't watch baseball without a beer or two." He gestured to a stained couch that had seen better days. "Take a load off—be right back. Save the rocker for me."

They balanced on the edge of the seat. While Bennie gazed at the screen, Justin popped the locks on the briefcase and pulled out a silenced Beretta M9A3 pistol. He motioned toward the TV. "Turn up the sound."

"Who's playing?" Justin stood, pulled a curtain aside, and glanced out the window.

"Doesn't really matter to me," Smitty called from the kitchen.

"Tonight, I think it's the Yankees and the Mets." He returned to the living room, carrying a six-pack. He handed one to Bennie. "Where's your friend?"

"Right here." Justin stepped from the window and pointed his gun at Smitty's midsection. "Sit down."

"Hey, are you fellas pulling my leg? Someone from work put you up to this?"

"Sit." Justin grabbed Smitty's arm and shoved him onto the chair. "We paid you a lot of money to kill a woman—you failed. Now, you'll pay for it."

"Wait a minute. I was told to make it look like an accident." Smitty gulped, his eyes wide. "Gimme another chance. I'll make it right." He tried to stand, but Bennie rushed over and pushed him back in the rocker.

Justin shook his head and pressed the weapon's barrel against Smitty's temple. "Time to say goodbye."

"Do—"

Justine pulled the trigger.

Bennie stared at the blood seeping from a small hole in Smitty's forehead, "Let's get out of here." He glanced at Justin. "What—what are you doing?"

Justin aimed at Bennie's chest. "Did you think I would just forget what you did at the lake? You've crossed me for the last time."

"W-Wait! I'll—"

Pffft! Pffft!

18

B ell Haven to Old Town Trail
Old Town, Alexandria, Virginia

CESAR STRUGGLED TO HIS KNEES, grabbing onto a sapling to steady himself. After taking a deep breath, he pushed himself upright, swaying on unstable legs. *What happened?* He touched the side of his head and winced. When he pulled his hand away, he felt some sticky dampness.

Blood?

He staggered to a bench along the path and sat. *Wonder who attacked me?* Cesar examined himself. *No other injuries.* He glanced around.

Quiet—no hikers or joggers appeared along the trail.

Whoever hit me got my SIG and my wallet. Good thing my phone and spare car keys were in my coat pocket. Cesar stood and walked in the direction of his SUV. When he neared the parking lot, he studied the vehicles. He owned the inferno red Jeep Grand Cherokee. Two other

SUVs—neither belonged to AJ. Not spotting anyone, he hit the key remote and unlocked his vehicle.

Once inside, Cesar pulled out his phone—one missed call and a text. He opened the message from Javier. *AJ will be a no-show. Something came up at work.* He hit the call return button and waited for Javier to answer. "Hey, Jefe. Just saw your text and missed call. You won't believe this—I got clocked. Didn't see who it was, but they got my pistol."

"Are you okay?"

"Slight swelling on the side of my head. There was a bit of blood, but nothing serious. More injury to my pride, letting someone sneak up on me."

"No worries, Cesar. Happens to the best of us. Why not head to the emergency room for a once-over in case of concussion and then go home for the evening? We'll catch up tomorrow."

"If you don't need me, I'll do that. I better stop by the police station and file an incident report. Don't want my pistol being used in a crime and traced back to me without any previous mention to the police it was stolen."

"Better to be safe than sorry. Come in after ten."

AFTER BREAKING THE CONNECTION, Javier leaned back in his chair. *Hope Cesar's incident was a random event and not part of a concerted effort against us.* He glanced at his watch. *Better head out—AJ said she'd be waiting for me.* He reached into a drawer, pulled out a loaded SIG Sauer P226, a holster, and an extra magazine. After securing his weapon under his coat, he turned off the lights and headed out the building's back door for the fifteen-minute walk to the restaurant.

When Javier arrived at the Virtue Feed & Grain, a line of people waited for tables. He waved his hand to attract the greeter's attention.

When she spotted him, she waved back and motioned him forward. "Your friends are upstairs, Mister Smith. Please go ahead." She unhooked the rope barrier to allow him past.

"Many thanks, Anna. Have a fantastic evening."

She smiled. "Always."

Climbing the stairs, Javier spotted AJ and Charlie sitting in their normal alcove. Between them, a pitcher of beer and a bowl of popcorn rested on a small wooden table.

Charlie waved an empty glass in the air. "Ready for one?"

"How many have you had?" Javier glanced at AJ.

"We got tired of waiting for you." She reached over and squeezed his hand. "Relax—you're only one glass behind."

He turned to Charlie. "In that case, fill 'er up."

After receiving a glass of Minute Man, Javier raised it before taking a swig. "Aah. That hits the spot. So where are the others?"

"Sam called a few minutes ago—they're running late due to D.C. traffic." AJ pushed her empty glass toward Charlie. "Sam said to order whatever we're having for them."

"Works for me." Javier looked around and spotted a waiter.

A young man wearing brown chinos and a blue shirt nodded and headed toward them. He held an iPad. "Can I help you, sir?"

Javier glanced at the man's name tag. "Hi, Paul. Yes, we'd like Virtue burgers with the works, corn on the cob, onion rings, and French fries for six. Oh, better add a couple more pitchers of Minute Man."

Paul's brows rose in apparent confusion. "Uh .... Hungry?" He glanced from face to face.

AJ laughed. "Three more friends will be here soon. They should be here by the time the food's ready."

"Gotcha." Paul grinned. "I'll put your order in right away." He tapped the screen on his iPad. "Is there anything else?"

"Not at the moment. Thanks." Javier drained his glass. "Well, perhaps bring a pitcher now. We'll be ready for it in a minute or two."

"Right away, sir." Paul turned and headed toward the upstairs bar.

Approaching footsteps accompanied by laughter caused Javier and the others to turn.

Sam, Wild, and TJ grabbed empty seats and introduced themselves to Charlie.

"So, where's the beer?" TJ picked up the pitcher, poured the dregs into a glass, and tossed it back.

Charlie glanced at each of his new team members. "How'd weapons training go?"

Paul approached with two pitchers of beer, set them on the table, and departed.

TJ filled everyone's glass. "Not bad. I learned something new today."

Wild laughed. "Yeah. Which end to shoot from."

Everyone chuckled, with Javier almost choking on his beer.

"Who would've thought? I always figured I was right-eye dominant. At least I've never had an issue before with a pistol." TJ sipped his beer and nodded at Sam and Wild. "Ask them who had a perfect score on the pistol range, including in the night-vision chamber."

Sam grimaced. "So, my eyes don't work as well in the dark. I'm not a cat or an owl."

"Yeah, but you missed three times!"

"Out of sixty. But who had problems on the rifle range?"

"I still qualified." TJ grinned and focused on Javier and Charlie. "When we hit the rifle range, I took out a target every time I shot."

"Yeah, but you're supposed to shoot the ones in your lane." Sam laughed.

"So, what happened?" Javier glanced at Charlie. "Anything we need to be aware of?"

TJ shook his head. "Naw. At least, I don't think so. Once we zeroized our M4s, I kept missing the targets. The instructor had me switch—I began shooting left-handed, vice right-handed. Once I did that, I didn't miss again."

Charlie nodded. "Not a problem as far as I'm concerned. We'll only be carrying SIG Sauers anyway. The rifle training was part of the package, and it's always wise to understand everyone's capabilities and shortcomings. Could make the difference between life and death."

Paul and another waiter approached, each carrying large platters.

After they passed the plates, everyone stopped speaking as they dug into their meal.

Before long, the food had disappeared, and conversation picked up. Javier refilled everyone's glass.

"Our flight to Hamilton will depart from BWI tomorrow afternoon. Take about two and a half hours." Charlie studied his team.

"Be at the office by 0900, and we'll go over the comms gear and a few other things." He turned to Javier. "Anything else?"

Javier tapped a finger against his lips. "Nothing from me—it's your show." He raised his glass. "Here's to the success of The Brusch Agency's first contract."

Everyone followed Javier's lead before taking a drink.

Javier stood and pulled out his wallet.

"No worries." Charlie waved away Javier's offer. "We'll stay a bit longer and become better acquainted. Meet you at the office in the morning."

Javier nodded. "Okay. Have a good evening." He glanced toward AJ. "How about you?"

AJ grinned as she stood. "Let's go."

Outside on the sidewalk, Javier stopped. "Coming over or heading home?"

AJ smiled. "Nothing early planned." She linked her arm through Javier's. "Let's head to your place and see what mischief we can get into."

Javier pulled her close. "Sounds promising."

They both laughed as they set off.

A MAN WEARING A YANKEES' baseball hat slid down in his seat as Javier and AJ passed. *Enjoy your evening. You'll get what you deserve soon enough.* He made a pistol with his thumb and index finger and pulled the trigger. *We'll have our revenge.*

19

L. F. Wade International Airport
Hamilton, Bermuda

CHARLIE AND SAM strode through the terminal's exit into the intense sunlight. Squinting, they donned their Ray-Bans to protect their eyes.

Sam covered her head with her hands and ducked as a seagull screeched and swooped toward her. "I hate gulls—they're a pest. I had one shit on me once—what a mess."

Charlie laughed. "At least this one gave you fair warning with his squawk."

"True."

They headed to a nearby taxi rank, choosing a silver Hyundai van with a picture of the Bahamian flag on the doors, and handed the driver their luggage.

The driver turned to Charlie. "Welcome to Bermy. First time here? Do you need a hotel?"

Charlie glanced back at the building. "Thank you. Yes, our first time here, but we have a hotel. We're also waiting for two more people." He pointed. "Here they come."

Wild and TJ approached the taxi and tossed their luggage in the back.

After the driver closed the rear of the vehicle, everyone climbed inside.

As they pulled away, the driver tapped his horn and cut off an empty taxi. "*Arryone, I am Felix. Wopnin?*"

Charlie and the others glanced at one another before he turned to Felix. "Is that anything like what's happenin'?"

Felix laughed. "You're too smart for me. Most tourists don't have a clue what I'm saying when I use our island slang." A grin spread across his face. "All de onions will try it on you."

"Onions?"

"At one time, onions were a major export from Bermuda, so those born and bred here became known as onions. What hotel?"

"The Oxford House in Hamilton. How long will the trip take?"

Felix nodded. "An excellent bed and breakfast. Since there is only one road from de airport, traffic is always slow. Today? Perhaps twenty minutes, but maybe forty." He shrugged. "We find out."

They left the taxi rank, merging toward the exit. At the first roundabout, the van lurched to a stop. "Sorry. Must be a tourist in front of us." Felix laughed. "Once we get on De Causeway, we will pass him." He turned the radio on—steelpan music infiltrated the vehicle.

"Do you mind turning it down a bit?" Charlie laughed. "I love the music but not blaring in my ears."

"Oh, sorry." Felix nudged the volume lower. "How's dat?"

Charlie made a circle with his thumb and index vehicle. "Perfect."

When an opening appeared in the traffic, Felix gunned the engine, taking the first left onto The Causeway and whipping past the slow-moving car. He tapped his horn and waved. "De water we are passing is called Castle Harbour. We will take de North Shore Road to Hamilton."

Charlie glanced at the pastel-colored buildings interspersed with small clumps of trees hugging the road. As they continued toward Hamilton, various souvenir shops, independent businesses, and restaurants dotted the landscape.

The van swayed as Felix alternated between braking for vehicles to dashing into oncoming traffic to pass anything in his way. After a series of turns in Hamilton, the van screeched to a halt in front of the twelve-room Oxford House. He checked the clock on the dash. "Twenty-eight minutes. An excellent time."

Charlie let go of the panic strap. Does everyone drive like you?" He chuckled.

"No, sir." Felix shook his head. "I am one of da better island drivers." He put a hand over his heart. "Never been in an accident—so far."

Everyone climbed out of the taxi and converged at the rear of the vehicle to collect their belongings.

"How much?" Charlie pulled out his wallet.

"Let's see. Ten miles from the airport, so that is thirty-two dollars and sixty-five cents." Felix raised a hand and pointed at their roll-around suitcases and backpacks. "Plus, one dollar for every piece of luggage." He grinned. "Because I like you, make it forty dollars."

Charlie raised a brow at Felix's creative math, pulled out two twenties and a five-dollar note, and handed the money to him.

"*Chingas!*" Felix pulled a business card from his shirt pocket. "If you need a taxi or a guided tour while you are in Bermy, give me a call, and I give you de business rate." He shook their hands. "Enjoy!"

Shouldering his bag and picking up his small suitcase, Charlie led the way between the palm trees guarding the entrance to the beige and white building.

Sam stopped at the bottom of the steps and glanced around. "Just like an English manor—but with fantastic weather!"

They stepped inside. In front of them, a winding staircase made of dark wood, with green carpeting down the center. A wrought iron railing ran along each side. To the left, a small sitting area filled with various chairs upholstered in cream and gold.

Behind and to the right of the stairs was reception. A young woman with long black hair sat at the table, typing on a keyboard. Her face beamed when she saw Charlie and the others. "Hello. May I help you?"

Charlie placed a reservation confirmation note in front of her. "Good afternoon, miss. We have rooms booked for a week."

The woman picked up the paper, turned back to the computer, and typed in the reservation number. "Yes, sir. You are confirmed and will be upstairs, overlooking the gardens." She activated four key cards. "If you care to put your belongings in the rooms, when you finish, I'll have tea, scones, and strawberry jam ready for you on a table outside."

Charlie smiled. "My mouth is already watering."

They climbed the stairs and located their rooms.

Charlie entered his. Inside, a four-poster bed took up most of the far wall. Floral curtains and pillows contrasted with the checked and striped chairs. A door to the side led into the bathroom. He dropped his suitcase on the bed and went to the phone on the desk. Punching in a local number, he waited for someone to answer. "Hello? We're here."

A cultured British accent filtered through the phone. "Excellent, I shall be with you in about thirty minutes."

"We'll be in the garden." Charlie broke the connection, picked up his backpack, and headed downstairs. He joined the others at a table for five shaded by an orange sun umbrella and a palm tree. Two carafes sat in the middle of the table, with plates of scones and other pastries on each side.

Sam munched on a profiterole. "I asked for some coffee as I know you don't like tea. The red pot is for you."

"Thanks." Charlie helped himself to a scone, spreading butter and jam on the warm surface. Steam rose as he poured a cup of coffee, the smell waking his senses.

The team sat in silence, eating and drinking. A warm breeze carried the scent of the ocean to them.

"Excuse me." A man with a cream-colored suit and multi-colored bow tie approached them. Tanned, with a white goatee, mustache, and wire-rimmed glasses, a Panama hat was perched on his head. He carried a large manila envelope.

"The Brusch Agency party, I assume?" He spoke in a soft, bass voice.

Charlie stood. "Doctor Yates?" He motioned to the empty chair. "Please join us."

"Thank you. But, please, call me Cedric. Doctor is too stuffy a title for such a beautiful place." He sat and placed his hat in his lap. "Besides, my doctorate is in history—hardly worthy of the title except in academia."

"You remind me of someone." Sam smiled and snapped her fingers. "I know who—"

"Yes, my dear." Cedric sighed. "I get asked quite often by American visitors if I'm related to the gentleman who founded Kentucky Fried Chicken." He shook his head. "I'm afraid not."

Everyone chuckled.

"Actually, you remind me of a great uncle." Sam laughed. "I believe he was from Cambridge but spent most of his time in Egypt working as an archaeologist."

"A much more rewarding career than slinging fried chicken, I'm sure."

"Would you like some tea?" Sam gestured toward the pot.

"Thank you, my dear. Perhaps, later, as I just finished two cups before coming here." Cedric turned to Charlie and slid the envelope across the table. "Before we discuss the contents, I must remind you that Her Majesty's Government frowns on the importation of firearms and other harmful goods." He glanced over the top of his glasses. "Of course, if the American consulate general provides something to you, who am I to object?"

Charlie smiled. "No plan to obtain weapons from the consulate." *Although it's been approved if we need them. No need to share this with Cedric.*

Cedric nodded. "Excellent. Now for our business. There is reliable information the American drug smuggler operates from at least three of the one hundred and eighty-one islands comprising

Bermuda. No specific locations for him here, which is called the Main Island, but in the envelope is a possible address for him on St. George's Island and another on Somerset."

"Any photos?" Charlie popped the metal clasp holding the envelope closed.

"Yes. Not very good ones, I'm afraid, but they're the best we came up with from CCTV. He's a cagey operator and seems to be aware of every camera, so they are all profile shots."

Charlie rubbed his chin. "Anything else we should be aware of?"

"Yes. Just this morning, I received snippets of information from London. Seems like he's using Maverick as a nickname. Also, he's been in contact with someone in the U.S. recently. This person speaks English and Spanish. He goes by the name of Alberto or Roberto— we're not sure which. Also, we don't know if that is the individual's given name or his surname."

"Thanks. Any information is better than none, and this gives us something to start with." TJ glanced around the table. "Don't know about the rest of you, but I'm looking forward to the chase."

"That's all I have right now." Cedric stood. "I'll be in contact whenever new information becomes available." He dropped a business card on the table. "Here's my mobile number. If you need my assistance, give me a ring." He put his hat back on and gave a small wave as he left.

"What's our first move, boss?" TJ grimaced as he finished his now-cold coffee.

Charlie turned to the others. "Take it easy for the remainder of the day. We'll get started first thing in the morning. Two groups—TJ and Wild, you'll head to St. George's Island. Sam and I will check out Somerset. I'll send Javier an email now and catch up with everyone later."

After Sam, TJ, and Wild departed, Charlie pulled out his comms gear. Once he connected the laptop to an Internet hotspot via a VPN, he began typing.

. . .

To: Cobra

From: Viper

In position. Contact established with local liaison. Potential locations for target, identified as Maverick, will be checked out tomorrow. His U.S. connection is called Alberto or Roberto, but nothing firm.

AFTER HITTING SEND, Charlie closed down his equipment and leaned back in the chair. *I have a bad feeling—better to swing by the consulate and pick up the SIGs we were promised. Don't want to head into a situation naked.*

20

T he Brusch Agency
        Old Town, Alexandria, Virginia

AJ SNATCHED a small package from the front seat, climbed out of her new Toyota RAV4 Hybrid, and slammed the door. She glared at Javier's Hummer before she stomped up the three steps to the back door of the building.

After letting herself inside, AJ kicked the door shut. Jaws locked, she hurried along the corridor to Javier's office. She walked in and dropped the parcel on a chair.

Javier rose from behind his desk. "Hel—"

"Sit." Hands on hips, AJ fixed an icy stare on Javier's face.

He sat.

"Have you lost your mind?" AJ shook her head as she flopped onto a chair. She reached over and picked up the package.

"What are you talking about?" Javier crossed his arms.

"Oh. I don't suppose you know anything about one of your employees following me?"

"Uh .... Well .... I guess." Javier's face reddened.

"Yeah. Don't think I can look after myself? You never learned anything about me when we worked together on our joint mission?"

"Well .... Look. I really care about you—a lot, and ever since I received the photo of headless bodies and then your accident, which seemed suspect, I assumed—"

"Remember the saying about making assumptions?" AJ rolled her eyes. "I understand you did what you thought was best, but don't you think it would have been better to include me in the decision?"

"I understand." Javier snapped his fingers. "Wait a minute. How did you find out I had someone following you?"

"I spotted Cesar a couple of nights ago. He did a good job of staying hidden and not making it obvious but remember I'm highly trained." She grinned. "Besides, the director thought the accident was a bit strange, too. He assigned a security officer to follow me—not all of the time, but when necessary. The guy tasked as my support spotted Cesar and clobbered him." AJ picked up the package from the other chair, leaned over, and tossed it on Javier's desk. "My guy filled me in this morning and gave me a present."

"What's that?"

"Cesar's weapon, his wallet, and a few condoms." She raised a brow. "Since when are condoms part of a surveillance package?" AJ smiled.

"Uh." Javier's face reddened again.

"No worries—just having some fun."

"Okay. But it's tough knowing someone might be gunning for you."

"We just need to coordinate things." AJ stretched out her legs. "I'll ask for assistance from you if I think I need it. Can you summon Cesar? I have a suggestion on how we should proceed."

Javier nodded, reached for the intercom, and hit a button. "Hey, Cesar. Can you come to the office? Bring Sindee with you."

"Sure thing, boss. Be there in a couple of minutes."

Moments later, a quick knock on the door frame.

Cesar and Sindee stepped inside and took empty chairs.

AJ glanced at Cesar and gestured to the side of her head.

He turned and showed her his bruises.

"Sorry he hit you so hard, Cesar." AJ suppressed a smile. "Until he found your ID, my security detail didn't realize you weren't out to cause me harm. So, he took steps to neutralize you."

"I'll survive. My pride was injured more than my body. Your guy was good—he was next to me before I realized anyone was there."

"So, what's up, Javier?" Sindee smothered a yawn. "Sorry. Heidi and I were up very late arranging furniture and unpacking stuff in our new apartment."

Javier tilted his head toward AJ.

"How's it going? Moving into a new place can be such fun." AJ rolled her eyes and pretended to stick a finger down her throat.

"I think I'd rather have my tonsils out than make another move." Sindee laughed. "At least with Heidi, I have a cool roommate."

AJ chuckled as she glanced at the others before turning serious. "As you're all aware, someone is sending a message to us. First, with the photo of six headless corpses, and possibly with my accident." She used her fingers to describe air quotes. "Plus, the attempt to kidnap Sindee when they took Heidi instead."

Everyone nodded.

"I think we should go on the offensive—try to grab someone and find out who is behind this."

"What do you propose?" Cesar rubbed the tender area of his head. "Do I need a helmet?" He grinned.

"Sindee, I realize you're not trained for this, but here's what I was thinking. If you're willing to be bait, we can put you on the street, strolling from here to your former apartment building. The difference is, we'll use at least two people to keep an eye on you, and they'll be able to intervene if something happens."

"Who will be with me?"

"I will. We'll pretend we're a couple in love." Cesar laughed.

AJ rolled her eyes." Oh, great. Just what we need—another Casanova."

"Not to worry, AJ and Sindee. I was just having some fun."

Sindee nodded. "Okay. I'm game—as long as someone has my back."

"How do you plan to run surveillance?" Cesar glanced at Javier. "I want to get whoever is behind this."

"It needs to be someone not associated with our agency." Javier drummed his fingers on the desk. "Can't involve local law enforcement either. If we catch anyone, they'll be obligated to read them their rights and haul them away. If they clam up, we'll be no closer to finding out who is behind this and what they want."

"I think the Snakes are out, too." AJ pursed her lips. "Not many options, are there?"

"Not legal ones." Javier gestured at Cesar. "How about one or two of your buddies you mentioned before? If we could find two and keep you in a support role, it might work."

Cesar nodded. "Sure. I can speak to a couple of guys who would be perfect for this. They used to be involved in following foreign diplomats around D.C., so this should be a simple job for them. When do you want to start?"

"What happens when we catch someone?" Sindee focused on Javier before switching to AJ.

"Simple. I know a cabin we can use in northern Virginia—an excellent interrogation center—no one will hear a thing." AJ's eyes narrowed. "There's a room already soundproofed, and the nearest neighbor is about a quarter of a mile away. The agency uses it for debriefing foreign nationals."

Javier raised a hand. "We need to plan the details—who, where, and when. What vehicles will the surveillance team use? What about weapons? Comms?"

AJ nodded. "Everyone armed, of course—except for Sindee. No time to run her through a quick firearms course, so she needs to appear as normal as possible. Standard comms gear The Brusch Agency purchased. Perhaps a couple of trackers in case things go haywire and Sindee is taken."

"But ...." Sindee looked around the room. "I'll be safe, right?"

"Of course, you will. But we need to plan for every contingency."
AJ turned to Javier. "When do you want to start?"

"ASAP. Cesar, contact your guys and get them lined up. Suggest no more than three consecutive days—both in the morning and evening."

"Will do, boss." Cesar stood. "If you don't need me anymore, I'll make some calls now."

Javier nodded.

After Cesar left, Sindee turned back to Javier. "If this works, how will you be able to do it without causing serious harm?"

Javier grinned. "Simple persuasion. AJ and I are both trained in extracting information without physical injury. We'll tag team if necessary."

"What if that doesn't work?"

"Better you don't know the specifics." AJ's voice hardened. "The individual or individuals will be given a choice—the easy way or the hard way. Makes no difference to me, but I've witnessed how persuasive Javier can be, and no one will hold out for long."

"Got that right." Javier cracked his knuckles. "I won't plan to do anything illegal—I don't think—but they'll wish they were dead."

21

S t. George's Parish
  Bermuda

A TALL, slender man, dressed only in Bermuda shorts and sandals, gazed out the open sliding doors of his two-story sanctuary perched on a prominent elevation across the South Shore. He sipped his iced Dark 'n Stormy as he rubbed the two puckered areas of skin on his lower right torso, the result of a recent altercation with a competitor.

"Good morning, sweetheart."

Phoenix Vanidestine turned at the husky words spoken in a posh British accent by his long-time girlfriend, Zaine Greenly. "'Bout time you woke up—it's almost noon."

"I needed my beauty sleep."

He chuckled. "You're always a beauty."

Zaine ran her hands through her long, straight blonde hair before stepping closer and taking his drink. She wrinkled her nose after tasting the Gosling Black Seal Rum and ginger beer. "Ugh. How can you drink this stuff?"

"What's wrong with it? This is Bermuda's national drink!"

"True. But you're not from Bermuda, so why not drink something that tastes better?" She ruffled his curly black hair. "Take me water skiing today."

Phoenix shook his head. "Can't. Too busy. There's—"

"I know, I know. Business. But you're the boss, so why aren't you making the decisions?"

"I might be the boss of this part of the operation, but we're just a small cog in the overall organization. Someone above me is calling the shots, and he wants his merchandise."

Zaine crinkled her nose. "I'm beginning to think you don't love me anymore. You spend more time with those guys than you do with me."

Phoenix wrapped his arms around her and gave a slight squeeze. "You're the most important person in the world to me. However, I still have to earn a living."

"Why can't you have a normal nine-to-five job instead of one that takes you away at all hours?"

He shrugged. "You should have realized I'd be bored doing some mundane job."

"Yeah, I guess." Zaine rubbed Phoenix's bullet-wound scars. "I just worry the thrills you seek might lead to your death."

"Not to worry." Phoenix puffed out his chest. "I'm golden— nothing can harm me." *I hope.* "Let's have brunch before I head to—"

"Your pocket's buzzing." She patted his backside.

Phoenix grinned, pulled his cell phone from a back pocket, and accepted the call. "Yeah?"

"We're waiting for you to check the shipment. Are you sure you don't want me to take care of things?"

"No! Nothing leaves the warehouse until I've examined the merchandise. You know that." *If I check it, I'll find out if anyone has added an unwanted tracking device.* "I'll be there in a couple of hours." Phoenix cut the connection and shoved the phone back in his pocket.

"Problems?"

"An overzealous employee. Nothing I can't handle."

"How about an omelet before you go? There's ham, cheese, mush-rooms, and hot peppers."

Phoenix drained his glass. "Sounds perfect. Put in plenty of chilies."

~

AFTER PHOENIX CLIMBED into his Blue VW EOS convertible, he tapped the horn and waved before turning onto the narrow road.

When he was out of sight, Zaine walked through the house and sat in a lounge chair overlooking the bay. While she was cooking, Zaine had placed a bag with her essentials next to the chair. She donned her Ray-Bans and thumbed through her cell phone contacts to the one she wanted. She pressed dial and waited.

Someone picked up. "Hello?"

"Daddy, he just left."

"Excellent, my dear. Thank you. I'll make the arrangements."

Zaine broke the connection, replaced her phone in the bag, and pulled out a copy of *Tears of Fire* by Gordon Bickerstaff. She smiled as she found where she left off and began reading.

~

PHOENIX TURNED UP THE RADIO. Reggae music broadcast by Irie 98.3 blasted from the speakers. He tapped his fingers on the window edge as he zipped through the streets.

He drove along Coot Pond and turned onto a narrow tree-lined road leading to Fort St. Catherine's. Phoenix took a right onto a path not much wider than his car and headed toward a disused pier on Gates Bay.

As he came over the ridge, he stopped.

Below, a sleek blue and white Cigarette Top Gun 38 boat bobbed in the water, with a single passenger holding an AK-47. Two ropes secured it to the rickety wooden pier. A white Renault Kangoo Panel Van sat on the sand by the dock. Two men pulled small parcels from the back of the vehicle and carried them onto the boat.

Phoenix smiled as he continued down the incline and parked near the van. After surveying the area, he headed along the pier and jumped onto the *Childhood Dream*.

The passenger stood and approached, a smile plastered on his face. "About time, Jefe."

They fist-bumped. "Hey, Jose. I had other business to attend to."

"Bet her name was Zaine." He chuckled.

Phoenix raised his brows. "How much today?"

"Twenty kilos. It's all stowed away."

"What are the guys loading?"

"Bermuda souvenirs." Jose shrugged. "The usual—miniature bottles of pink sand, tote bags, key rings, and posters. They'll be sold in the Miami store."

Phoenix nodded. "As soon as you're ready, take off. I'll let the man know the shipment's on the way."

Blam! Zing!

Phoenix ducked and yanked a pistol from underneath his shirt. "Where'd the shot come from?"

Jose knelt next to him, his pistol aimed toward the bluff. "I don't see anyone."

Thwack!

A second shot sent fiberglass shards into the air.

The two workers who had carried boxes below dashed onto the deck. They yanked their AKs from across their backs and sprayed the hillside.

Bang! Bang!

A shot tore across the top of one man's head while the second round drilled through the other man's nose. The impact knocked them overboard. They floated facedown, blood spreading out from their bodies.

"I need to get out of here!" Phoenix jumped onto the dock. "Cover me!"

Bullets followed him, throwing up splinters and small columns of sand as he rushed along the dock and back to the car. He emptied his pistol at the unknown assailants as he struggled with the keys.

"Wait!" Jose stood and jumped to his feet.

Three bullets stitched across Jose's chest. He fell onto the pier, his blood glistening in the mid-afternoon sun.

His head lolled to the side, his eyes staring at—nothing.

Phoenix pounded on the dash and screamed. A cloud of black smoke billowed from the exhaust as the engine finally turned over.

No other shots came, as if the perpetrators had disappeared.

He raced up the incline, narrowly missing a tourist bus, as he turned left toward Coot Pond.

"Damn! Damn!" He slapped the wheel as the vehicle screeched to a stop. As soon as the road cleared, he gunned the engine, fishtailing onto the main road heading into St. George's. *Who was behind this? I'll kill them!*

THE RINGING PHONE brought Zaine back to reality. She checked the number and accepted the call. "Yes, Daddy?"

"All taken care of, my dear. You shouldn't have any more difficulties with command and control."

"Thank you, Daddy. Phoenix was too soft with his cousin—Jose was getting in the way." Zaine chuckled. "Are you coming for dinner?"

"Wouldn't miss it—I'll bring the wine."

22

Hideout
Centreville, Virginia

ALBERTO SMILED as he pocketed his cell phone. *Twenty kilos—more than enough to keep us financed until we exact revenge.* He pushed away from the table, the chair legs screeching as they scraped across the floor. *Time for tea.*

While the water boiled in the electric kettle, he pulled a tall glass from the cupboard. He dropped in a teabag, pouring the water when it was ready. Alberto stirred for a moment before lifting out the bag. Once he added four sugar cubes and gave it a final stir, he returned to the table.

Hmm. Better send an update. Alberto opened his laptop before taking a cautious sip of his drink. *Perfect.* He began typing:

To: Ismail

From: Abdul

Twenty bags of sugar on the way for our party. Ingredients should arrive in two to three days. Need your cooking expertise to maximize profits. Excess revenue will be shared with our brethren. Please advise chef's arrival information.

AFTER SENDING his message and closing the laptop, Alberto resumed sipping his tea. *Where are Justin and Bennie?* He glanced at his watch. *Should be here by now.*

ALBERTO HEARD A NOISE OUTSIDE. He scurried to the window and glanced outside. *At last.* He returned to his seat.

Justin pulled the SUV into the driveway and killed the engine. He pursed his lips as he stared at the house. "Hope Alberto believes me since I don't have a backup plan. If not, there'll be trouble."

After pounding his fist on the steering wheel, Justin hopped out of the vehicle and dashed to the rear of the house. He checked the door.

Unlocked.

He pushed the door open and stepped into the kitchen.

Alberto turned and stared at him. "About time. Where's Bennie?"

"Uh. He's ...." Justin straddled a chair opposite Alberto.

"Well? Was the job completed?"

"Yes." Justin grimaced. "But ...."

"But, what? Did something go wrong?"

Justin swallowed. "You could say that. The trucker—he sensed something was wrong before he answered the door. H-he had a gun. He shot Bennie in the stomach and ran back into the house."

Alberto crossed his arms and frowned. "What did you do?"

"I chased him through the house into the kitchen. Before he opened the door to the backyard and tried to escape, I shot him—

twice. Afterward, I put his body and Bennie's in the SUV and went to one of the decadent home improvement stores, where I bought chains and concrete blocks." He grinned. "No one will find them. They're both at the bottom of the lake now."

"Are you sure the bodies won't resurface?"

"Positive. I put a cement block on each leg and wrapped the chains through the holes and connected them to loops on their jeans."

Alberto shook his head. "You better hope they don't surface." *I'm sure Bennie and Justin couldn't set off a vest without help.* "Get cleaned up. I'll make arrangements to replace Bennie." *Might be time to get rid of Justin, too.*

"Yes, Alberto." Justin stood and left the room.

Still shaking his head, Alberto reopened his laptop. He stared at the ceiling as he contemplated who to contact.

To: Farooq

From: Abdul

Require your assistance as soon as possible. Need two or three of your best men for a hazardous job. Money no object but success is vital. Multiple targets.

AFTER SENDING HIS MESSAGE, Alberto grabbed a Diet Coke from the fridge and went into the living room. He drank half of the can before glancing at a wall clock. *Almost time for the game.* He rushed into the bathroom to relieve himself. *Wonder if once I've exacted revenge, I should send a message to the infidels. Perhaps place some of Walter's devices in one of the stadiums?* He returned to the living room, sat on his recliner, clicked the remote, and selected a sports channel.

∾

JUSTIN STEPPED from the shower and dried himself. *I think I fooled Alberto, but I need to keep an eye on him. His desire for revenge might be our undoing. He's too obsessed.* Justin sighed. *I'm not sure what to do.* He put on a clean t-shirt and jeans and headed downstairs.

"Yes!' Alberto celebrated a home run by his favorite team, the Detroit Tigers, as Justin joined him. "I've requested a replacement for Bennie—someone better suited to our mission and won't be tempted by American decadence."

Justin nodded. "Bennie was too soft. When will the person arrive?"

"I don't know. I'm still waiting for a response. In the meantime, I want you to head to Miami. A shipment should arrive soon—twenty kilos." Alberto grinned. "While we tend to personal business, we'll continue to weaken the infidels with our low-priced cocaine."

"Where do you want me to take it?" Justin rubbed a hand over his head. "Should I cut it, or are you bringing someone else in?"

"Take it to the other house. Walter will keep an eye on it while we wait for Ismail's man to arrive. He'll decide what to mix it with. Make sure there's plenty of flour, baking soda, cornstarch, and talcum powder for him."

Justin nodded. "Will do. Anything else? If not, I'm heading out for a burger. Should I bring you back something?"

"Nothing else right now." Alberto paused the game. "Wait. Bring me two Whoppers. I'm not hungry now, but I will be tonight."

"Be back soon."

"Okay." *Perhaps it's time for you to join Bennie. Can't have any more mistakes.*

~

AFTER JUSTIN LEFT, Alberto retrieved his laptop during the seventh-inning stretch. He checked for messages. There were two:

. . .

To: Abdul

From: Ismail

Sorry, my chef can't arrive for at least a week. He's busy with a local celebration and relocating the bakery. As soon as he's free, I'll send you his arrival information.

ALBERTO NODDED. *As expected. The federales must be closing in on Ismail's group again.* He opened the second email.

To: Abdul

From: Farooq

Three of my finest will arrive in your area next week after they travel through Europe. They'll contact you once they enter the U.S. You've paid well in the past and are a faithful follower of Allah. The only payment required will be the team's expenses. Keep them with you as long as you require.

ALBERTO TURNED his attention back to the ballgame. He cheered as the Detroit Tigers scored three times in the top of the ninth and held on to beat the Washington Nationals, 9-7. After turning off the television, he leaned back in his recliner and gazed at the ceiling.

Images of the slaughter of Michael and their friends at the warehouse in Mexico flooded his mind. Tears seeped from his eyes as he recalled holding Michael in his arms as he stiffened and began his journey to Allah.

"Aaaaah!"

Alberto jumped from the chair and rushed to a framed photo of Michael with him at their training facility in Colombia. He removed the back of the frame, allowing six pictures to fall into his hand.

One by one, he stared at each photo, stopping at an image of Javier. Alberto repeatedly stabbed at the paper with a forefinger. *Soon,*

Coronel, I shall remove your image from this earth as if you never existed. Allah shall have his vengeance, and my friends will rest in peace.

He flicked to another photo and grinned. "But first, you must watch your woman die. Afterward, I'll cut you until you beg for death. Allahu Akbar!"

23

The Brusch Agency
Old Town, Alexandria, Virginia

RETIRED CIA ANALYST Phil Price leaned back in his custom-built ergonomic chair and grinned. *You can run, but I'll always find you!* He popped the top of his Mountain Dew and took a swig. *Just like old times—except the pay's much better!*

He swiped a hand through his thinning gray hair and typed a note to himself before turning back to the details he had uncovered. *I have to be certain.* Placing the tip of his index finger on the computer screen, he scanned the last report. He slapped a hand on the desk. *You're mine!*

Phil hit print and grabbed the paper. After a final read, he jumped out of his chair, dashed out of the room, and ran down the hall. Pausing to catch his breath, he knocked on a closed door.

"Come in."

Phil opened the door and stepped inside. "Sir, I ... uh ... have ... some—"

"Take a deep breath and relax." Javier grinned as he gestured toward a chair. "Take a load off and stop calling me sir."

"Yes, sir. I mean, Javier." Phil sat. "I uncovered some information you might find interesting."

"Go ahead."

"I was researching the connections with the Islamic State trainers named Michael and Alberto. As you know, Michael died in the warehouse attack in Mexico, but no one knows what happened to Alberto."

"What are your sources of the connections?"

"Uh ... well .... I forgot to tell the IT office I retired." Phil gave a slight smile. "Seems I still have access to several databases—at least through some backdoors I left. Not anything supersensitive, but enough for me to investigate these men."

Javier struggled to maintain a straight face. "I see." He rubbed his chin and pursed his lips. "Can anything come back on you? I'd prefer we not end up in a cell together."

Phil shook his head. "Unless the security guys are specifically looking for me, I doubt anyone will notice. Besides, I told AJ I was doing this."

"What did she say?"

"She just rolled her eyes and told me to stay out of trouble."

"I agree with her. Don't tell me any more about your methods, so I have some plausible deniability if the authorities begin an investigation."

Phil placed an index finger over his mouth. "My lips are sealed. Shall I tell you what I found out?"

Javier nodded. "Please."

"Okay." Phil perched on the edge of his chair. "Before I retired, we learned Islamic State referred to Alberto as Abdul Rahman. He's from Argentina."

"What about Michael?"

"This is where it gets interesting. Michael was known as Mahmood. They also called him the Cockney." He waved the printout in the air.

"From London?"

Phil nodded. "Yes. We knew the phone numbers used by both men. They've been silent since the warehouse attack. But …."

"But?" Javier raised a brow.

"Both men were in regular contact with a number in Madrid. The user of the Spanish number was confirmed as a recruiter for Islamic State."

"I seem to recall some of this from AJ."

Phil grinned. "Yes, but I wanted to bring you up to speed before I give you the latest information."

"Don't keep me in suspense. What'd you find out?"

He glanced at the report. "Calls between the Madrid number and one in Virginia began a few weeks before you retired. Not often, but once or twice every ten days or so."

"Who owns the Virginia number?"

"I'm still working on it. Perhaps Alberto is here looking for you?"

"A good guess." Javier sipped from a cold cup of coffee on his desk and grimaced. "I should have finished this earlier."

"Do you want me to get you another one?"

Javier shook his head. "No thanks, Phil. My own fault."

"There's also something else."

"What is it?"

"I hope you don't mind, but I had someone look at the photos Lieutenant de Santa Anna took after the warehouse attack. My friend's a photo analyst. He compared the body purported to be Michael's with the headless pictures you received."

"Did he find anything of interest?"

Phil nodded. "Yes. He compared Michael's photo with the others. He's ninety percent sure one of the pictures you received is of Michael's body."

"How did he make this determination?"

"It's not my forte, but he examined the hands in both photos and extrapolated the size of the torso." Phil stared at Javier. "Someone is sending you a message."

"Hmm." Javier drummed a beat on his desk before grinning. "Great work, Phil. Keep at it, but stay out of trouble."

"You got it. As soon as I find out anything else, I'll update you. In the meantime, I need to work on the information that came from Bermuda, so I'm on top of things."

"Keep me posted."

After Phil left, Javier pulled the keyboard of his desktop closer and typed a message:

To: Snakes

From: Cobra

Suspected Islamic State recruiter possibly in contact with the escaped fighter from the Mexico encounter. I might require your services to beef up our security. Will keep you posted.

AFTER SENDING THE EMAIL, Javier picked up his cup and headed out of the office in search of fresh coffee.

WALTER CLIMBED out of a silver Honda Accord. He donned a pair of sunglasses and pressed the key fob to lock the door. Satisfied with the responding beep, he strolled along the street. He gazed at the various buildings bordering the tree-lined street, continuing past the home of The Brusch Agency.

Once he reached the next corner, Walter turned back. When he approached The Brusch Agency again, he stopped, bent over, and pretended to adjust a shoelace. He glanced around—no one appeared to be paying any attention to him.

He headed along the driveway toward the back of the building. Walter focused on the doors and windows on the ground floor. *Plenty of windows, but only two doors. Excellent.* He continued his trek around the building, stopping before he reached the parking lot. *Another security camera—hard to spot since it's tucked under the eave. I hope there's a gap in the coverage.*

At the rear of the property, Walter identified two parking spots dedicated to The Brusch Agency. A black Hummer sat in one of them while the other was empty. He headed back to the street and returned to his car.

Jumping inside, he grabbed a notebook and pen from the passenger seat and drew a diagram of the building, marking the security cameras he had spotted. Finished with his crude drawing, he tapped the pen against his lips. Walter added the parking spots, leaned back, and smiled.

"All they have to do is open one of the doors." He clapped his hands. "Boom!"

Walter laughed as he fished his cell phone out of his pocket. He scrolled through the numbers and selected one.

After three rings, he heard a voice say hello. "Alberto. I'm putting together my plan. Revenge will be yours soon."

"Excellent."

24

T he Oxford House
Hamilton, Bermuda

A SLIGHT OCEAN breeze cooled the relentless morning air. Charlie closed the newspaper, drained the last of his coffee, and reached for the carafe. He glanced at the other team members seated around the table as they finished breakfast.

"Hey, Charlie, give me a top up." TJ pushed his empty cup across the table.

"Sure. Anyone else?"

The others shook their heads.

Charlie filled TJ's cup and then his own. "As soon as everyone's ready, we'll get our mission underway to find this Maverick character. Sam and I will collect our package from the consulate and meet you here. TJ and Wild, pick up the rental cars Sindee reserved for us—be easier than relying on public transportation."

"Shall I find a taxi for us?" Sam pushed her plate away.

Charlie shook his head. "It's only two klicks. We'll walk and pretend we're tourists. Bring your camera. The slight ocean breeze will keep things tolerable. Any other questions? If not, let's do it."

DRESSED IN MATCHING TOPS, shorts, and mirrored sunglasses, Charlie and Sam strolled from the B&B toward the harbor. Each had a backpack slung over a shoulder, while Sam had a camera strap around her neck.

After turning left on Front Street, Sam pointed to a sign. "Look! Do you think we'll have time to take a cruise on the *Reef Explorer*? I've never been on a glass bottom boat before." She pulled the camera from around her neck and took several photos.

Charlie chuckled. "Sounds like a plan to me. What about the sunset cocktail pirate cruise? We can all dress up." He glanced around—no one nearby. "Mission first, fun later."

Sam put her camera away and linked her arm through Charlie's. "Of course, dear."

Screeech! Screeech!

Both ducked as seagulls divebombed, their calls shattering the morning calm.

"Must be looking for breakfast." Sam grinned. "Next time we're out for a walk, I'll bring something to feed them."

Charlie glanced at her, a brow raised. He whispered, "Don't overdo the tourist bit. Let's go."

They continued their stroll along Front Street. On their left, three and four-story buildings painted in pastel colors lined the street. They crossed the street and walked along the promenade near the edge of the inner harbor. Trimmed hedges, flowers, and palm trees lined the path, while a waist-high fence kept unsuspecting tourists and locals alike from falling in the water.

"Perhaps tonight we'll check that place out." Charlie tilted his head toward a beige and white building with an awning-covered terrace on the second floor.

Sam laughed. "Yeah, Flanagan's Irish Pub. Do you think they'll have Guinness?"

"Duh! Of course. However, I was thinking more along the lines of listening to the locals' chatter and see if we can pick up some intel."

Sam slapped a palm against her forehead. "Of course—mission first."

"All the time. But we'll need to eat and nothing wrong with a drink or two—for authenticity, of course." Charlie winked.

As they continued their walk, the promenade narrowed. Gone were the hedges and flowers, replaced by a long pink and white edifice.

"What's this place? I don't see any sign."

Charlie gestured along the street. "Access to the cargo docks is just head. This is probably their admin building."

They passed another tall hedge running along the edge of a series of metal shipping containers before the promenade resumed.

"We better hustle. Not sure when the American Citizens Service unit shuts for lunch."

Ten minutes later, they stopped in front of the American consulate general. Green and white bollards were embedded in the sidewalk along the length of the compound. A whitewashed brick wall supported green iron bars. They rang a buzzer near the pedestrian access point and entered the one-story security building.

A stern-faced Marine stood behind a bullet-resistant partition. "How may I help you, sir?"

Charlie and Sam held up their passports. "We're here to pick up a package being held for us at the American Citizens Services. I have a letter confirming this." They slid their passports and the letter into a slot in the wall.

The Marine scrutinized their documents. "No need to go inside the chancery. You were expected today, so the Gunny brought your package here." He gestured to his left. "Step to the door, and I'll open it for you."

They did as instructed. Inside, Charlie and Sam found themselves in a small featureless room. A sturdy box, secured with red and white tape, sat on a table in the corner. An exit door on the opposite wall bore the usual alarm warnings.

Sam waved at the Marine, who watched them through a side window from his post. "Are you going to open it?"

"And show the Marine the contents?" Charlie shook his head and picked up the box. "We'll open it back at the B&B. Let's go."

They raised their hands in salute to the Marine and left the building. Charlie and Sam walked to a nearby taxi stand and returned to Oxford House.

AFTER PAYING THE FARE, they went inside to Charlie's room. He placed the package on the bed and pulled a knife from his backpack to cut the tamper-proof tape.

Someone knocked on the door. Charlie motioned Sam to check who it was while he picked up the package and dashed into the bathroom.

Sam glanced through the peephole before opening the door.

TJ and Wild strolled inside and sat on the room's two easy chairs while Sam climbed onto the bed with her back against the headboard.

"Where's the boss?" TJ scanned the room.

"Right here." Charlie approached the bed, carrying the now opened box. "Christmas time!" He grinned as he handed SIG Sauer P226 pistols to the other three. "Fifteen-round magazines are in the package. Help yourselves—three each. Take a holster, too."

Wild reached inside the box and pulled out a black metal rectangle, no larger than a coin. "What's this?"

"It's a Tail It GPS tracker. Should be a dozen in the box—six for each team. If you find something worthy of tracking, activate it, place the device in a hidden spot, and you're good to go."

TJ took the tracker from Wild. "What's the range? How do we track it?"

"Since it uses GPS, the range is limitless. We'll use a smartphone App for tracking."

Sam pursed her lips. "Is it easy to damage? What if it falls in water?"

"All excellent questions. The Tail It tracker is shock resistant and waterproof. The only negative I've experienced is battery time. Since we won't be able to retrieve and recharge, they'll work for up to two weeks, which should be sufficient for our needs."

Sam grinned. "Cool."

Charlie glanced at TJ and Wild. "What about our vehicles?"

Both men grimaced.

"Not as cool as the tracker." TJ pulled a set of keys from his pocket. "Tourists aren't allowed to use gasoline or diesel-powered vehicles in Bermuda. However, they do have four-wheeled electric vehicles. Here are the keys to your Tazzari." He tossed them to Charlie.

He nodded. "I spotted what must be the Tazzari in front of the B&B parked next to a small Hummer."

"With my height, I couldn't fit in your vehicle, so we rented an electric Hummer HXT for us. The agent said we'd be able to cover the twenty-one-mile length of Bermuda four times on a single charge. You'll cover a bit more distance with yours."

"Okay, you and Wild better head to St. George's Island. We'll check out Somerset and meet at Flanagan's Irish Pub on Front Street tonight about six for happy hour and dinner."

"Roger, boss."

SAM AND CHARLIE stood next to their black and gray vehicle with bright orange wheels. "Can I drive?"

Charlie raised a brow. "Ever driven on the left side of the road before?"

"No, but there's always a first time."

Charlie shrugged and tossed the keys to Sam. "Try not to kill us."

They squeezed into the small vehicle.

Sam started the engine. "Well, navigator. Show me the way."

Charlie laughed. "Head to Front Street and turn onto Crow Lane. We need to follow the main road to Somerset."

"Okay. Just tell me when to turn."

Charlie glanced at the map on his smartphone. "Not long after we're on Railway Trail, the road will fork. Keep to the left."

Sam gestured through the windshield. "There's a sign ahead mentioning South Road and Middle Road."

"Stay on South Road. Both end up in Somerset, but we'll return on the other one to mix up our route as much as we can."

They continued their journey. On either side of the road, houses and walled compounds were juxtaposed between stretches of trees. Telephone poles ran along the righthand side, while on the left, glimpses of the water could be seen.

"Slow down." Charlie tightened his seatbelt. "Appears to be a blind curve, and this is a narrow road."

"Not to worry—"

"Watch out!" Charlie reached over and jerked the wheel to get them back in their lane and out of the path of an oncoming delivery vehicle straddling the centerline.

"*Yeeeeah!*"

Sam let go of the wheel.

He overcompensated as she did so.

The Tazzari plunged over the edge.

25

S t. George's Parish
   Bermuda

A FRUSTRATED PHOENIX climbed out of his Volkswagen, slammed the door, and stormed inside the house. "Zaine! Where the hell are you?"

"On the lounge chair overlooking the bay." Zaine's voice drifted in from the patio. "Why? What's wrong?"

He grabbed a beer from the fridge and sat on a chair next to her. "I've had a shitty day—someone attacked *Childhood Dream* as the guys loaded the cargo." He chugged half the bottle. "I think someone tried to kill me—they got Jose."

"What?" Zaine took Phoenix's hand in hers and squeezed it. "Are you okay? Poor Jose."

Phoenix clenched his teeth. "I'm fine, but I'll find the bastard who organized this."

"What'll you do?"

"No one does this to me. I'll kill him." He drained the remainder of the beer. "Grab me another."

"Just one more." She stood. "Daddy's coming for dinner tonight."

Phoenix groaned. "Again? He ate with us last week."

"So? I enjoy his company."

"He's not even your father."

"No, but he's lonely. Besides, he's filthy rich."

ROLAND RUSSELL, called Daddy by Zaine, stepped into the house, holding a heavy package. He kissed her on the cheek as he handed the reusable bag to Phoenix. "Here's the wine I promised—two bottles of white and two bottles of red. What's for dinner, dear?"

"Nothing fancy—cottage pie followed by sherry trifle."

"Excellent. My favorites." Roland wiped the side of his mouth with a finger. "My mouth's drooling at the thought."

Phoenix removed the red wine from the bag and placed it on the island before shoving the white into the fridge to chill. "Want a beer?"

"Sure." Roland gazed out the window at the bay. "I can't get over this view. It mesmerizes me every time I'm here. Are you sure you won't sell?" *Be a great place to keep an eye on incoming and outgoing shipments.*

Phoenix pulled two bottles from a cooler, popped the tops, and handed one to Roland. "Not a chance. I spent months finding the perfect place to live, and I won't give it up."

"Oh, well. Can't hurt to keep asking." He raised his beer in the air. "Cheers."

"Cheers."

ROLAND PUSHED BACK his empty plate and patted his stomach. "Outstanding, my dear. Your cottage pie is the best in Bermuda."

"Don't tell her that, Roland. Compliments go to her head." Phoenix drained the remains of his red wine.

Zaine stuck out her tongue at Phoenix. "Says the person who can't cook."

"Ahem. Be nice, children. Tell me, how are things going with your import-export business?"

"Competition remains stiff, but we're holding our own." Phoenix glanced at Zaine. "We ran into a serious problem today—resulted in the death of one of my employees."

Roland rubbed his chin. "What happened? Were the police involved?"

"As the men loaded cargo onboard the *Childhood Dream,* one of them slipped and fell between the pier and the boat. Before we pulled him out, a wave shoved the boat, pinning him against a pillar. The collision broke the man's neck. Since it was an accident, we didn't contact the police."

Good. Might have been rather awkward if they involved the police. "How horrible! Will it delay your shipment?"

Phoenix shook his head. "I don't think so. We planned to go to Miami in a few days. I think we'll still make it since most of the cargo is loaded."

"Don't forget to take my island jewelry." Zaine smiled. "The Miami outlet is screaming for more merchandise."

"If they ever find out your jewelry is handmade by underpaid street children in Brazil, they'd drop you in a heartbeat."

"I won't tell them." Zaine shrugged. "Besides, look what it did for me. Until a photographer showed my photos to a modeling agency, I made jewelry, too. Somehow, I survived—it didn't kill me, and I'm stronger for it."

"True, but you'll always bear the internal scars of what you went through." Phoenix reached for her hand and squeezed it. He turned to Roland. "What's your agenda for the next few days?"

"A meeting with the governor, another one at the bank. If there's time, I plan to do some big-game fishing." Roland glanced at his watch. "Speaking of time, would one of you be so kind and ring for a taxi? Since I was bringing wine and figured we'd be doing some drinking, I didn't want to risk driving and getting caught by the police."

"I'll do it, Daddy." Zaine stood and picked up her phone from the island.

"Wish I had time to go fishing with you, Roland." Phoenix stretched out his hands. "I'd love to tackle a few marlins or tuna." He chuckled. "Or spend the afternoon watching my line."

"Perhaps next time."

"It's a date."

Both men laughed as they shook hands.

Minutes later, a horn sounded outside.

"Your taxi's here, Daddy." Zaine kissed him on the cheek. "Come again, soon."

"I will, dear. Thank you for a delightful evening."

ROLAND HOPPED out of the taxi and entered Flanigan's. He studied the packed bar area before heading upstairs in search of his contact.

"Hey, Roland. Over here, buddy." A stocky bald man dressed in tight-fitting jeans and a black shirt stood. Bicep muscles threatened to split the seams of his shirt. His deep bass New York accent seemed to part the crowd.

Roland weaved his way to a table overlooking the street. He grasped the huge hand extended toward him. "Jaden. Good of you to come."

Jaden smiled, showing three missing teeth. "As if I could resist, man. Are things okurrr?"

"So far." Roland winced as he pulled his hand from Jaden's. "Might have a job or two for you."

"What do I need to schlep and where? Will there be guap?" He rubbed his thumb against his fingertips.

Roland laughed. "Cut the New York bullshit, Jaden. You're as British as I am."

"Just practicing. Who knows—there might be a talent scout

looking for a dude as handsome as me." Jaden chuckled as he rubbed the long scar down the left side of his face.

"All I need you to do is head to Miami and watch for the arrival of this boat. It should arrive in three days." Roland slid over a photo of the *Childhood Dream*. "No intervention, but I need to know who's onboard, where they go, and who they meet. Use as many of your friends as necessary. As usual, I'll cover all expenses, and you'll receive your regular bonus."

Jaden flagged down a waitress and glanced at Roland. "Want anything to eat or drink?"

"Just a beer."

Jaden ordered fish chowder and two beers. After the waitress departed, he turned back to Roland. "Any other jobs on the horizon?"

"Yes. One you'll enjoy." Roland smirked. "Once my brother is avenged, there are three other matters for you to take care of. Afterward, your debt to me will be paid in full."

Jaden nodded. "Michael was like a brother to me. It'll be my pleasure to tie up any loose ends. What are their names?"

Roland stared across the street at the dark water. "Alberto, Phoenix, and Zaine. How you do the job is your choice."

Jaden ran an imaginary knife across his throat. "Excellent. I shall not fail."

T

he Brusch Agency
Old Town, Alexandria, Virginia

A SPRING EMITTED a high-pitched protest as Javier leaned back in his chair. A thump followed as he rested the heel of his boots on the edge of his desk. He savored his first cup of coffee as he reread the email from Dougie:

To: Cobra, Snakes
From: Adder

DIDN'T TAKE LONG for you to need bailing out. I have some leave coming up, so I'll head your way to assist with your security. The others will follow if you require help for a longer period. Please provide weapons and plenty of beer. Say hello to Mrs. Smith.

. . .

JAVIER FINISHED HIS COFFEE, dropped his feet to the floor, and typed.

To: *Adder, Snakes*
    From: *Cobra*

WHAT CAN I SAY? *I'll need you to keep out of sight as much as possible. Don't want to scare them away—better to deal with things now rather than spending time looking over my shoulder. Weapons, lodging, and all the beer you want are on me. You can pay for your own food—would cost more than the rest.*

AFTER SENDING HIS RESPONSE, Javier picked up the phone, punched a single digit, and waited for Phil to answer.

"Uh, yes, boss. What can I do for you?"

"Any word from Bermuda?"

"No, sir. The last contact mentioned Charlie and Sam were heading to Somerset while TJ and Wild were checking things out at St. George's. Should I request an update?"

Javier pursed his lips. *Something's wrong—not like Charlie to skip SITREPs.* "Yeah. Someone should have sent a situation report by now."

"Will send a request right away." Phil cleared his throat. "Remember I mentioned I still had access to some CIA databases?"

"Yeah. Did anyone catch you?"

"No, but the security guys cut my access." He chuckled. "Not a problem—when I was doing the last software update, I added a backdoor."

Javier smacked his forehead. "Is this going to come back on us?"

"Negative. Since I was one of the authorized members of the IT team, I had full access. I doubt anyone will go sniffing around to find out if I left anything."

"I suggest using this access only on the rarest of occasions—and don't tell me when you do."

"You won't hear it from me."

"I hope not." Javier broke the connection. He stood, picked up his cup, and went in search of more coffee.

Before he reached the door, someone shoved it open.

"Good morning, Mr. Smith." AJ's eyes sparkled as she handed a travel mug to Javier. "When are you going to hook up the Smarter Coffee machine I gave you for The Brusch Agency? Everything's ready—just waiting for you."

"As soon as I find the time. It has loads of bells and whistles I need to understand first."

AJ raised a brow. "Uh-huh. You live here—you can find the time. Men—always an excuse!"

"Now, wait a minute." Javier raised his hands in surrender. "If you quit your job and came here to work, as I've hinted on several occasions, we could sort a few things out."

"Yeah, right. I know what you mean." AJ smiled. "Anyway, it was a slow day at the office, so I thought I'd stop by and find out what's going on. How's Phil working out?"

"Couldn't be better—but he had an excellent role model."

AJ kissed Javier on the cheek before they sat in front of his desk. "You might be a smooth talker, but it won't keep you out of trouble."

Javier shrugged. "What can I say? By the way, Dougie says hi."

"How's he doing? I miss the Snakes."

"He's going to use his accrued leave and will be here in a few days to provide extra security. You know I don't like sitting on my hands when we should be proactive. I want Sindee and Cesar on the street ASAP to see if we can flush out whoever seems to have it in for us. Dougie will remain here while they walk the area."

AJ nodded. "Great idea. Assume Cesar will be armed in case of trouble? Too bad we couldn't get Sindee through a weapons course quick enough."

"Uh ... I discussed weapons basics with her, so she'll be carrying a SIG P365."

"Are you nuts? She might be more of a hindrance than helpful."

"Perhaps, but it seemed like the right thing to do." Javier frowned. "What's up?"

"Charlie and his team missed their latest SITREP. I don't like it—something's up. I can feel it."

AJ rubbed her hand on Javier's arm. "Things are quiet for me at the moment. I can get away for a few days and go check things out."

Javier shook his head. "If that photo with the six bodies missing their heads is supposed to represent us, I don't want you in a possible dangerous situation in case something happens to Charlie and the others." *Better we find those looking for us and deal with them.*

"Excuse me! I'm a big girl and can look after myself. Remember Colombia and Panama?"

"Got me there. I'm just a worrier—at least when it pertains to close friends. I don't have a lot of them, so I can be a bit protective." A smile spread across his face. "Let's wait and see if Charlie gets back to us. Might be nothing." *But I doubt it—something's up.*

PHIL RUSHED DOWN the hall to Javier's office. Out of breath, he pushed the door open without knocking. "Boss. I—"

Javier and AJ turned at the interruption. He waved Phil inside and pointed to a chair.

"Sorry to interrupt. I found something that might be important. At least, MacKenzie and Makayla did."

AJ glanced at Javier. "Stealing my team?"

"Just a helping hand. What did they find out, Phil?"

"There's a small shipment headed to Miami. Might not be anything of interest to us, but it's coming from Bermuda."

"How did they find this out?"

"Uh. I'm not supposed to tell."

AJ rolled her eyes. "Phil, spit it out."

"Yes, boss. One number contacted another and mentioned the

shipment. The number they're monitoring is the one in previous contact with Islamic State in Spain."

Javier smiled. "Pass on my thanks to MacKenzie and Makayla. Keep at it—we need as much intel as possible."

"Will do, boss." Phil stood and hurried out of the room.

Javier turned to AJ. "Well, Mrs. Smith. Are you game for a short vacation in Florida?"

AJ smiled. "What did you have in mind?"

"Once we know more, it'll be time for you and me to get from behind our desks." Javier chuckled. "We're going hunting!"

Across the street from The Brusch Agency, a city cherry picker sat underneath a streetlight. In the bucket, a man wearing a hardhat and dressed in coveralls worn by the Arlington Department of Public Works finished changing the burned-out bulb. Before replacing the cover, he installed a small surveillance camera and connected it to the lamppost's electrical supply. "Perfect."

As soon as he finished, Walter lowered the boom, hopped out, and climbed inside the truck. He drove away, tapping on the steering wheel. *As soon as I have a good idea of the number of people working at the agency and their comings and goings, they're going to receive a surprise.*

He laughed. "A deadly one." His cellphone rang, and he accepted the call. "Hello?"

"Is it done?"

"Yes."

"Excellent. I grow impatient."

"If Allah wills, soon The Brusch Agency will be no more."

27

S t. George's Parish
  Bermuda

WILD DROVE their electric Hummer HXT along Kindler Field Road past the Bermuda Airport. He tapped a hand on the steering wheel in time with the Reggae music playing on Irie 98.3 FM.

TJ perched his long legs over the window edge as he studied a map of Bermuda on his phone. "Keep following this road—I'll tell you when to turn."

"Yeah, right. Make sure you give me plenty of notice—last time we were almost past the turn when you freaked me out with your waving and shouting, 'Turn!'"

TJ shrugged. "What can I say—I'm still getting my bearings. You should have paid extra for the built-in sat-nav."

"Charlie said not to overspend."

"Do you always do as you're told?" TJ laughed.

"Only when the mood suits me."

"Well, turn right at the roundabout onto St. David's Road, or we'll be going the wrong way."

Wild coasted to a stop as he checked for traffic. He pulled out—

Beeep!

Wild slammed on the brakes.

The driver of the car coming from the right gave a V-sign to Wild as he drove past. "Asshole!"

"Do you want me to drive?" TJ grinned. "Remember to look to your right first while we're here."

"No, I'm okay—just need to concentrate." The road clear, Wild drove into the roundabout and took the second exit. "How far?"

"We'll be on this road until we're on the other side of the island." TJ punched a number on his phone. "Gonna check with Charlie and Sam to find out how they're doing." The phone rang several times. "Hmmm. No answer. Maybe they're already in position checking out their address."

"Send them a text later."

"Great idea." TJ yawned as he squirmed in his seat to get comfortable. "Hey—careful around the curves. Never know if someone will be on your side with these narrow roads."

"Relax, TJ. You're like my mother—always nagging when she's in the car with me."

TJ rolled his eyes. "Must be a reason for it. Hey, hang a left—we're coming up to Cashew City Road."

"Gotcha." Wild turned and followed the road around a grassy recreation area. "I hate one-way systems. Too easy to get lost."

"Never mind—watch for a yellow house—should be a sign for 'Dun Roamin'."

As they came over a rise, Wild pointed to the left. "There it is— bright enough yellow, isn't it?"

"Yeah. It screams at you. Drive past and find a place to park." TJ reached into his backpack, retrieved his binoculars, and placed them on the console.

Wild drove to the end of the street and backed into a parking spot where they had a clear view of the property. He turned off the engine and picked up TJ's binoculars.

TJ sent a text to Charlie: *In position.* He watched as a black SUV towing a boat backed down the public launch ramp. Once the boat was in the water, the driver drove into a nearby spot for vehicles with trailers. Meanwhile, a car parked next to them. A family climbed out, carrying hampers to one of the picnic tables.

"Looks like a good place to hide in plain sight." TJ gestured toward the arriving family. "With people coming and going, we should be able to remain unnoticed."

Wild lowered his glasses. "No sign of a young guy at the property. An elderly couple just came outside. He's using crutches, and one pant leg is pinned up at the knee. The woman is carrying a tray with a pitcher and sandwiches. They're heading to a table overlooking the water."

"Wonder if the address is wrong?" TJ pulled a camera from his backpack. "I'll check it out." He climbed out of the Hummer.

"What're you doing? Charlie instructed us to monitor the property, not go knocking on any doors."

TJ laughed. "Don't worry—keep an eye out." He turned and took a snap of the picnic area and the boat launch. "I'll be back."

"You're crazy."

He strolled toward the lemon-yellow house. As he neared the property, TJ spotted the couple sitting under an umbrella. "Hello!" He waved at the couple. "Do you mind if I ask you a question?"

The couple glanced at each other before nodding. The woman pointed to the gate. "Come in and join us."

He entered the property and walked across the grass. "Sorry to intrude. This is my first time in Bermuda. A friend of mine in the States gave me your address. He said his best buddy lives here."

"Please, sit down." The woman gestured to an empty chair. "My husband is Jack, and I'm Matilda." She peered at him through thick glasses. "Would you like some lemonade? I made it this morning."

"No but thank you. I'm Tom. I'm a police officer from Baltimore. My friend mentioned his friend's name was Maverick."

Jack raised a brow. "Are you chasing Maverick? He's been a handful since he was a youngster. What's he done now?"

"No, sir. Just looking to say hello while I'm here. Perhaps he can show me some of the nightlife."

"He could do that." Jack laughed. "However, Maverick hasn't lived here for years. He lives with his girlfriend here on St. George's." He clicked his fingers. "Strange name—Zaine something."

"Now, Jack. Be nice." Matilda laid a hand on her husband's arm. "Our son's name is Phoenix. He earned his nickname because he always had a mind of his own and didn't care to be one of the crowd."

"Do you know his address?"

"He lives in a big blue house on the cliff overlooking the South Shore. Don't remember the number, but you can't miss it."

"Thank you." TJ stood. "Sorry to have bothered you. I better go and let you enjoy the rest of the day." He shook hands with both of them.

"Stop by anytime while you're in Bermuda." Matilda smiled. "We're here most days."

"I'll do that. Thanks again for your hospitality." TJ headed back to the gate, turned left, and hurried to the Hummer.

"Well?" Wild raised his hands in a questioning manner.

"Right property, but he no longer lives there." TJ grinned. "However, his parents told me where to find him." He opened his phone and shook his head. "Still nothing from Charlie. Wonder if something's happened?"

"Keep trying. There must be a reason he hasn't responded."

CHARLIE LEANED back against his seat. He wiped his forehead and looked at his hand. *Blood.* He glanced at Sam before gazing at the hood of the car, crumpled and jammed into a tree that arrested their forward momentum down the hill. *Good thing we hit it. If that tree hadn't been in the way, we'd have gone over the cliff.* He turned to Sam.

Her head rested on the steering wheel, both arms hanging limp.

"Sam. Can you hear me?"

"Uggh! What ... what happened?"

"Don't move—we've been in an accident. I—"

Da da. Da da. Da ....

"Listen—help's arrived. They'll take care of us."

Moments later, paramedics and police officers surrounded their vehicle. Someone yanked Charlie's door open. "Are you okay, sir? Can you move your head?"

"I'm fine—just a cut on my head. See to my friend—she's in worse shape."

"My colleagues will see to her. Just relax." The man helped Charlie out of the car. Two others assisted him up the hill to a waiting ambulance.

As a paramedic attended to Charlie, a scream pierced the air. "Sounds like your friend is in a lot of pain. Don't worry—they'll get her out of the vehicle. Then you're both off to the hospital." He finished bandaging Charlie's cut. "They'll stitch you later, but the emergency room staff will take care of your friend first."

"What's wrong with her?"

The paramedic shook his head. "I don't know. I overheard one of my colleagues say she might have a broken clavicle to go along with a deep gash along the hairline. Too soon to know if there are any other injuries."

Four responders pulled an empty gurney out of the ambulance and placed it next to the damaged rental.

Sam's head was positioned in a neck brace. The paramedics had strapped her down to prevent further injury. The responders placed Sam on the gurney and carefully lifted her into the ambulance.

The man who treated Charlie took his arm. "You can ride with her. The police will meet you at the hospital and take a statement after your treatment."

"Can I use my phone in the ambulance? We have friends with us on our vacation, and they'll be worrying about us."

"Of course."

After Charlie climbed in, the paramedic shut the door. The siren kicked in as they headed away from the scene. Charlie opened his phone and saw TJ's text. He responded with three words:

Accident. Hospital. Now.

28

H ideout
Centreville, Virginia

ALBERTO PUMPED a fist into the air, broke the connection, and slipped his phone back in his pocket. *At last. Once Michael's death is avenged, I can return to my beloved Argentina.* His hand wavered over a Budweiser. *I need to leave this accursed country before I'm corrupted beyond recovery. May Allah forgive me in my moment of weakness.* He grabbed a Coke from the fridge and strolled into the living room.

He sat in his recliner and picked up the TV remote. As he searched for a baseball game, his phone rang. "Hello?"

"As-alaikum-salaam, Abdul. Farooq gave me your number. He passed along his prayers for your successful mission."

Alberto hesitated. "Wa-salaam-alaikum. Please refer to me as the name by which I am known here."

"Forgive me, Alberto. My friends know me as Hamza. We arrived earlier today."

"Who else is with you?"

"Farooq said you required two or three men to take care of ... unfortunate circumstances. I brought Jabbar and Kamal with me. They are both well versed in dealing with problems, as am I."

Alberto chuckled. "Did Farooq give you my address?"

"Yes."

He glanced at a wall clock. "Be here in two hours. After dark. Knock twice and then three times." Alberto disconnected.

~

THREE HOURS LATER, Hamza drove into Alberto's driveway and killed the engine of their rental. He stepped from the vehicle onto the manicured property illuminated with motion-sensor security lights, patting the holster hidden under his jacket to ensure his pistol remained secure.

Jabbar and Kamal followed.

A sensor activated a light on the wall toward the back of the house.

The three men pulled their pistols as they rushed to the side of the building and approached the door.

Hamza knocked twice, paused, and knocked three times, ducking back into the shadows until a man's silhouette appeared in the doorway.

Alberto stepped out the door under the light. "I am Alberto. Please, come inside."

The men approached, putting their weapons away.

Alberto held the door open, allowing the visitors to enter.

Once in the kitchen, Hamza held out his hand. "As-salaam-alaikum, Alberto. Farooq passed along his prayers for your successful mission. I apologize for our delay in arriving. We had a flat tire and at first, could not find the spare. Then I drove into the wrong driveway on a nearby street. A man came out of the house with a gun and chased us away."

"Wa-alaikum-salaam. May Allah's blessings be upon you." Alberto grasped the proffered hand, a hearty smile on his face as he maintained direct eye contact with Hamza. "Delays should always be anticipated. At least the man didn't call the police."

"Yes. He threatened to call them, but we left."

After a prolonged shake, Alberto turned to the others and repeated the traditional greeting. Once they finished, he gestured to the table holding a teapot and a plate of dates, stuffed grape leaves, and slices of feta cheese. "Please sit. You will be hungry and thirsty after your long journey. After you refresh yourselves, we shall discuss your target." *They could be brothers—same short black hair, dark eyes, slender build.*

While the others ate, Alberto opened a folder and rifled through the contents. Satisfied, he closed it and poured himself some tea.

After the men satiated their thirst and hunger, Alberto gazed into their unshaven faces. "Thank you for coming to my assistance. By killing my friend, the infidels have shamed me and dishonored Allah."

"What would you like us to do?" Hamza thumbed a set of prayer beads.

"Your task is simple." Alberto pushed the folder across the table. "While we prepared to do Allah's work and destroy the infidels, they attacked us without warning in a Mexican warehouse. Our brother, Michael, was killed." He pounded the table. "His death must be avenged!"

Hamza opened the folder and pulled out several photos. He spread them across the table. "Are these our targets?"

"Yes." Alberto pointed to Javier's picture, taken outside the Pentagon. "He is the leader."

"Who is the woman?"

"His whore. She and the others do what the leader tells them to do."

Hamza sifted through the remaining photographs. He held up one showing a building. "Is this where they work?"

Alberto nodded. "Yes. Walter also thinks the leader lives there since he spends most of his time inside. Walter installed a few surprises around the property, but I won't be happy until I can spit on the infidel's body."

"Allah will guide us, and they will die like dogs." Hamza glanced at Jabbar and Kamal. "Perhaps we can teach the whore some manners before she departs this world?"

"No. Allah didn't teach us to behave like animals."

Hamza frowned. "Okay. When shall we start?"

"As soon as possible." Alberto pointed at the folder. "You'll find a piece of paper with the infidel's business name and address. I also included the address where Walter will brief you on what he's set up. I don't want him further involved—he's my bomb maker, and I have several tasks for him to complete."

"I have heard of a bomb maker with two missing fingers by his real name but have never met him. If Walter is the same person, I look forward to it."

"Call him first before going to the address. He booby-trapped the property in the event the authorities uncover his real identity and try to capture him."

"Good advice."

Once the men departed, Alberto opened his laptop to check for messages. He spent several minutes weeding through the spam and insignificant emails before finding the one he hoped for.

To: Abdul

From: Ismail

Chef delayed indefinitely. Local celebration completed but relocation of the bakery is taking longer than anticipated. Will advise chef's availability as soon as I find out.

ALBERTO GRIMACED. *Delay won't hurt. Better to deal with one issue at a time.* He typed a short response:

. . .

To: Ismail

From: Abdul

Chef's delay works better for current circumstances. Sugar delivery postponed due to inclement weather. Will advise any further changes.

AFTER CLOSING HIS EMAIL, Alberto dialed a number in Miami. After six rings, voice mail kicked in. "What's the holdup with the shipment? Haven't heard anything."

Once he hung up, he returned to the living room. Before the call from Hamza, he spotted on the TV menu the Detroit Tigers were playing the Baltimore Orioles. He shook his head. *The Americans and their cute names. Too much decadence here for me, but I'll enjoy it while I can, may Allah forgive me.*

HAMZA DROVE by Walter's address. *Curtains closed. No signs of activity.* "We will go around and come in from the opposite direction. Watch for anything to show he is at home."

"Thought I saw a light flick on and off." Jabbar pointed. "That's the signal." He turned back in the front passenger seat and glanced at Hamza.

"I will turn around at the end of the street."

Minutes later, Hamza pulled into the property and stopped in front of a garage.

Another light flashed on and off. "Let us go."

The men climbed out of the car, pistols in hand.

Hamza knocked on the door and stepped back.

A faint voice responded, "It's open."

Hamza pointed at Kamal and gestured him forward.

Kamal inched toward the door. Twisting the knob, he gave a shove and dove for the floor.

"Get up and come inside."

Alberto's new team entered the house.

In front of them, Walter leveled a shotgun in their direction. "At this range, I can't miss. Ever been hit with double-aught buckshot? Identify yourselves before my finger slips."

Hamza stepped forward. "Alberto sent us. He mentioned Michael —said you would understand."

Walter nodded. "Who are you?"

"I am Hamza." He pointed at the others. "My colleagues—Jabbar and Kamal. You have information for us."

Walter lowered his weapon. "Follow me to the basement."

Downstairs, Walter took them to a makeshift table made of plywood and sawhorses. He gestured to the model of a building. "There's your target—the left side of the property. Two entrances— front and back. The main target lives in the building."

Hamza nodded. "How many others?"

"At least five people present during working hours. Do you want me to take you there?"

"No. We need to learn our way around before we strike. This is not a suicide mission, so we must find multiple ways to leave the city."

Walter gestured to several photos taped to the back wall. "Pictures of your targets. Study them. Take note there are two parking spots in the back. A Hummer is parked there most of the time— belongs to their leader."

Kamal studied the pictures. "What about alarms?"

"Latest technology, so you'll set them off as soon as you enter."

"Better weapons?" Hamza raised his pistol.

Walter crossed his arms. "AR-15s. I also made a few explosive devices for you."

"Excellent. We will rest here tonight and head to Arlington in the morning to examine the target for ourselves."

"When do you plan to attack the infidels?"

"If Allah's grace shines upon us, within a week, The Brusch Agency will be no more."

29

St. George's Parish
Bermuda

PHOENIX AND ZAINE sat on the outdoor swing chair overlooking the ocean. Each held a glass of juice as they enjoyed the warm breeze drifting across the water.

He turned to Zaine and took her hand. "With Jose's death, I'm not sure who to trust." He wiped a sweaty brow as a nervous tic pulsated under his right eye. "We might need to relocate." *At least I should.*

"Do you have a location in mind?" She studied Phoenix's face.

"Perhaps Puerto Rico?" He shrugged. "Haven't given it much thought, but it's something to consider." He drew her close. "I don't want you hurt."

Zaine tapped his arm. "If we decide to move, perhaps the Bahamas or Florida? Sales of my jewelry are doing well in both."

"Uh-huh. Sure. First things first. I want to find the person responsible for Jose's death."

"What will you do—turn them over to the police?"

He smirked. "Something like that." *I'd rather kill them.* "The other guys are moving the *Childhood Dream* to a new berth—not as remote, but it'll be easier to keep an eye out for anyone sneaking up on us."

"Where? Perhaps I can help finish the loading—at least my new island merchandise."

"I'm waiting for a call—they'll let me know when—"

Phoenix yanked his buzzing phone from his pocket. He stared at the number and grimaced. *Mum or Dad. What do they want?* He hit the accept button and put the call on speaker. "Hello?"

"Maverick, Dad here. Glad to hear your voice. We keep waiting for you to drop in and introduce us to your new girlfriend."

Phoenix glanced at Zaine and rolled his eyes.

She covered her mouth to smother a laugh.

"Yes, Dad. We'll come by soon. Is that all you wanted?" *I hope so.*

"Actually, no. A man stopped by the house a couple of days ago looking for you. Said a mutual friend suggested he look you up while he was in Bermuda on vacation."

"What? Did he identify himself?"

"Yes. Said his name was Tom, and he's a police officer in Baltimore."

What the hell? I've never been there. "Did he say which mutual friend? Are you sure he said Baltimore?"

"Positive. Have you done something wrong—again?"

"No, Dad. Look, I gotta go. Love to Mum. I'll call to arrange a night together and will bring Zaine with me."

"Okay, Maverick. Take care of yourself."

Phoenix broke the connection and turned to Zaine. "I wonder if this strange visitor is somehow tied into the attack on the *Childhood Dream* and Jose's death." He stood and paced.

"What should we do?"

"Until I know where the boat is berthed, we can't do much. Pack a bag—we might need to keep a low profile for a bit. Bring only what you need."

"B-But ... aren't you overreacting?"

"Listen, Zaine! Why would a cop be nosing around? Not like I've been a Boy Scout all my life, but I haven't been in any serious trouble." *At least lately.* "Your merchandise is legit, but mine can land me in jail. Is that what you want?"

Zaine shook her head. "No. I just thought—"

"Let me do the thinking." He glanced at his watch. "Grab your stuff—I want to leave in thirty minutes."

"Where .... Where are we going?" She froze, staring with wide eyes and raised eyebrows.

Phoenix lifted his hands to the sides of his head and squeezed. "Let me concentrate!" He raced to a closet and yanked out a backpack. "We'll get in the car and drive around until Jesús calls."

Zaine backed away from him. "Why can't I just stay here?"

"Are you crazy? If someone's after me, they'll use you as bait." He pulled a pistol from his bag. "Better to be with me so I can protect you."

"If your car is gone and mine's in the garage, no one would know I'm still here." Zaine pursed her lips. "Where will we go?"

Phoenix tugged a curtain back and peered outside. "We'll sort out where we're going later. Better to stay hidden than become a target."

"O-Okay. I'll be right back." She dashed into the bedroom.

Phoenix followed and dumped a couple of changes of clothes in his bag. He pulled out a second pistol, two magazines, and a roll of money from the nightstand drawer. After shoving them in with the clothes, he turned to Zaine. "C'mon! Let's move!"

He raced out of the house without waiting, jumped in his VW EOS convertible, and started the engine. He glanced toward the house. *Where is she?*

Phoenix turned the car around so he could head out the gate. *Still no sign of Zaine.* He slammed a fist on the horn.

The door opened, and Zaine appeared, dragging an overloaded suitcase. She shut the door and hauled the bag toward the car.

Phoenix jumped out and grabbed her case. "I said to pack the essentials. We have plenty of money to buy whatever else we might need."

"I did pack my essentials." She glared at him. "A woman's essential needs are greater than a man's. If there had been time, I would've packed a second bag."

Phoenix rolled his eyes. "Just get in the car." He stuffed the bag in the small trunk and climbed in beside her. "Let's go."

AFTER DRIVING around the island for a couple of hours, Phoenix pulled into a service station advertising food and stopped at one of the fuel pumps. He pulled a baseball hat over his forehead as he fished out his wallet and offered several notes to Zaine. "Go inside and find something to eat and drink. None of that tofu stuff—real food." He reached in the back seat. "Wait! Don't forget your sunhat."

She jerked the money and the hat from his hands and went inside.

Phoenix filled the tank and climbed back into the vehicle. He turned away from the street as a police car pulled into the station and stopped. *They can't be on to me yet.*

An officer climbed out of the vehicle and went inside.

Phoenix slouched in his seat.

Moments later, the officer returned and began pumping fuel.

Phoenix exhaled. *Just filling up.*

Zaine appeared ten minutes later, carrying two paper bags. She handed one to him. "Careful—hot pizza slices." Opening the door, she sat in the passenger seat, placing the second bag between her legs. "I bought a few sandwiches, Coke, and water."

Phoenix pulled out a paper plate covered in foil. "Smells good. What kind?"

"They only had pepperoni ready. Said it would be another ten minutes for vegetarian."

"Pepperoni's my favorite." He unwrapped his and took a large bite. "Great!" He started the engine and pulled back onto the main road.

Zaine bit into her slice. "Where to?"

"We'll keep cruising for now. A police car just passed, but I don't think they're looking for us. Hand me a water, would you?"

She reached in the bag, pulled out a bottle, and handed it to Phoenix. "A bit paranoid, perhaps? Are you sure we need to do this? Why not dock somewhere?"

Phoenix glanced at her. "Do you want to end up like Jose? I sure don't."

"Okay. What about your house in Somerset? Perhaps we could go there."

He shook his head. "Not yet. I want the boat berthed somewhere so we can check things out. After it's dark, we'll go to Somerset. If it seems safe, we'll spend a night or two. Otherwise, we'll sleep on the boat."

"Whatever you think is best." She sighed.

"I'm not—"

Phoenix yanked out his ringing phone and glanced at the number. He accepted the call and put it on speaker. "About time, Jesús. Where are you?"

"Sorry it took so long. Pier 41."

"You couldn't find a quieter location?" Phoenix sighed as he pulled over, doing a U-turn when the traffic cleared.

"We got a slip at the far end away from the entrance—an easy spot to make a quick getaway."

"Uh-huh. Copy that. Be there in ten."

After Phoenix found a place to park at the marina, he grabbed their luggage from the trunk. He turned to Zaine. "Act normal—don't draw any attention to us. We're just another couple off for a day or two on the water."

She nodded. "Okay." She gestured toward the marina's minimart, where a couple had just stepped outside. "Isn't that—"

"Stop it! No time to talk. Let's move." Phoenix guided them along the walkway. He smiled when he spotted the *Childhood Dream*.

Jesús stood on the deck and waved as they approached.

"Permission to come aboard." Phoenix laughed.

"Granted, boss. Are we heading out now?"

"No. We'll check over the cargo first and cast off later. Did you stock provisions?"

Jesús rolled his eyes. "Of course. Oh, someone dropped off a package for you."

"When?" Phoenix turned and scanned the marina. "Anyone we know?" His shoulders tensed.

"Naw. It was a guy from Five Star Home Delivery. He delivered to several slips, not just here."

"I didn't order any package." Phoenix glanced around. "Let me stow our gear, and we can—"

Zing!

He ducked as a bullet passed near his head, gouging a path through the transom. "Get down!" He hugged the deck and yanked a pistol from his back.

Several shots rang out.

Phoenix and Jesús hugged the deck. Both pulled out their pistols, seeking targets.

"Aiyeeeee!"

Phoenix turned at Zaine's scream.

She took a step backward and tumbled off the boat.

He leaned over the transom—no sign of her.

"Zaine!"

T he Brusch Agency
Old Town, Alexandria, Virginia

DOUGIE RANG the doorbell and waited. He turned and scanned the area. *Upmarket street.* No response, so he pushed the buzzer again.

"Hold on!" a voice shouted through the intercom.

Moments later, someone threw a deadbolt back, and the door swung inward. "Come in. Sorry about that. We don't let anyone in the front door without checking them out on the monitor." The clean-shaven man wiped a hand through his dark red hair before pointing to a screen above the door. He held out his hand. "I'm Elton."

Dougie dropped his pack on the floor, grinning as he shook hands. "I've heard about you. Something about I shouldn't call you ET?"

"I see you've been talking with the boss." Elton laughed. "You must be Dougie, one of the Snakes."

"That's me—also known as Adder. Is Javier in?"

Elton nodded. "He's expecting you." Elton shut the exterior door. "Follow me." He led Dougie along a corridor, stopping to point to an open door. "Our break room—plenty of coffee, tea, soft drinks, bottled water, and munchies. Help yourself."

"Thanks—perhaps later."

Elton escorted Dougie to a closed door at the end of the corridor. He knocked once and entered, motioning for Dougie to step inside. "Found him, boss." Elton slipped away.

Javier jumped to his feet and came around the desk. "About time, Dougie. Did you slither here?"

Both men laughed.

"Take a load off." Javier pointed to a chair. "Glad you made it. Something's come up, and I need to leave—tonight."

"Where are you heading?"

"Miami. AJ's going with me."

"Business or pleasure?"

Javier raised a brow. "If I'm lucky, a bit of both. I've been doing a lot of thinking about AJ. She seems, you know, a little out of my league. I sometimes wonder what she sees in me."

"Must be your charm because it's definitely not your looks." Dougie punched Javier on the arm. "In all seriousness, I think you make a great couple."

"Thanks, I guess." Javier rubbed his elbow. "Hey, do you remember the photo with the headless bodies?"

Dougie nodded.

"It's getting personal. Not sure who's behind it, but there have been too many strange things happening. We caught someone on camera casing the property last week."

"What was his excuse?"

Javier shook his head. "We have several clear shots of the man's face and profile. I don't think he's aware we spotted him. We left him alone for now, although Cesar, another of my employees, bugged his car. If he's working with a crew, we're hoping he'll lead us to others. In the meantime, we're going on the offensive."

"How's that?"

"Someone tried to kidnap Sindee but went into her next-door neighbor's apartment by mistake. Tonight, Sindee and Cesar will be heading out from here and walking the nearby streets to see if they can pick up surveillance. If we can determine who they are, we'll decide whether to shadow them or bring them in. If we're unable to identify them, we'll have no choice but to capture him or her."

"Sounds like a plan." Dougie rubbed his chin with his thumb and index finger. "Do you want me to tag along in the background?"

"It's a thought, but let's start out slow and easy. Don't want to chase any bad guys away—yet. Our goal will be to capture someone so we can find out who's behind this."

"Understood. When do I meet Sindee and Cesar?"

"Later. They're both out shopping—getting something together to wear this evening."

"Why not wear their regular clothing?"

"For the most part, they will be, but Sindee needed a seasonal jacket to conceal her shoulder holster. Cesar also wanted to check out their comms gear and let Sindee practice her surveillance techniques. He'll pick out an unsuspecting shopper and monitor Sindee's efforts. This'll be the first time she's used the equipment, and we want her to be comfortable."

"Can she shoot?"

Javier glanced at the ceiling. "Why me?" He snorted. "Of course, she can—at least she knows the basics. Otherwise, I wouldn't provide her with a weapon. I'm retired, not brain dead."

"Just checking." Dougie chortled as he patted the side of his motorcycle jacket. "Perhaps she should get one of these."

"I don't think she'd appreciate being considered a motorcycle momma." Javier shrugged. "But that's up to her." He nodded toward the door. "Why don't you head out to reception, and ET will take you on a tour of the building."

"Sounds fine to me."

∽

CESAR SAT at a round plastic table in the food court. The remnants of his lunch rested on a tray while he held a newspaper with both hands, scanning the area over its top. He keyed his comms gear. "Beauty, this is Angel, over."

He yanked out his earbud after a burst of static. Shaking his head, he replaced the device. "Beauty, this is Angel. Come again?"

"Sorry, Angel. I'm still getting used to this equipment."

"Understood. Pick out someone to follow but don't let them see you."

"Roger that, good buddy."

Cesar cringed. *She's been watching old movies again.* "Did you identify someone?"

"Yes. A blonde-haired woman with a red and blue floral dress. She has a large shoulder bag. Coming your way."

Cesar glanced over the paper again. "Got her. Remember what I taught you. Don't get too close. No sudden responses if she happens to turn back. Allow—" He stopped as the woman walked past his table. Spotting Sindee, he nodded. *Good—doing as I said.* "Excellent job, Beauty. Keep following her until she leaves the mall. If she gets in any vehicle, get the make, model, color, and license plate number. I'll wait here for your report."

"Uh. Ten-four, Angel."

Cesar dropped his paper on the table, stood, and deposited the remains of his meal in a nearby trash can. He went back to the counter, purchased a Diet Coke, and returned to his newspaper.

Twenty minutes later, Sindee plopped in a chair next to Cesar. She slid over a piece of paper. "Here's the info on her car, including the plate number." A smile spread across her face. "How'd I do?"

"You dun good." Cesar chuckled. "Need to drop the ten-fours and good buddies from your comms. Might work in the movies, but unnecessary."

Sindee nodded and sipped on the drink she had purchased before joining Cesar. "Anything else?"

"Your choice of top, jeans, and shoes are all appropriate." He grinned. "However, I'd find a less gaudy pair of sunglasses. The cat eyes on the lens are cute, but you don't want anything which might stand out."

"I'll buy a toned-down pair before we leave."

"As soon as you finish, we'll pick out some new glasses for you. We'll meet our temporary boss later today. I understand he's less concerned about procedures as long as the mission succeeds." *Hope he's still that way.*

Sindee stood. "Lead on, oh wise one."

They both chuckled.

Javier and AJ climbed out of the taxi at Reagan National Airport. After paying the driver and collecting their luggage, they headed inside the terminal.

"Ugh! Look at the line!" AJ rolled her eyes. "I hate waiting—should have skipped bringing luggage to check. We'd already be on our way through security."

Javier glanced at her. "Might I remind you, Mrs. Smith, we couldn't take our weapons in carry-on luggage."

"I know. It's just—" AJ threw her hands in the air. "Can't help it if I'm impatient."

"Relax." He gestured at the line. "It's moving at a fast clip, so we shouldn't be here too long."

When it was their turn to check in, Javier put AJ's hard-sided suitcase on the belt.

The bored airline staff member snapped her gum. "How many bags?"

"Two—one each for checking in." Javier glanced at AJ. "A backpack each for carry-on."

"Anything we need to be aware of in your checked baggage?"

AJ pulled out her CIA identification. "Yes. My unloaded SIG Sauer P226, along with three full magazines, are in my bag." She nodded toward Javier. "Same with my husband's luggage."

The attendant pushed a button, and a luggage tag snapped out of the machine. After attaching it to the first bag, she nodded for the second one. When she finished, she handed the luggage tags to Javier. "Have a nice day."

As they walked toward security, AJ linked her arm through Javier's. "Let's go, hubby. You can buy me a drink before we board."

As DUSK DESCENDED, the front door of The Brusch Agency opened. A couple stepped out and glanced around.

"Psst! Wake up, Ivan." Robert sat in the driver's seat of the fifteen-year-old red F-150 extended cab pickup. He shoved his dozing partner while keeping his eyes fixed on the rearview mirror that he had repositioned to monitor the front of the building. "We're on."

Ivan studied the man and woman. "They seem innocent enough."

"The smart ones always do, but we'll find out what they're up to." Ivan yawned. He took several photographs as the couple crossed the street and walked away from them. "Give them some distance before turning around and following them."

"Roger that." Robert started the engine, waited for an opening in the traffic, and did a U-turn. He pulled into an empty spot. "Let's wait until they reach the corner before moving any closer."

Ivan pursed his lips. "Pass them—I'll get a profile shot when they pass under the streetlights." He placed a Glock 17M in his lap before focusing the telephoto lens of his camera.

"Coming up." Robert pulled out, dropping his speed as he coasted through the intersection. "Well?"

Ivan checked the shot. "Perfect."

"Good. We'll pull up another block and wait for them to catch up."

The couple continued their walk, arms linked together.

Laughter echoed across the street.

"Wonder what's so funny?" Ivan twisted a silencer onto his pistol.

"Don't know, but things are gonna get serious in a hurry." Robert pulled a mask from a pocket, covering his face below his eyes.

Ivan did the same before easing his door open. He glanced at Robert. "Ready?"

"Let's do it."

31

King Edward VII Memorial Hospital
Paget Parish, Bermuda

WILD TURNED off Point Finger Road before reaching the six-story King Edward VII Memorial Hospital and followed the signs for the KEMH's Acute Care Wing parking lot. "Charlie said he'd meet us in the ACW's main lobby."

"Hope Sam's doing okay. Charlie's text didn't say much."

"He doesn't say much at the best of times."

TJ nodded. "Let's find out."

They climbed out of their Hummer, crossed a street, and entered the building.

Charlie sat in the lobby, a stoic expression etched across his face. He spotted Wild and TJ approaching and rose to meet them. "Thanks for coming."

"How's Sam?" TJ held a bouquet of mixed flowers in his hand.

"I spoke with the doc a little while ago." Charlie ran a hand through his blond hair. "She's been in a coma since the paramedics brought her in. The doctors plan to rerun the tests tomorrow."

"Geez!" Wild glanced from Charlie to TJ. "Can't they do something?"

Charlie shook his head. "If the docs had induced the coma to keep her immobile and out of pain, they could bring her out. Sam cracked her head against the windshield, causing a concussion. She was conscious when the paramedics pulled her from the vehicle but slipped into her current condition. I hope we'll know more soon."

"What should we do?"

"Let's see her." Charlie pointed to a sign for the elevators. "She's on the fourth floor."

When they entered the elevator, Charlie pushed the button for the third floor.

"Hey, boss." TJ scratched his head. "I thought you said she was on the fourth floor."

"She is. But as a former British colony, Bermuda uses the same numbering system for floors as the UK. In the States, we would say first or main floor when entering a multi-floor building, but here it's the ground floor, and their first floor equates to our second. Got it?"

TJ pursed his lips. "I think so."

"Never mind." Charlie laughed. "Let's go to her room."

They rode in silence. When they arrived at the correct floor, Charlie led them along a shiny tiled hallway. Photographs of local tourist spots decorated the cream-colored walls. He waved to one of the staff at the nurses' station before stopping in front of a door.

The person smiled and returned Charlie's wave.

"The regular staff know me now, so I don't get stopped every time I return to the floor." He stopped in front of a door. "All rooms are private, so we won't be disturbing any other patients." Charlie pushed the door and entered, followed by TJ and Wild.

Among the various diagnostic devices and an IV stand, Sam lay motionless on a bed near the single window, her head wrapped in a white bandage, with a red sling holding her left arm in place. A blue chair sat in the corner next to the head of the bed, while two others were positioned along the opposite wall. The only sounds came from the machines monitoring Sam's vital signs.

Wild and TJ approached Sam, squeezed her hand, and stepped back.

TJ wiped away tears trickling down his face. He placed the flowers on the edge of the bed and left the room.

Charlie stepped up to the bed, leaned down, and whispered a few words to Sam. When he finished, he motioned for Wild to follow him.

They joined TJ in a seating area near the entrance to the patients' terrace garden.

Charlie glanced outside and headed to a table at the far end away from the entrance.

Moments later, Wild and TJ followed him.

"What did you say to Sam?" Wild raised a brow.

"I told her to stop sandbagging, we needed her." Charlie chuckled. "I also mentioned I had a hundred bucks on her waking up today."

"What? You're kidding me, right?"

Charlie grinned. "Of course. I told her we were all here for her and to get well soon. What else could I say?"

"Remind me never to get sick or injured with you around." Wild laughed.

"I just hope she regains consciousness soon." TJ stretched out his legs.

"Here's the thing." Charlie sighed. "The doc thinks someone should be with Sam at all times. If she comes out of the coma, memory loss is a possibility, and having a familiar face might be the cue her brain needs to jumpstart her recall." He drummed his fingers on the table. "Not sure the best way to handle this as we still need to continue with the mission."

TJ glanced at Wild. "You're the team leader, Charlie. I recommend you keep Sam company and get over your cuts and bruises."

"All I did was twist an arm and a leg in the crash, plus a couple of scratches. Nothing broken." He waved a hand in dismissal. "I'm fit and raring to go."

"I suggest you keep an eye on Sam, and we'll amp up our efforts to find the bad guys." He scanned the empty terrace. "Okay?"

Charlie nodded. "Did you uncover anything so far?"

"Yeah. The address in St. George's was a minor hit. Maverick no longer lives there, but his parents do. They volunteered he still lives on the island, along with his girlfriend, Zaine."

"Excellent work. Don't suppose Maverick's parents had his current address?"

"Sort of. They didn't know the number, but they've pointed us in the right direction. Said he lives in a blue clifftop house overlooking South Shore."

"Okay. Suggest you and Wild check the place out. I'll hang around here for now unless you uncover some actionable intel. Keep me posted."

"Will do." TJ lumbered to his feet, along with Charlie and Wild.

They stopped at the elevators.

"Good hunting, guys."

Wild and TJ nodded as the elevator door closed.

CHARLIE HEADED BACK to Sam's room and sat in the chair. Squeezing her hand and touching her shoulder, he leaned back and closed his eyes. Tears trickled down his cheek. *Come back to us, Sam. We need you.*

AFTER LEAVING THE HOSPITAL, Wild and TJ headed back to St. George's Island. Before long, they came to a standstill, the road blocked with vehicles of all descriptions. Several drivers honked their horns.

TJ stood and stared ahead.

"See anything?"

"Looks like two vehicles collided at the intersection. Turn back and find a way around this mess."

Wild pulled a Y-turn and then an immediate left on a side road they just passed. He weaved through the streets until he reached Harrington Sound Road, heading toward St. George's. "Do I head toward the airport?"

"Negative." TJ studied the Google Earth map on his Android. "Hang a right up ahead and follow the signs for Tucker's Town. It'll take us to Shore Lane, where you'll take another right."

"Gotcha."

Twenty minutes later, Wild pulled into Shore Lane. He slowed as they glanced at each property.

"Check it out!" TJ pointed at a two-story blue house with a white roof and shutters. "Maverick must be loaded! This house will be worth millions."

"I'll say. Now what?"

"Stop in front of the house. If anyone approaches, we'll pretend we're lost."

No sooner had they parked when a white-haired woman appeared. Dressed in a bright yellow dress and an apron, she held a pair of pruning shears in her hands. "Looking for Phoenix and Zaine? They aren't home."

"No." TJ waved a hand to encompass the area. "We're on vacation and just traveling around the islands."

"I've heard that one before." The woman laughed. "You both look like you're some type of law enforcement officials." She nodded toward the house. "I could tell you plenty about the shady characters coming and going. At least Phoenix and Zaine are decent to the other Shore Lane residents."

Wild gestured toward TJ. "As soon as we figure out our next stop, we'll be on our way."

"Uh-huh. Well, they left in a hurry a few hours ago. Didn't even wave when they sped past." She jerked a thumb over her shoulder. "I live there. When you finish whatever you're doing, stop in for some fresh lemonade." She glanced at each of them in turn. "No shenanigans, mind you, my husband won't stand for it."

"Thank you, ma'am. What did you say your name was?"

She smiled. "I didn't." She waved and walked away.

Wild turned to TJ. "Now what?"

"Seems like we received an invitation to check things over. Perhaps we'll find something to confirm the information Cedric provided." He opened the door and climbed out. "Let's do it."

They approached the house, scanning the area for any sign of activity.

Nothing.

Wild climbed the brick steps and rang the bell.

A chime echoed through the house, but no one appeared.

He tried again.

Still nothing.

Wild pulled a small leather packet from his pocket and knelt in front of the door. He removed two small picks from the package and inserted them in the lock.

"What are you doing?"

Wild grunted. "Just ... a—"

Click.

"You said we had an invitation." Wild put away his lockpicks and smiled. "But we don't have a key." He pushed the door open and stepped aside. "After you."

"Holy ... Check out that view!" TJ grinned. "What I'd give for a place like this."

"C'mon. Let's go exploring."

They strolled into the first room on the right. A table for twelve dominated the green and white room. Two floor-to-ceiling windows provided ample sunlight and stunning views of the ocean.

"Could feed an army in here." TJ glanced at the simple yet elegant chandelier. "Good place to put one of the GSM bugs."

Wild nodded. "Take care of it, and I'll continue wandering around. Meet you at the front door."

Twenty minutes later, they stepped out of the house and entered a sheltered courtyard garden.

"I left a bug in the master bedroom." Wild grinned. "At least I think it was the master. It's bigger than my whole apartment. There's an upper family room, so I hid one there, too."

"I put one in the library and another in the living room. Maverick's a boating enthusiast—almost every book in the library was about sailing and speed boats. Plenty of pictures on the wall, too. Several featured a yacht called *Childhood Dream*."

"I think this whole place would be anyone's childhood dream. Let's see if there are any vehicles in the garage. The nosy neighbor said they left together, but perhaps we'll find another car and can put one of the trackers on it."

TJ nodded as they left the garden and strolled through the property to the garage. Tall enough, he peeked in the window. "One car."

"Excellent." Wild tried the handle of a pedestrian door—it turned. "Be right back."

TJ sat on a nearby bench overlooking the ocean.

"Yeeow!"

Wild flew out of the garage, a dark shape behind him.

"Grrrrr! Woof! Woof!"

Wild tripped and tumbled into the grass.

Teeth bared, the shape jumped into the air, intent on catching its prey.

Wild scooted away but was pinned to the ground when the animal landed on him.

Jaws snapping, saliva dripping, the beast's massive head descended.

board the *Childhood Dream*
Bermuda

ZING! Clunk! Thwack!

As the gunfire tapered off, Phoenix continued to duck with each shot while he searched the waves, hoping to spot Zaine. *Gotta find her.* He turned to Jesús. "Get the boat moving but stay near the shore and the docks. Zaine's here. Somewhere." He wiped a tear from his cheek.

"Right away, Jefe." Jesús scurried to cast off. He started the engine and backed out of the berth.

Phoenix cupped his hands around his mouth. "Zaine! Zaine!" He scanned the area, ducking as he tried to look below the floating docks. *Where is she?*

Thirty minutes later, Jesús pulled back into their berth. "No use, Jefe. If she was nearby, we'd have spotted her."

"I—I know." He pointed along the shore. "Head that way. Perhaps she's still alive and swam away from the boat." *Or she's dead.*

When they returned to their berth after a fruitless search, two police officers stood on the dock waiting for them.

Phoenix turned toward Jesús. "Take care of the boat. I'll find out what they want." *Hope they're not after us.* He jumped onto the dock and approached the men. "What can I do for you, officers?" He studied their shoulder boards—a constable and a chief officer.

"We received reports of gunshots in the area, so we're investigating," the chief officer said. He glanced at the *Childhood Dream.* "Sir, how many others on board?"

"Just one. Do you want to check?"

The chief officer motioned to the constable. "Yes, so we can rule you and your boat out. Did you hear anything?"

Phoenix crossed his arms and forced his fingers to be still. "Nothing like gunshots. We were out on the water—the engine was giving us fits. There were sounds similar to backfires, but we couldn't spot where they originated." *What do they suspect? I hope they leave soon.*

The constable returned and shook his head.

The chief officer pulled a business card from his wallet. "Just for the record, would you please provide your names and the name of the boat to the constable." He extended his hand. "Here's my contact information. Give me a ring should you think of anything else."

Phoenix glanced at the card before giving the officer a mock salute. "Sure thing."

THE POLICE OFFICERS scanned the marina as they returned to their vehicle. The constable climbed in behind the steering wheel. After the chief officer settled in the passenger seat, the constable glanced at him. "Sir. I didn't mention this in front of the boat's owner, but when I was aboard, I spotted three areas on the starboard side where bullets might have ricocheted."

"Why didn't you mention it at the time, Constable?"

"Well, sir, the man on the boat saw me inspecting the gouges. He said they were caused when they were in the port loading cargo and a crane tipped and damaged the boat."

"Hmm." The chief officer pursed his lips. "When we return to the station, run their names through the system and see what pops up. Find out everything you can about their boat, too. Let's make sure their story checks out. I'm not sure what it is, but something doesn't seem right."

"Yes, sir."

HANDS clasped one of the supporting boards of the dock as Zaine remained stationary in the water. When Jesús and Phoenix's voices faded, she ventured away, keeping herself as low as possible. She crossed under another section of the pier, turning her head left and right as she searched for—

The rumble of a diesel engine broke the calm.

Zaine hurried back under the dock.

"Psst! Zaine!"

I recognize that voice. It's Valeria! Zaine edged out from under the dock. She spotted her friends and waved.

Valeria gave Zaine a thumbs up.

The boat veered closer and coasted.

"You like a drowned rat." Enrique pushed a rope ladder over the port side of *Lost Souls* and reached down.

Zaine laughed as she grabbed his outstretched arm and climbed aboard. She hugged her friends, a smile etched across her face. "I thought Phoenix and Jesús would never stop looking for me." She looked around. "Where are the cops?"

"They wandered toward the other end of the pier." Valeria handed Zaine a towel. "I think you're mistaken about Phoenix's love for you. He called your name many times as they searched."

"Perhaps. When I spotted you at the minimart, I almost told him who you are."

"Better he doesn't find out." Enrique maneuvered away from the dock and headed toward Somerset.

Zaine finished drying her hair and sat next to Valeria. "Who did the shooting? One bullet gouged the side of the boat where I jumped overboard."

Valeria glanced at Enrique. "Wasn't us. We used blanks."

"Then who?"

"I don't know." Valeria frowned. "But we'll find out."

JESÚS LOCATED an isolated and disused pier toward the end of the main island. After securing the boat, he turned to Phoenix. "Now what, Jefe?"

Phoenix raised a hand as he held his cellphone in the other. "Just a minute—it's ringing."

A gruff voice answered. "Hello."

"What the hell were you thinking?" Phoenix clenched his phone until his knuckles turned white. "I didn't want her injured—just scared."

"It wasn't me—someone else was shooting at them, too. I aimed well above their heads."

"You idiot! She fell overboard, and we couldn't find her. She might be dead—I don't know. The police showed up, too." Phoenix sighed. "Unless someone finds her—alive—you won't receive a penny for the job."

"Now just a min—"

Phoenix cut the connection and stared at the phone. "Asshole." He waved toward Jesús. "Stay with the boat. I'm going to find a taxi. Be back as soon as I can."

THE CONSTABLE PRINTED out three documents before rushing along the corridor. He knocked on the chief officer's door. "Sir!"

The officer lowered the report he'd been reading. "Yes, Constable. What is it?"

"I checked out the two guys on the boat." He grinned. "Both have been visitors to our station for drug-related charges. Minor offenses, for possession, but the owner—Phoenix Vanidestine —is believed to be involved in smuggling." The constable placed two documents on the chief officer's desk. "The deck hand is Jesús Valdez."

"Excellent work, Constable. Anything else?"

"Yes, sir. I checked with the Ministry of Transportation. It appears the *Childhood Dream* makes a trip to Miami every three to four weeks."

"How did the ministry determine this? I didn't think they tracked boats to this level."

"For the most part, they don't. However, the American Coast Guard queried the ministry for more information regarding the boat's owner and repeated cargos. They provided the ministry with arrival and departure details."

"I see." The chief officer skimmed the final document and set it aside. "Wait another day, so they think we bought their story. I'll contact the emergency response team, and we'll make an unannounced return to the *Childhood Dream*."

"Yes, sir."

∾

ZAINE JOINED ENRIQUE and Valeria at a small restaurant in Somerset. Since it was still early, the place wasn't busy.

"Want a glass of wine?" Enrique held a bottle of Marlborough Sauvignon Blanc.

"Yes, please."

He filled a glass and passed it to her before topping up Valeria's.

She sipped the cool wine. "Perfect." Zaine glanced at each of her friend's faces. "I'm worried Phoenix is trying to get rid of me—not just break up but make me disappear."

Enrique nodded. "Have you considered tipping off the authorities about him being a drug smuggler?"

"No way." She crossed her arms. "If he found out, I'd definitely be on borrowed time."

"Zaine, we've known each other for over a decade, ever since you hired us to help import jewelry from Brazil." Valeria laid a hand on Zaine's arm. "I think it's best for you to leave for a while."

"Where should I go? My life is here."

"There's more of the island jewelry in our warehouse. Why don't we take some to Miami ourselves? We could make a vacation out of it, too."

Zaine nodded. "Sounds like a plan." *I wonder if I should tell Daddy?*

As dusk descended, Phoenix returned and climbed aboard the *Childhood Dream.* "C'mon, Jesús. Let's get moving."

Jesús rushed up the steps from below. "Where we going?"

"Back to the marina. The taxi took me past the docks. No one lurking about, so I think it's safe to return, and we can get out of here."

"Okay, Jefe."

After they cast off, Jesús started the engine and turned the boat around.

Phoenix leaned on the stern and pulled his phone out. Skipping through his contact list, he punched a number located in Virginia. He let the number ring twice and disconnected.

Moments later, his phone rang. He checked the number and accepted the call. "It's me."

"You're late. Was there a problem?"

"Yes—some personnel issues. They're sorted out. The shipment is ready, and we'll depart for Miami tomorrow morning."

"Excellent. Keep me posted on any changes—and don't be late again."

Phoenix listened to the dial tone after his contact broke the connection. He creased his brow. "Arrogant bastard. If I didn't need his money, I'd find another customer." He put the phone in his pocket and turned to watch the shore lights.

I'll miss the good times I had with Zaine. Am I making a mistake? My life will be empty without her. He grasped the railing and leaned over, staring into the abyss.

"Zaine .... Where are you?"

33

Miami International Airport
Miami, Florida

"WELCOME TO MIAMI. American Airlines flight 1938 has now arrived at gate twenty-three. It's a balmy day with temperatures in the high eighties. Enjoy your stay."

After the captain's announcement, Javier let AJ scoot past him before he yanked their carry-on cases from the overhead bins. He stepped aside as an elderly woman bumped into him, bashing her wheeled bag into his shins.

"Excuse me, ma'am. Do you need any help?"

The woman glared at him. "Mind your own business, sonny. I can take care of myself. If I need any help, I'll ask for it."

Javier smothered a grin. "Yes, ma'am."

The woman stepped behind AJ, who had already joined the line of passengers waiting to disembark. AJ glanced over her shoulder. "Hurry up, Javier. Time's passing."

"Yeah, yeah." He shook his head. "No need to rush—the door isn't open yet—no one's going anywhere."

AJ laughed. "I know. But we still have to collect our check-in baggage before getting the rental."

Once the aircraft door opened, the passengers surged through the jetway and into the terminal. AJ and Javier followed the signs for baggage claim. Upon entering the area, they joined other passengers surrounding their flight's carousel.

The murmur of the impatient crowd increased in volume before the belt alarm sounded and warning lights flashed. Several passengers pushed forward.

Javier spotted their bags and pointed. "Didn't take long. Let me grab them." He pushed between two passengers standing by the carousel with empty carts. "Excuse me." Astonished their bags arrived together, he reached forward, picked them up, and rejoined AJ.

"Check the locks." AJ glanced at the other passengers. "If there's no sign of tampering, we should be ready to go."

Javier examined the cases. "Still locked. Let's find our car and head to the hotel."

Fifteen minutes later, after picking up the keys and getting directions to their rental, AJ and Javier approached a beige Chevrolet Equinox. He opened the driver's door and began to climb in.

"Keys." AJ glanced at Javier.

He shook his head. "Uh-huh. Not a chance. I've been with you before on a mission when you drove—remember Panama? I wore out the panic strap trying to hang on."

AJ laughed. "Chicken. I thought you were a tough guy."

"I am. But self-preservation is high on my list of priorities." He shrugged and tossed her the keys. "Just to show you I can handle it—you drive." *I can always keep my eyes closed.*

"Excellent change of strategy. Just sit back and relax—we're on vacation, remember?"

"Only until we hear from Phil." He hopped into the passenger seat. "What are you waiting for? The 19th Hole restaurant should be open at the hotel, and I'm hungry."

AJ climbed behind the steering wheel and started the engine. "So, what else is new? You're always hungry."

"Can't help it if my metabolism requires a steady supply of nutrition."

"Yeah, right." AJ revved the engine and sped toward the exit. "Sit back and relax—only about five miles to the hotel."

WITH JAVIER BRACING FOR IMPACT, AJ rocketed to a stop in front of the hotel, the rear of the Equinox skidding.

A valet rushed forward and opened AJ's door. "Welcome to the Biltmore." He snapped his fingers, and a staff member rolled a cart near the SUV. "My friend will take care of your luggage. If you give me your keys, I'll move your vehicle to a suitable parking spot."

AJ handed him the keys. "Thank you."

The valet handed a parking receipt to her. "Enjoy your stay."

Javier and AJ entered the lobby and approached the check-in desk.

A tall, slender man dressed in a suit smiled. "Good day. Welcome to the Biltmore. Do you have a reservation?"

Javier stepped forward. "Yes—Smith. We're booked in the Terrace Suite." He placed a black American Express card on the counter.

"Outstanding, sir." The clerk picked up the card, ran it through a reader, and handed it back. "You're all set, sir." He gave directions to the elevators. "Your luggage will be brought to your suite shortly. Enjoy your stay at the Biltmore."

As they walked away, AJ squeezed Javier's arm. "A suite? Who are you trying to impress?" She chuckled.

"I figured we'd relish the luxury while we're waiting. Who knows when we'll get another chance like this?" Javier pointed toward their right before enveloping her hand with his. "C'mon. This way leads to the 19th Hole."

They strolled through the hotel grounds to their restaurant of choice. Once they were seated, Javier scanned the menu. He glanced at his watch. "Too early for the main courses. Think I'll go with a Cuban sandwich—and lemonade. What about you?"

"Same for me. I—"

Javier pulled his cellphone from his shirt pocket, glanced at the number, and accepted the call. "Hey Phil, what do you have for us? There's no one around us, so I'll put you on speaker."

"Hi, boss, and ... er ... boss."

"Hiya, Phil. AJ here. How's retirement treating you?"

"So far, so good, but—"

"Give us the intel, Phil. You can talk with AJ later." Javier silenced the speaker.

"Sorry, boss. I've been working with the M and M twins. A boat identified as the *Childhood Dream* is heading to the Florida coast from Bermuda. Should be there in about twenty-four hours."

"Did you get a destination?" *Hope so—we can wrap the mission up and still enjoy ourselves.*

"Sort of."

The sound of rustling paper came over the speaker.

"Sorry, dropped my lunch. We don't have a specific location, but at least the name of the river—we think—the Miami."

"Just a minute." Javier muted the call.

A waiter placed their sandwiches and drinks on the table. After receiving headshakes when he asked if there was anything else, he departed.

Javier returned to the call. "We're back. Go ahead."

"Sixteen rivers feed Biscayne Bay. The largest of these is the Miami River, which flows past the airport. Of course, there's no telling which tributary the *Childhood Dream* will be using."

"Hmm." Javier took a bite of his sandwich, chewed, and swallowed. "Anything else?" He turned to AJ and mouthed, "Biscayne Bay."

She nodded and continued studying her iPad.

"Not yet. As soon as we learn more, we'll send the details."

"Great work, Phil. Tell M and M the same. We'll—"

AJ glanced up and turned her iPad around for Javier to see.

"We're about nine miles from Biscayne Bay. After we finish lunch, we'll do some reconnoitering. Talk later." Javier broke the connection and picked up his fork, gesturing toward AJ. "Let's eat, grab our backpacks and weapons from the suite, and take a drive."

"I'm driving because—"

"Absolutely not. My turn." Javier shook his head before grinning. "You can be the navigator."

"Do I have a say in this?" AJ smiled.

"Not today."

A VALET BROUGHT their vehicle to the hotel's entrance and handed the keys to Javier. "Enjoy your afternoon, sir."

"Thank you." Javier deposited their backpacks behind the driver's seat and climbed in. He turned to AJ. "Ready, navigator?"

"I want to protest—this is a setup." She laughed. "Turn right and follow the signs for Granada Boulevard. I'll tell you when to turn."

"Don't get us lost." He chortled.

AJ rolled her eyes. "Not a chance."

Thirty minutes later, Javier pulled off Granada Boulevard and followed the road toward Isla Dorada Boulevard. "Where to now, oh wise one?"

She gave him a playful slap on the arm. "Find a spot to pull over. We'll work our way through the trees to the water's edge." She reached over the seat and grabbed her backpack. "Well, what are you waiting for?"

"Just admiring the view." He took his eyes off AJ, edged onto the shoulder, and stopped.

AJ hopped out and scanned the road. "Seems quiet. Let's take a look, shall we?" She headed into the trees.

"Sounds like a plan." He secured his backpack over a shoulder and followed AJ through the packed copse.

They weaved through the trees until they reached the water's edge.

Javier pulled his binoculars from his bag and panned the area. "Man, plenty of places for a small boat to come in. This might be a nightmare."

"Agreed. Hopefully, Phil and the twins will come up with some additional intel."

Snap!

Javier and AJ turned at the sound.

A short, wiry man with a scraggly beard held a rifle, pointed toward them. He spat tobacco juice onto the ground and wiped his mouth with the back of his hand. "Whatcha y'all doin' on my property? Can't you read?"

"We didn't see any signs."

"That's what all them druggies say." He raised his weapon. "Don't move, or I'll blast you to kingdom come." He fished a phone from a pocket of his dirty cut-off overalls and hit a button. "Hey, Vern. Come a-runnin'! I done caught me two of them highfalutin smugglers!"

34

Shore Lane
Bermuda

"TYSON! STOP GROWLING!" A silver-haired man walked around the side of the garage and stopped. He used one cane to support himself and waved a second one at the boxer dog. "Tyson, you bad boy!"

The dog jumped off Wild and ran to his alpha male, tongue flopping and tail wagging.

Keeping an eye on the dog, TJ helped Wild to his feet.

"I'm sorry, young man. Tyson greets everyone the same way, but he wouldn't hurt anyone."

Wild dusted off his clothes as he glanced at Tyson. "No problem. A friend of mine has a boxer who acts the same way. I just didn't expect to get jumped here." He grinned.

"Is there anything I can help you with?" He jerked a hand over his shoulder. "I'm Jim. I live next door and keep an eye on my neighbors' homes when they're away."

"We're here on vacation. A friend of ours suggested we look up Maverick while we're in town."

"I see." Jim pursed his lips. "Don't know anyone named Maverick. Phoenix and his girlfriend, Zaine, live here."

"I think Maverick was a nickname from his youth—might not use it now."

Jim rubbed his hand over Tyson's back. "Makes sense, I guess. Anyway, they aren't home. They left this morning."

"Many thanks, sir." TJ smiled. "Any idea when they'll be back? We're in Bermuda for a week, so we can come back another time before we return to the States."

Jim shook his head. "They usually tell me, but they seemed to be in a rush. Do you want to leave your name and number?"

"That's okay—we'll try our luck another time." Wild reached out to Tyson and let the dog sniff his hand.

Tyson licked the proffered hand and glanced back at Jim.

"Good boy, Tyson. Friend."

"We'll be on our way, Jim. Thanks for the info." Wild extended his hand.

"Stop by any time. If no one appears, come next door and sit a spell—I can always use the company." Jim turned to Tyson. "Let's go home, boy." They headed across the lawn toward a door set in the garden wall. With a wave, Jim opened it and followed Tyson through.

"Well, that's two people confirming Phoenix AKA Maverick lives here." Wild glanced around. "Nosy neighbors—will make it difficult to keep eyes on the property."

"We planted enough listening devices, so we should find out when he returns." TJ jerked his head toward their vehicle. "Nothing else we can do here, so let's go back to the hospital and give Charlie an update. We'll be able to check on Sam, too."

Wild nodded.

∼

TJ AND WILD tapped on the door to Sam's room at the hospital.

The door crept open. Charlie stood in the doorway and placed a finger against his lips. He stepped into the corridor and closed the door. "Sam came out of her coma about three hours ago. She's resting now."

TJ and Wild high-fived. "When can she leave?"

"Not right away. The doctors want to monitor her for a few more days. However, I managed a few words with her before she fell asleep. I told her you had stopped by. She said for us to come in when our time permits, but the mission comes first."

TJ rubbed a hand across his head. "What should we do?"

"I'll stay here overnight, and we'll play things by ear. How'd it go with checking out Maverick's property?"

"Guess who made a new friend?" TJ nudged Wild. "A guy named Tyson."

Charlie raised a brow. "Too much information."

TJ burst into laughter. "Not a problem—Tyson is a boxer dog owned by a neighbor. Maverick and his girlfriend weren't home, so Wild picked the lock. We placed a few listening devices in the house and stuck a tracker on the car in the garage."

"Excellent work." Charlie crossed his arms. "What's your plan now?"

"I dunno, boss." Wild mimicked Charlie's arm crossing. "We don't know where Maverick is at the moment. Any suggestions on our next move?"

"Yeah. Take a break and listen to the devices you planted. Perhaps you'll pick up something useful." Charlie pursed his lips. "Why not check out Flanagan's Irish Pub on Front Street? Someone mentioned it was one of Maverick's hangouts, and we were going to go there anyway before the accident."

"Good idea." TJ nodded. "We can listen to them while we're there. I could go for a decent meal and a pint—or two."

Charlie laughed. "Have a pint of Guinness for Sam and me, but don't overdo it. No telling when some actionable intel will come along."

"Got it, boss." Wild jerked his head toward Sam's door. "Keep us posted on her condition."

"Will do." Charlie smiled. "Now, get back to work. I'll rejoin Sam and watch her sleep. If there's any change, I'll send a text."

CHARLIE RESUMED his seat next to Sam's bed. He picked up his bag and rummaged for a peppermint candy. He dropped the wrapper in the trash can next to his chair and popped the candy in his mouth.

"Hey. Got one of those for me?"

Charlie turned and smiled when he saw Sam's open eyes and a hand stretched toward him.

"Sure thing." He retrieved one for her and held the partially unwrapped peppermint toward her.

Sam stuck the candy in her mouth. "Divine—much better than Jell-O." She glanced around the room. "Where are TJ and Wild?"

"Still on the mission. They came by a few minutes ago. They're heading to Flanagan's. I told them to have a pint of Guinness for us."

"Can't wait to have one for one myself." She smiled and closed her eyes.

WILD AND TJ parked on Front Street and followed the rock music to Flanagan's. They joined a line of customers waiting to enter.

TJ leaned against the railing on the steps. "Good thing we called for a reservation."

"I checked their website, and reservations aren't required but recommended for seating on the balcony. Figured we'd want to keep an eye on things but not be blasted by the music."

"Great minds think alike." TJ turned as a waitress wearing tight jeans and a Flanagan's t-shirt walked down the steps. "Excuse me. We have a reservation for two on the balcony—Smith and Jones."

"Yes, sir. Please follow me, and I'll take you to your table." She led them into the pub, weaved through customers onto the balcony, and took them to a reserved table overlooking the street. "Here we are. I'll take your drink order if you know what you want."

Wild pointed toward TJ. "We'll both have a Guinness. Also, could we order Steak and Guinness Pie?"

She nodded. "Of course. I'll put your order in and be right back with your drinks."

Wild admired the view as the waitress departed.

TJ laughed. "What's caught your eye, son?"

"She reminds me of someone—except cuter. I just like her walk, as if she owned the place. It has a 'hello, I'm here' quality to it." Wild glanced around. "What's taking so long with our drinks?"

"Relax. As Guinness says, 'Good things come to those who wait.' It takes about two minutes to pour a proper pint."

Wild rolled his eyes. "When did you become such a connesewer?"

"You mean connoisseur?"

"That's what I said."

TJ laughed. "As it happens, I've been to several proper Irish pubs in Boston and Dublin. Anyone who's an aficionado of fine lagers, bitters, and stouts knows this." He nudged Wild. "Shh. Here she comes."

After the waitress left, Wild and TJ clinked glasses and tested their Guinness.

TJ smacked his lips. "Perfect." He pulled a pair of earbuds from his pocket and attached the cord to his phone. "Might as well get to work."

Wild nodded. "Agreed."

TJ clicked on the connection for a listening device in Maverick's library and leaned back in his chair, balancing on two legs.

Silence.

TJ continued to listen as he sipped his stout.

Without warning, he heard voices through his earbuds. He dropped his chair back to the floor and turned to Wild. "Holy shit! Take a listen." He backed up the recording and removed the cord to his phone before handing it over.

Wild plugged in his earbuds and hit play.

"I'll kill you." A male with a deep voice spoke with a British accent.

"No. Wait! I'll—"

Bang! Bang!

After footsteps faded away, silence ensued.

"What the—"

TJ nodded. "I thought the property was empty."

"Me too. So, who just got shot?"

TJ shook his head. "Beats me." He stood, drained his glass, and pulled out his billfold. "I think we should check things out." He dropped money on the table. "C'mon."

As they entered the bar area, the same waitress approached carrying a tray. "Is something wrong?"

Wild nodded. "Yes. There's an emergency. Could you put the food in carry-out containers? We left money on the table."

"Sure. Hope it's nothing serious."

"Might not be, but better to check it out in case there's a problem."

"Oh!" Her eyes widened. "Give me a minute—I'll be right back."

While TJ retrieved the money he dropped on the table, Wild waited for the waitress.

She returned moments later carrying two cartons. "Sorry, you have to rush away."

Wild grinned as he handed her the money. "Me, too. We'll come back another time when we can relax. Keep the change. See you soon."

TJ and Wild dashed down the stairs and ran to their vehicle.

While Wild drove, TJ continued listening. "More shots. Screams, too. Not sure what's going on." He reached down, pulled a pistol out of his bag, and checked the magazine. "Better be prepared."

"Check mine, too." Wild swerved around a slow-moving vehicle and blew the horn. "Outta the way!"

As Wild maneuvered through traffic toward Shore Lane, TJ

spotted flashing lights. "We might be too late. Two police cars and an ambulance ahead."

Wild nodded. "We'll still check things out. Perhaps we'll find out what happened."

"Yeah. And whether they're dead or alive."

35

T errorist Hideout
          Centreville, Virginia

THE FOLLOWING MORNING HAMZA, Jabbar, and Kamal climbed into their rental car. They headed out of Centreville, with Hamza keeping a close eye on the speedometer and remembering to use his turn signals. Their destination—The Brusch Agency in Old Town, Alexandria.

Kamal sat in the back, checking his AR-15. Satisfied, he reseated the magazine and chambered a round. He stroked the barrel as he gazed through the window. "Hope we see action—I'm ready to kill someone."

"Relax, Kamal." Hamza adjusted the rearview mirror so he could see his counterpart. "Our mission is surveillance—no shooting unless fired upon. I like that you are ready, but I need you to relax."

Kamal picked up one of Walter's bombs from the floor. "How about we hook this up to one of their vehicles?"

"I agree with Kamal." Jabbar stared out the window, catching glimpses of passing motorists. "It's time to instill fear in the infidels. Too long we've waited without taking action."

"Will both of you calm down? Farooq put me in charge because he knew you were hotheads and would take matters into your own hands." Hamza sighed. "Prepare your weapons and study the photographs Walter gave us. First, we will monitor the property and confirm the information he provided." A devilish smile etched across his face. "When I say the time is right, we shall bring the wrath of Allah upon them."

"That's more like it." Kamal pulled a knife and whetstone from a bag. He rubbed the serrated blade against the whetstone. "We'll be ready."

~

CAUGHT in the morning rush hour, they arrived in Alexandria an hour later. Hamza drove along the street, pausing in front of the building housing The Brusch Agency. "Take a quick look. I will circle again and find a place to park."

Jabbar lifted the picture of the property from the seat and compared it with the building. "Yes, we have the right one. Drop me off at the next corner, and I'll walk back toward you."

"Okay, but do not loiter. Find somewhere to watch the building without being noticed." Hamza passed a camera with a telephoto lens attached. "Take pictures of anyone coming out of the building."

"Why can't I just use my cellphone?"

"We need closeups to verify we are watching the right people." Hamza paused at the next intersection. "Besides, I told you to use the camera."

Jabbar took the camera and jumped out, ignoring the horns of inconvenienced drivers. He punched the crosswalk signal button every three seconds until the white walking man light indicated he could do so.

Meanwhile, Hamza and Kamal circled the block. Hamza slid the car into an empty spot as he rejoined the main street. He turned to

Kamal. "Find a good place to keep hidden while you monitor the building from this direction."

Kamal nodded. "Where will you be?"

"I will stay here." He pointed at a green and white sign. "Parking limited to two hours with no return within an hour. We must not draw attention to ourselves, so I will abide by their silly rules, but we will take matters into our own hands soon."

"When? Tonight?"

Hamza nodded. "Perhaps. Depends on what you and Jabbar learn. Take photographs as I instructed Jabber. We'll compare them later."

"As you wish."

Alone, Hamza tipped a baseball hat over his eyes and dozed.

Two hours later, Jabbar and Kamal returned to the vehicle. Hamza started the engine and pulled out, flipping a finger out the window when a car approaching from the rear slammed on its brakes, and the driver blew the horn. He grinned. "The finger—a very useful tool. So, did you get any pictures?"

Jabbar glanced at Hamza. "I took four—at least that many are clear."

"I managed six." Kamal grinned.

"Okay, we will stop somewhere to eat and compare your artistry with the photographs provided by Walter." Hamza continued along the street, turning right at an intersection where he remembered seeing a fast-food restaurant. He pulled into the parking lot. "We will eat here. They used to advertise billions and billions sold."

They climbed out of the car and entered the restaurant. As they waited in line, Jabbar pointed at the menu. "Hamza. We cannot eat here. It's unclean!"

"What do you mean?"

"Look—they sell hamburgers. Ham is from the pig, and we are forbidden to eat it."

Hamza laughed. "Relax, Jabbar. When we were in London, you ate beef burgers, right?"

"Yes, because they came from a cow."

"There is no difference. American hamburgers are the same as British beef burgers." Hamza chuckled. "If it makes you feel better, order a cheeseburger."

"Is it made from cheese?"

Hamza shook his head and sighed. "No. They place cheese on the hamburger."

"I am so confused."

"Never mind. Why not find an empty table outside, and I will order for all of us."

After placing and receiving his order, Hamza joined the others. He passed out the food and strawberry shakes. "Did you compare your photos with Walter's?"

"Yes, Hamza." Jabbar unwrapped his cheeseburger and sniffed. "Smells okay." He took a bite and chewed. "Tastes okay too. Three of my pictures matched."

Hamza nodded. "Excellent. How about you, Kamal?"

"Four—three are the same as Jabbar's." He grinned as he sucked the straw in his shake.

"Fantastic. After we eat, we will find a place to park and rest until later. I want to return to The Brusch Agency after they close."

As dusk settled in, Hamza and the others stopped in front of The Brusch Agency. Since they were closer to the building than during the morning, Hamza used his cellphone to photograph Jabbar and Kamal with the building in the background. As he took several snaps, the front door of The Brusch Agency opened, and a couple stepped out.

Arm-in-in arm, the man and woman strolled past the three men without glancing at them. They walked around the building and disappeared.

"Are they our targets?" Jabbar caressed the butt of his pistol through the shirttail covering his jeans.

"I think the woman is—I do not recognize the man." Hamza pulled several pictures from his pocket and sifted through them. "Just the woman."

Moments later, a car drove from behind the building, turned right, and disappeared in the traffic.

Hamza gazed at the building. Most of the lights were off. "Let us go around back. If anyone is watching, we will pretend we are lost."

When they reached the back of the building, a black Hummer occupied an open slot on one side. An SUV and a black F-150 pickup were parked in spots on the other side of a short sidewalk.

Hamza gestured. "Put one of Walter's bombs on the decadent black vehicle. The cost of something like that could feed my entire village for a month."

"What about the others?" Kamal pointed to a Jeep Cherokee and the F-150 pickup.

"Yes, attach a device to each of them. When you are finished, we will return to the car."

DOUGIE LEANED back in the plush leather chair in the security office on the second floor of The Brusch Agency and rested his feet over a corner of the desk. He sipped a cold Dr. Pepper as he monitored the six screens attached to CCTV cameras hidden on the front, back, and side of the building.

"What the hell?" He panned in on activity near the Hummer. "What are those guys doing?" He recorded their images to a thumb drive as he continued to monitor the intruders.

One of the men slid under the front of the vehicle, and another handed him a small bundle. A third man glanced around, apparently unaware their efforts were being recorded for posterity.

When the man under the Hummer rejoined the others, Dougie hit two switches.

The first switch activated two spotlights, while the second turned on blue and red flashing lights. All were aimed at The Brusch Agency's two parking spots.

Dougie hit a third switch and spoke into a microphone. "Hug the ground and don't move. Any attempt to flee will be met with deadly force."

One of the men darted away, glancing back at the others.

Dougie hit a fourth switch. Gunfire echoed behind the building.

"You don't listen too well. I said, don't move." Dougie hit the fourth switch a second time.

The man attempting to flee fell to the ground and remained still.

36

H ideout
Centreville, Virginia

"*MIERDA*!" Alberto slammed his phone on the table. "Farooq promised his men were the best. Where are they? No one answers." He opened a folder prepared by Walter and flicked through the photographs and reports a third time. "There must be something useful here."

Alberto tossed the pictures aside and started skimming through Walter's observations regarding their targets. *If Farooq's men cannot do the job, I'll take revenge into my own hands. Time to leave this cursed country and return to my beloved Argentina.*

His phone rang. *Walter.* Alberto accepted the call. "What?"

"Have you heard anything from the team in Alexandria? They were supposed to check in an hour ago."

"Nothing so far, Walter. You're the only one of my loyal followers who is competent."

"Thank you, Alberto. What do you suggest I do?"

"Stand by. I'm going through your previous reports now. Perhaps you mentioned something which will allow us to move forward and avenge Michael. If there's no update from them in the next hour or so, I shall deal with matters myself."

"I'll call back if I hear anything."

Alberto broke the connection. He resumed his examination of Walter's reports. He reread one of them. *A possibility?* He lifted the photo Walter took at the restaurant and shook his head. *Not one of them, but it will still send a message.*

DOUGIE CALLED Sindee as he watched the intruders behind the building.

"Hello?"

"Sindee, you and Cesar head back here ASAP. There are three guys pinned down behind the building. I need your help."

"Hang tight. We're only a block away."

"Meet you in back." Dougie flicked the console switches to the middle position, dimming the lights in the parking area. He checked his SIG Sauer and scrambled downstairs to the back door. He emerged on the dark side of the light but could still see the intruders, although they wouldn't see him.

One of the trespassers remained still on the ground. The other two crawled toward their weapons.

"Don't move, assholes." Dougie pulled his weapon from its holster. "You fell for the weapons-fire recording, but the bullets in my pistol are real, and I won't hesitate to pull the trigger."

The men remained motionless.

Dougie approached and kicked their weapons away.

Two cars pulled to a stop next to Dougie. Doors slammed as the occupants rushed forward, weapons drawn.

Sindee joined Dougie. "Hey. We brought reinforcements. They're Cesar's friends and were tailing us in case we ran into difficulty trying to flush these guys out."

"Oh, man!" Cesar nudged the unmoving culprit with the toe of his boot. "Smells like he died—at least he shit himself." He glanced around.

The other men cuffed the intruders, dragged them closer, and dropped them on the ground.

"What do we have here?" the taller man asked. Both men wore jeans and FBI windbreakers. "Anyone you know?"

Dougie shook his head. "Negative. Caught them on the surveillance cameras. Might need a bomb squad—I think they attached something under Javier's Hummer. By the way, I'm Dougie."

The taller man shook hands and pointed to his partner. "He's Robert, and I'm Ivan. We were lending some unofficial assistance to Cesar during our downtime." Ivan grinned. "Seems like you have things well in hand."

Robert clicked his phone shut. "Just called for the bomb squad and paramedics. I notified the Alexandria Police, too, since this is their jurisdiction."

"Thanks, Robert." Ivan turned to Dougie. "We'll hang around a bit to run interference with the local cops."

"Thanks." Dougie sat on a wooden bench next to the back of the building. "An interesting night, for sure." He glanced at Sindee. "Are you alright?"

She nodded.

"I hope you're ready for a long night."

"I will be after some strong brew. If you don't need me here, I'll get a pot of the good stuff going."

Dougie nodded. "Great teamwork, Sindee. Thanks." He watched her head inside before turning his attention to their captives.

Red and blue flashing lights appeared as four vehicles joined the others.

Two paramedics grabbed their equipment and rushed to the downed man. After a quick examination, they stood, shaking their heads.

Dougie approached. "What's the verdict?"

"He's a goner—the coroner will determine the formal cause of death, but I think it's clear." The red-haired man gestured to the body. "Appears to be a knife sticking in his gut." He glanced at a dark, damp area. "Looks like he bled out."

"Hmm." Dougie pursed his lips. "Must have had the knife in his hand when he fell to the ground. But why bring a knife? Did he think he'd get close enough to stab someone?"

"We'll call the coroner's office." The paramedics shrugged, returned to their vehicle, and departed.

A member of the bomb squad approached, holding a handmade device. "Found this under the Hummer. Pretty sophisticated, but nothing we couldn't handle. We'll take it away with us."

"Many thanks." Dougie extended a hand. "Appreciate your quick response."

The man gestured toward the FBI. "Thank them—they called us out." The man walked toward his vehicle.

Alexandria police officers shoved their prisoners in the back of two squad cars before one of the officers approached. "We'll need statements from everyone." He gestured toward the top of the building. "Does that camera work, or is it for show?"

"It works—everything's been recorded."

"Excellent. We'll need a copy. One of my men will monitor things here until the crime scene investigators arrive. In the meantime, why don't we start our interviews?" He gestured toward Cesar, Ivan, and Robert. "You, too."

Dougie nodded and pointed toward a door. "Let's go inside. Coffee? Donuts? My team just put on a fresh pot."

The officer laughed. "Smartass."

ALBERTO WAITED until after midnight before he climbed into the decade-old blue Buick he bought from an ad in a store window. A bit rusty around the wheel wells and a dent in the driver's door, but the engine still purred as if new. He pulled out of the driveway and headed toward the Beltway.

Still no answer from Farooq's men. Alberto glanced at the newspaper on the seat beside him. Underneath, a loaded pistol with an attached silencer. *Should be enough to handle the job. I should have done this long ago.* He gripped the steering wheel tighter as he merged with light traffic and headed toward Arlington.

Twenty minutes later, Alberto weaved through the city streets until he found the property tucked behind a row of young maple trees. He turned off the engine, keeping an eye on a beige and white townhouse across the street.

Alberto hunkered in his seat as a late-night dog walker approached. After the man and his terrier passed, Alberto glanced around.

No one else.

He grabbed the pistol and eased the door open. Once on the sidewalk, he studied the row of townhouses.

No lights.

Satisfied, Alberto crossed the street and climbed three steps. He rang the bell and eased away from the door. Looking up, he spotted a light come on in a room on the next floor.

He waited before pushing the bell again.

"Hold on! I'm coming."

Alberto heard the man turning locks inside. He stepped closer.

The door opened. "Something the matter?"

Alberto pointed toward his car. "My ... wife. I think the baby is coming. Can you help? I don't know where the hospital is, and I lost my phone."

"Just a minute." The door closed for a moment before the man reappeared, a phone in his hand. "I called for an ambulance. Let's take a look."

With a single movement, Alberto raised his arm.

Pfft! Pfft! Pfft!

The shots tore into the man's body. He clutched at the holes in his stomach, trying to stem the tide of rushing blood before he gasped once, fell to the ground, and lay still.

Alberto fired a fourth time, piercing the man's forehead before hurrying across the street. He climbed into the Buick and drove away. Three blocks later, he pulled into an all-night restaurant. He entered and followed the signs for the restrooms.

After washing his hands and wiping his face with damp towels, Alberto studied his reflection. He grinned. *At last! The message is sent. Now to find the others. They'll meet the same fate, and Michael's spirit shall be free.*

T he Brusch Agency
        Old Town, Alexandria, Virginia

PHIL SWATTED at the buzzing by his head as he continued to poke at the keyboard. "Blasted fly. How did it get in here?" He glanced around, but couldn't spot the insect, although the buzzing continued.

A message popped up on his desktop screen. *Answer your phone, idiot.*

Phil scanned the room before activating his phone. "Sorry, Makayla. I thought the buzzing was a real fly."

"Why couldn't you use something more creative than a fly to identify my calls? You gave MacKenzie a tweeting bird."

"I'll find something else for you. Anyway, you buzzed?" Phil laughed.

"Please—enough with your humor or lack thereof. MacKenzie and I continued our call chaining analysis of the number located in Virginia."

"Anything of use for Javier?"

"Yes. We're scraping details together. The number we mentioned before in Madrid is confirmed as being used by an Islamic State supplier named Farooq."

"What does he provide?"

"He appears to export men and weapons in support of terrorist operations."

Phil typed himself a note. "Okay. Go ahead."

"Through an indirect link, someone named Hamza received instructions from Farooq to assist a person in Virginia. We've identified this individual only as Alberto—at least so far."

"Excellent." Phil tapped on his keyboard. "Anything else?"

"You think we're magicians?" Makayla chuckled. "So happens there is. Alberto is expecting a shipment to arrive in Florida aboard a boat called *Childhood Dream*."

"What?" Phil pulled up a separate file and skimmed the page. "This ties in with what Charlie and the others are doing for the DEA in Bermuda. Well done to you and MacKenzie. Things are coming together. Is there anything else?"

"Not right now. Will let you know."

"Okay. I better call Javier right away."

"Don't forget to remind AJ we're still waiting for her return." Makayla broke the connection.

Phil called Javier. After six rings, it switched to the messaging service. "Javier, Phil here. I have some great news to share. Give me a call as soon as you receive this message."

AJ AND JAVIER glanced at each other and raised their hands. They remained still, watching the young man covering them with a hunting rifle.

Javier's phone rang. In an automatic reflex, he began to reach for it.

"No! Now, didn't I tell ya not to move?" The man raised his weapon. "I should shoot ya for disobeyin' a direct order." He cackled.

Snap!

The man turned, aiming his rifle in the direction of the sound.

"Don't shoot, Robbie. It's me—Vern." A young man with glasses wearing torn jeans and a dirty T-shirt stepped into the clearing. "Is this them smugglers you mentioned?"

"Yep! Ain't they a sight for sore eyes? How much do ya reckon we'll get for turning them over to the DEA?"

Vern stopped about three feet from Robbie's left and trained his .22 rifle on them. "Well, they don't look like them big names on the DEA website. Too bad—we could be rich!"

Robbie cradled his rifle in one arm, yanked a plug of chewing tobacco from his back pocket, and shoved it in his mouth. "Sho'nuff." He worked his jaws around the plug. "Bet we might get a few hunnert for them—each."

"You're pulling my leg. They must be worth more than that—maybe even a thousand each." Vern grinned. "What you gonna buy with your share?"

"A neighbor said he'd sell me his beat-up pickup for five hunnert." Robbie spat. "How 'bout you?"

"I'm savin' up fer a bit—want to go to one of them fancy schools and become edumacated."

Javier and AJ shared a bemused look.

He nodded toward Vern.

AJ returned the gesture, indicating Robbie.

"While you two make your plans for the reward money, can we drop our hands?" A smile etched across Javier's face. "You have us cornered—where will we go?"

Robbie turned to Vern as he scratched his head. "Whaddya think, Vern?" He spat again.

Vern lowered his weapon. "He's right, Robbie. Look around—where can they go except into the water? We'd drop them like pheasants if they tried for the trees."

"Reckon, you're right." Robbie lowered his weapon. "Y'all can lower your hands, but no funny bizness."

Javier and AJ dropped their hands and lunged at their captors.

AJ grabbed the barrel of Robbie's rifle and yanked, pulling it out of his hands.

He screamed and dropped to the ground. "Don't shoot! I'm too young to die!"

"Roll over."

Javier swept Vern's feet from beneath him with a scissor kick. After Vern fell, Javier grabbed his .22 and tossed it away. He pulled out flex-cuffs, tossed some to AJ, and secured Vern's hands.

AJ and Javier helped the now-trussed men to their feet and placed them back-to-back.

Javier glared at them. "How old are you? You're too young to be taking on smugglers if that's what we are."

"We—we'ze yunguns, mister. Jest turned twenty. Pappy will tan our hides for losing our guns, lessen you kill us." Robbie swallowed and tried to scoot away as Javier approached.

"Don't kill us, mister." Tears trickled down Vern's face. "We was jest having a bit of fun with ya'll."

"Don't you understand you both could end up in a shallow grave for trying to take on smugglers?" Javier studied their faces. "Do you live around here?"

"Yessah." Robbie raised his tied hands and pointed toward a large, two-story brick house across the inlet. "My pappy lives there. He told us we needed to earn a livin' if we wanted to make somethin' of ourselves."

AJ glanced in the direction Robbie gestured. "Forgive my ignorance, but how did your father buy that property?"

Robbie grinned. "He done played the lottery for a long time, always buying his ticket from the same bar. Last year, he won the Florida jackpot."

"That figures. Wish I was so lucky."

Javier shook his head. "Better to stay in school and finish your education." He pulled out his identification wallet and showed it to them.

AJ did the same.

Robbie and Vern's eyes widened when they saw AJ's CIA identification. They stared at each other.

"Y'all ... y'all not going to send us to that terrorist place, Gigantimo?"

AJ laughed. "You mean, Guantanamo Bay?" She shook her head. "No, we won't do that." She turned to Javier. "What do you think?"

"Hmm." Javier rubbed his chin. "Perhaps we could put them to work. Won't pay as well as a DEA reward but should keep them out of trouble." He turned to Robbie and Vern. "We need your help. Can you write?"

Both men nodded.

"Okay. We'll release you. I'll put a number in your phones."

AJ reached into her bag and pulled out a knife.

Robbie and Vern backed away until she reached for the zip ties and cut them.

"Pay attention." Javier pointed at them. "I want you to send me everything you can remember about suspicious boats in the area—descriptions, how many people, what they looked like. Did you see any cargo? Any names of the boats, too."

"Whatcha needin' all that fer?"

"We're on assignment for the DEA, and we're looking for a particular boat—*Childhood Dream*."

"Hey, Robbie. We knows that boat." Vern turned to Javier. "It came here three weeks ago. It's what gave us the idea to help the DEA."

"Well, by helping us, you'll be assisting the DEA. We'll put in a good word with them. Who knows? They might give you the money you're looking for."

Robbie and Vern looked at each other and grinned. They chimed, "Awesome!"

Javier's phone pinged again. He accessed his voice mail and listened to Phil's message before calling him back.

"Phil, I got your message. Something more to pass on?"

"Yes, boss." He filled Javier in on the information he received from the twins.

"Excellent. Get in touch with Charlie and let him know."

"Will do, boss. What are you going to do now?"

"AJ and I are going to do some fishing." He chortled. "We have two new helpers."

"Who?"

"A couple of locals who insist they've seen the boat we're interested in. We'll put them to work locating it the next time it comes ashore. In the meantime, we have some unfinished vacation time to use up."

"Should I call you if any new information comes in?"

"Of course. AJ and I can relax anytime. Right now, the important thing is to find the *Childhood Dream* and put an end to the owner's illegal business."

38

S hore Lane
Bermuda

THE HUMMER COASTED to a stop underneath the overhanging branches of an ancient Bermuda Cedar tree on Shore Lane. Wild and TJ eased their doors open and climbed out. They pulled on their backpacks before pushing the doors closed with a soft click.

After glancing in both directions along the road, they donned their night-vision goggles and shouldered their packs. With the ease of panthers, they threaded their way toward Maverick's house, avoiding the streetlights and keeping in the shadows as much as possible.

TJ raised a hand as they neared the property.

Both men halted, reached up, and adjusted their goggles. With another glance around, they climbed the wall and dropped onto Maverick's driveway.

A silver Kia Rio sat in front of the garage.

Wild extracted a tracking device from a side pocket on his backpack and crept toward the vehicle. After placing the tracker under the rear bumper, he signaled for TJ to move toward the house's main entrance.

TJ pulled his SIG Sauer from a shoulder holster and stood beside the door.

Wild joined him. He tried the handle.

Unlocked.

He turned to TJ and raised a hand in the air. He whispered, "Did someone beat us here?"

TJ shrugged before he pushed the door and stepped inside. Both hands tight around the pistol grip, the barrel of his pistol followed his eyes' trajectory.

Wild mimicked TJ's movements.

Their NVGs cast an eerie green glow as they scanned the interior.

TJ pointed toward the living room and edged forward.

Chairs overturned, end tables knocked on their sides, paintings torn from the walls—all signs of a struggle and a search of the room. In the center, a dark splotch covered the top of a glass coffee table.

Wild teased a pair of blue nitrile gloves from a pouch on his backpack. After squeezing his fingers into them, he stepped forward, touched the sticky substance, and sniffed his finger. A sweet, metallic pungency assaulted his sentences.

Blood.

"Psst." TJ waved at Wild. "Over here—got a body."

Wild scooted around the table and joined TJ. "Recognize him?"

TJ shook his head as he nudged the still form before bending down. "Let's see if he's carrying any ID." He fished out a wallet, opened it, and glanced at a driver's license. "Jaden Adams—from Bermuda."

Wild crouched by the body and checked for wounds. "Long, bloody gash by his left ear." He continued his search. "Ah. A hole in his side. A separate bullet crease, too."

TJ handed the wallet to Wild. "Put this back in his pocket, and let's clear out of here."

They retreated from the property. After checking the coast was clear, they worked their way back to the Hummer. Once inside, TJ turned to Wild. "We heard three shots on the listening device."

Wild nodded. "We know where two of them went. Suppose Adams fired a shot before someone killed him?"

"Perhaps. Not our place to find out." TJ motioned for Wild to start the vehicle. "C'mon. Time to leave before someone calls the cops. It'd be awkward for us to explain our presence."

"Agreed." Wild started the engine and pulled a U-turn. "Where to?"

"The guest house to clean up—then the hospital. We need to talk with Charlie, and I don't want to use the phone."

WHEN THEY ARRIVED at Sam's room, Charlie was sitting in a chair in the corridor sipping on a Coke. "Sam's asleep—let's not bother her." He stood and pointed toward the patients' garden terrace.

After they sat, Charlie glanced at TJ and Wild's faces. "What's up?"

"We picked up shots on one of the bugs we planted at Maverick's house." Wild rubbed the side of his face. "We checked it out—someone killed a guy named Adams."

"Were you out of your minds?" Charlie glared at each of them. "What if someone spotted you?"

Wild dropped his head. "Guess we weren't thinking."

"Damn straight! Can't be helped now. Too late to call Cedric. We'll let him know first thing in the morning."

"How's Sam?"

"She's doing good, TJ. If she's still stable tomorrow, they'll discharge her." Charlie frowned. "However, the docs say she needs to take it easy for another week or two. So, I'll be taking her back to Virginia."

"What about us?" Wild gestured to himself and TJ. "Do we continue or what?"

"We'll make a decision about you once I speak with Javier. I assume the mission will proceed as planned. However, since we don't know Maverick's whereabouts and time is passing by, I'm not sure where to send you." Charlie stood. "Why don't you head back to the guest house and get some sleep. We'll talk tomorrow."

THE NURSE COMPLETED her check of Sam's vital signs and smiled. "Everything is where it should be."

Sam returned the nurse's smile. "When can I leave?"

"The specialist will stop in when he does his rounds. If he's satisfied, you'll be discharged today."

"Good. No offense, but I'd rather be anywhere than in the hospital."

The nurse chuckled. "That's a good sign. Most of our patients on the road to recovery say the same thing." She turned toward the door as it opened.

Charlie stuck his head inside the room. "Everyone decent?"

The nurse glanced at Sam. "Safe to enter?"

Sam nodded and grinned. "C'mon in, Charlie. We won't attack you."

He entered the room carrying a green and white duffle bag. "Thought you might want this in case they let you out."

The nurse crossed her arms. "My patient isn't going anywhere until the specialist approves her re—"

Someone knocked on the door before it swung inward. As the doctor approached Sam's bed, the nurse handed a tablet to him. He scanned the latest results and smiled. "Excellent. Young lady, I'm going to release you, but you must promise no more driving in Bermuda."

Everyone laughed.

The specialist raised his hand. "However, it might take two or three hours for the paperwork to make its way through the system before you'll be allowed to leave."

Sam groaned. "Just like the military—hurry up and wait."

"Patience, Sam." Charlie placed a hand on her arm. "Once everything is approved, I'll take you to the guest house, and you can relax outside."

"Works for me—you'll have to wait on me hand and foot, so I don't overtax myself." Sam raised her arm embedded in the sling. "Better find some good food, too. I hate hospital food, and I'm starving."

Charlie smirked and rolled his eyes. "Whatever."

FOUR HOURS LATER, Charlie, Sam, Wild, and TJ sat under the sun umbrella back at Oxford House, sipping on freshly squeezed lemonade. The remains of tuna and cheese sandwiches rested on a plate in the center of the table.

"I had a busy morning on the phone while waiting for Sam. My first call was to Cedric." Charlie glanced at Wild and TJ. "I told him about you finding a body in Maverick's home. He said Jaden Adams worked for a guy known only as Daddy in an undefined enforcer role. So far, there's been insufficient evidence to pin any crime on Adams."

"Who is this Daddy?" Wild pursed his lips.

"Cedric said he's a minor player in the Bermuda drug smuggling trade, but he's as slippery as an eel. Has friends in high places. Apparently, he's a friend of Zaine, Maverick's girlfriend, but nothing definitive."

Wild and TJ nodded.

"I also spoke with Phil and Javier. Seems Maverick's boat, *Childhood Dream*, is expected in Miami. Javier wants you both there to help support him and AJ."

Sam half-raised a hand. "What about me?"

"Bad news, I'm afraid." Charlie shook his head. "For me, too. Javier instructed me to escort you back to Virginia for continued rest and recuperation."

"Why? What about the mission?"

"There'll be plenty of other missions. With this one heading to the U.S., it won't be long before things are turned over to the DEA. Better for you to fully heal and prepare for the next adventure."

"I suppose—but I don't have to like it." Sam frowned.

"That's true, but you'll get plenty of opportunities as the business grows." Charlie glanced at his watch. "Since we never made it to Flanigan's as a group, I suggest we do so tonight. Our teams will separate tomorrow and continue as I outlined. Questions?"

The others shook their heads.

ROLAND DROPPED the binoculars into his lap. *Perfect. I'll have the others keep an eye on this group. Too bad they stumbled across Jaden's body. Not sure who they're working for, but an unplanned incident or two should clear the way.* He twirled his gold pinkie ring. *Might be time to find a few hungry sharks.*

39

S wizzle Inn
Baileys Bay, Bermuda

ROLAND GLANCED at the red and white building before stepping from the bright sunshine into the somewhat dimmer interior of the Swizzle Inn. With the facility always packed with tourists and locals alike, he enjoyed the friendly atmosphere. He wiped his eyes with a hand until they focused before he weaved through the crowded bar area and headed upstairs to the dining room.

He spotted an empty table for four against the far wall, a perfect place to people-watch. Roland flagged down a waiter. "I already know what I want—a grilled shrimp cocktail to start and the smoked St. Louis style ribs."

The waiter nodded. "Right away, sir. Would you like anything to drink?"

"Yes. Bring a jug of Rum Swizzle."

"Half or full jug?"

"Better bring a full one—I'm expecting someone to join me.

Please put my order in now—I'm hungry. The others can decide what they want when they arrive."

"Yes, sir."

After the waiter departed, Roland glanced at the five HD screens, each showing a different sporting event. Not interested in the current programs, he scanned the room for anyone he knew.

Someone laid a hand on his shoulder.

He turned, ready to jump to his feet, before recognizing the person.

"Daddy!" Zaine wrapped her arms around Roland as she kissed him on the cheek. "Sorry we're late." She turned to the couple who accompanied her. "Valeria, Enrique. This is Roland, better known as Daddy."

Roland chuckled. "At least to my friends." He pointed toward the empty seats. "Please, join me."

After they claimed places, Zaine studied Roland. "What did you want to discuss with me?"

"Can't I just eat lunch with one of my favorite people and her friends and enjoy their company?" *I wonder if she suspects anything.*

Zaine smiled. "Of course."

"I've been trying to reach Phoenix, but he's not returning my calls. Has he already headed to Miami?"

"I-I'm not sure where he is. Sometimes, he disappears for—"

The waiter returned with Roland's food. After setting it down, he asked Zaine and the others if they were ready to order.

Zaine gestured to Roland's meal. "I'll have the same."

"Me, too," Valeria and Enrique said in unison.

Daddy turned to Enrique. "What do you want to drink?"

"We'll have the same as you." He turned to the waiter. "Better bring another jug."

"Right away, sir."

"You were saying, my dear?" Roland plucked a juicy shrimp from his cocktail.

"Sometimes, Phoenix disappears for a few days at a time, but when he returns, he never tells me where he went or what he did."

Roland reached across the table and patted her hand. "No worries. I'm sure we'll hear from him soon. After all, how can he stay away from such a beautiful woman? Besides, he knows there's a business proposition I want to discuss with him." *Profitable for me, unlucky, or even deadly for Phoenix.*

Zaine blushed. "Thank you, Daddy." She filled a glass from the jug, sipped, and shook her head. She screwed her face into a comical reaction and grasped her throat as she pretended to choke. She spoke in a raspy voice. "I don't understand how you can drink this stuff." Everyone laughed.

Zaine drank more. "Once my taste buds get over the explosion of flavors, it's actually not bad, but the first taste was enough to make me gag."

"It is an acquired taste, but one which Bermuda is famous for." Roland refilled his almost empty glass.

Conversation disappeared as the four tucked into their meal. When they finished, Roland signaled for the waiter. "Check, please. Put everything on one bill."

"As you wish, sir."

Enrique waved a hand. "It's okay. We can pay for our own."

"Nonsense. I invited Zaine, and when she asked if you could join us, I agreed." Roland laughed. "If it makes you feel better, you can pay next time."

"You're on."

BACK IN HIS CAR, Roland prepared to pull into traffic when his phone rang. He accepted the call. "Yes?"

"It's me—Jesús. We're leaving for Miami in a couple of hours. I couldn't call sooner because Phoenix always seems to be watching me."

"Understood." Roland sighed. "Call me when you arrive. There might be something extra in your monthly envelope if things go according to plan."

"Have I ever failed you? I'll contact you when I can after we complete our journey."

"Excellent." Roland broke the connection. *Even with the loss of Jaden, things are coming together. Soon Phoenix and Zaine will be eliminated, leaving only Alberto to deal with.* He headed toward the marina.

～

THE POLICE constable knocked on the chief officer's door. "Sir."

The officer glanced up from his computer screen. "What is it, Constable?" He motioned his subordinate inside.

"As you ordered, I took two men to the marina for a further inspection of the *Childhood Dream*. We couldn't find it. When I checked with the harbormaster, he said the boat left yesterday, but he didn't know where it was going."

"I see." The chief officer pursed his lips as he rubbed his chin. "Ask the Marine Section to report any sightings of the boat. Better contact the U.S. Coast Guard, too."

"Right away, sir."

～

"WHO WERE YOU TALKING TO, JESÚS?"

"J-Just my girlfriend. I told her we were taking some fisherman out for a couple of days, and I'd see her when we return."

Phoenix locked eyes with Jesús. "Uh-huh. You better buy her something nice. Get some fish, too, so she doesn't become too suspicious." *What's he up to?*

"Great idea. Let me finish stowing everything, and we'll be ready to cast off and head to the States."

"I'll give you a hand. The sooner we dock in Miami and hand over this shipment, the better for all of us." *But if you happen to have an accident on the way back, there'll be a larger cut for me.*

"I checked the weather forecast." Jesús placed several packages inside a locker and secured the door. "Should be smooth going, but the American meteorologists reported a tropical storm is forming—which could end up being a hurricane. The waves are already five feet high, and the wind is gusting up to forty-five miles per hour."

"Keep an eye on the forecasts. If necessary, we'll sail around it—been through a few storms in the past and prefer to avoid them."

Jesús locked another locker. "Fine with me." He glanced around. "We're ready as far as I can tell."

"Excellent. Let's cast off."

SAFELY ENSCONCED in his yacht in Hamilton's marina, Roland checked for emails. Not finding anything of interest, he logged out. He climbed the stairs onto the deck and headed toward sun chairs at the stern. Plopping into one, he pulled out his phone, dialed, and let it ring until someone answered. "It's me."

"About time, brother." A deep male voice echoed through the handset. "What's the status?"

"The cargo should be in your area within twenty-four hours."

"Are they aware we'll be taking the shipment from them?"

Roland laughed. "No. They're too trusting and think because I'm called Daddy, I'll be kind to them. Little do they know."

The callee chuckled. "Once we take control, what do you want us to do with them?"

"Whatever you want—their use is at an end. They'll make good shark food."

"An excellent idea. What about the boat? Should we sell it?"

"Sink it in deep water. I don't want a trace of the *Childhood Dream* or Phoenix and his crewman discovered."

"Have you transferred the money?"

"Yes. It should be in your account later today."

"Excellent. Always a pleasure doing business with you." The man cut the connection.

Roland smiled as he placed another call. *They say everything comes to those who wait. We've been patient long enough.* The phone rang six times. He hung up and redialed.

"Yes?"

"Things are going according to plan. As soon as a few loose ends are dealt with, it'll be time to leave here—for good."

"Sounds good—partner. Any idea where you want to go?"

"Hmm." Roland chortled. "Fancy a vacation in Europe?"

40

H ideout
Centreville, Virginia

AFTER DITCHING his gun in a dumpster behind a strip mall in Annandale, Alberto pulled his hoodie right around his head as he avoided security cameras and returned to his hideout. *Success. No one will find me—I hope.*

Once inside, he ripped off his jacket, leaned over the sink, turned on the faucet, and filled a glass. Downing the water without taking a breath, he sat at the table. He held out an arm—steady as a rock. *Nerves of steel.* He smiled.

Alberto fished his phone from a pocket and dialed. "Walter, any update from Hamza and the others?"

"No. However, I just saw something on the TV. The talking head said three men were captured in Arlington—they had weapons and homemade bombs."

"*Mierde!*" Alberto slammed his fist on the table. "It must be them. They saw our faces and can identify where we're staying."

Walter ignored Alberto's outburst. "What should we do?"

"Let me think." Alberto tapped his fingers against the phone. "The only identity they can provide for you is your American name. But they know my real one. Hang on. I'm going to turn on the TV." He walked into the living room and picked up the remote as he perched on the edge of his recliner. He clicked on a twenty-four-hour news channel.

"The man died at the scene. Identification is being withheld at this time, pending the return of his spouse from an overseas business trip.

"In other news, we understand the three men captured in Arlington belong to a Middle Eastern terrorist organization. The FBI and CIA are reaching out to their international counterparts to learn more about the men. As soon as they—"

Who did I kill? The man we hired wasn't married. Alberto muted the TV sound. "Walter, are you still there?"

"Yes." He sighed. "I'm getting worried."

"I will never give up my mission to avenge Michael, but I don't want to risk being captured by the Americans, locked in one of their prisons, and tortured. Time to leave—we'll keep track of Michael's killers, and one day, they will meet their god." *There are plenty of Allah's followers willing to die for the cause, but not me—I have too much to offer.*

"Inshallah."

"Here's what we're going to do. First, buy some bleach and paper towels. Wipe every surface you might have touched. Don't forget to wash the bedding or throw it in a dumpster somewhere."

"But Alberto. I've been here for weeks. I'll have to wipe everything down."

"Do it. We must make things difficult for any forensics people. I'll do the same thing here. Next, destroy anything with your name on it. Get rid of everything not nailed down that could give away any clues." *I wonder if we should torch both properties? Something to consider.* "In the meantime, I'll send emails to Farooq and Ismail. We'll need to leave this accursed country by different routes. They can help us."

"I don't know ...."

"Just do what I tell you." Alberto broke the connection and rushed into the kitchen. He opened his laptop and began typing.

T *o:* Farooq
    From: Abdul

T *HE SITUATION IS HEATING up more than expected. We can't reach the men you sent, so it's better for Maheer and me to leave until things quieten. Can you assist with his departure? I'll make separate arrangements for myself.*

A *S SOON AS* he sent the message, Alberto began another one:

T *o:* Ismail
    From: Abdul

B *ROTHER, I am in need of your expertise once again. My plan is interrupted by unforeseen circumstances. I must leave and rejoin the others in our jihad against the infidels. Please arrange for someone to assist me at the place where we first met. I can get there on my own but will need your assistance to return to the Middle East.*

A *FTER SENDING THE MESSAGE,* Alberto scurried into the basement. He grabbed two gallons of bleach and a package of paper towels before returning upstairs. *I'll leave the kitchen and the bathroom to last. Better to sanitize the bedrooms and living room first. Once all the surfaces are done, I can go back through to sanitize and clean the floors.*

DOUGIE PARKED Javier's Hummer in the parking lot of the Alexandria Police Department and went inside. He approached a counter, his driver's license in hand. "Hello. I'm Dougie Dabney. Chief Clark is expecting me."

The officer glanced at Dougie's license, nodded, and stood. He pointed to the open upper half of a stable door. "Right this way." The officer opened the lower half and walked along a corridor. He stopped in front of an opaque glass door and knocked.

"Come in."

The officer opened the door and gestured for Dougie to enter.

The chief rose and shook hands before pointing to a chair. "Have a seat. I want you to understand I normally don't discuss any ongoing cases with civilians, but I'm making an exception because Javier is a friend."

"Understood, Chief. I greatly appreciate it. We know one perp died at the scene. Anything new from the other two?"

"Yeah." The chief picked up a folder. "The FBI took them into custody. Before the FBI hauled them away, the suspects tried everything they could to extricate themselves from their situation, although they shut up after talking with public defenders. They said the dead man was called Jabbar, and they identified themselves as Hamza and Kamal."

Dougie rubbed his chin. "Common names. Anything else?"

The chief glanced at the folder again. "Yeah. Said a Latino named Alberto hired them to do a hit on Javier's agency. They also identified the guy who made the bombs—someone named Walter. Seems these guys don't like last names."

"If their prints are in a database, the suspects will be identified." Dougie nodded. "Don't suppose I can read that file?"

The chief laughed. "No way. However, I'll give you one last nugget. Hamza tried to keep Kamal quiet, but before they lawyered up, Kamal gave us two addresses in Virginia. The FBI, state police, local authorities, and bomb squads will be making simultaneous raids this evening."

Dougie stood. "Appreciate your time and the info, Chief. I'll update Javier if that's okay with you."

"Sure. Tell him he buys the Kentucky bourbon the next time."

Dougie laughed. "Will do, and thanks again."

THREE HOURS LATER, a tired Alberto sat at the kitchen table, a Diet Coke at hand. He held a towel filled with ice against his warm forehead. *Almost done. A short break, and I'll get the kitchen cleaned up.* He opened his laptop and checked for messages—there were two.

To: Abdul
From: Farooq

THINGS ARE NO BETTER for me at this time. I'm unable to assist Maheer. Why not take him with you or, better yet, send him to meet Allah?

ALBERTO SLAMMED a fist on the table. *Figures. After all I've done for Farooq, he turns his back on me. I shall remember this. May he burn with the infidels.* Alberto deleted the message and opened the other one.

To: Abdul
From: Ismail

OF COURSE, I will assist you, my brother. Will anyone accompany you? I only ask so I can make proper arrangements. If possible, I shall meet you myself. When should I expect you?"

. . .

ALBERTO SMILED. *More like my brethren than the traitorous Farooq.* He typed a response.

To: Ismail
  From: Abdul

ALLAH BE PRAISED! Thank you, my brother. One other individual will be arriving with me. Barring any unforeseen problems, we shall arrive in three or four days. We must proceed with caution, so we don't alert the infidel authorities.

ALBERTO FINISHED his drink and called Walter. "Are you finished?"

"Almost. The cleaning is done as you ordered. I want to leave a little surprise for the authorities before I depart."

"Excellent." He took a deep breath. "We have a slight problem. Farooq has become weak like the infidels and won't provide further assistance."

"Huh? What should I do?"

"Relax. Finish your preparations. I'm almost done here. We shall meet tonight at Denny's in Breezewood, Pennsylvania, and discuss our departure."

"Until tonight. Inshallah."

~

A TEAM OF LOCAL POLICE, state police, and FBI agents met in a conference room at the Fairfax Police Station. Two bomb squad members also joined them. Unlike more boisterous gatherings, everyone remained stoic, waiting for the briefing to begin.

A tall, thin man with a receding hairline and wearing an FBI jacket over his suit stepped onto a raised platform. "I'm Special Agent in Charge, James Kirk." He glanced around the room as quiet laughs grew in intensity. "Don't blame me—it's my parents' fault. At least my middle name isn't Tiberius—it's William."

Laughter continued.

Kirk raised his hands for silence. "Enough. We're here for a serious matter. A group of international terrorists is gunning for one of our own. We've been fortunate in capturing two of them, which led to our group's creation. Under questioning, one of them revealed two addresses."

A hand shot in the air. "How reliable is their information?"

"We're not certain, but we can't ignore this. We'll split into two fifteen-person teams. One team, designated Bulldog-One, will head to a property in a rundown area near Culpepper, while Bulldog-Two will go to a residential district in Centreville."

Kirk glanced at his watch. "Details will be uploaded to your encrypted tablets and smartphones. We'll hit both properties in three hours—at 2100 hours. Since our response is being put together on the fly, the powers that be decided upon an integrated force." He pursed his lips. "Anyway, according to the information provided by the suspects, there's only one person at each place, but assume there are more. Bring them in alive—if you can. However, don't take any unnecessary chances. That's all." Kirk turned and left the podium.

ALBERTO FINISHED CLEANING THE KITCHEN. He kept a final bleach-soaked cloth to wipe down the door as he left. Depositing his personal belongings in the vehicle, he called Walter. "I'm leaving now."

"Okay, Alberto. I'm heading north in a few minutes."

"Obey the traffic laws. Meet you in Breezewood. Remember to dump all of your cleaning supplies and any excess clothing at different rest stops on the way."

ONE BY ONE, the fifteen men and women comprising Bulldog-One crouched low and dispersed, moving from bush to bush, keeping out of sight whenever possible as they approached the Culpepper property in force.

Once they surrounded the house, the overall team leader commenced a radio check with his five subordinate teams. "One. Status?"

"One in place. Ready."

The leader received similar responses from teams two through four. When he contacted team five, he was met with static.

"Team five. Where are you?"

Someone keyed a mic. A barking dog could be heard over the radio, the noise diminishing as moments passed.

"Sorry. This is five. A local dog didn't like the look of us and started making a racket. His owner came out of the house and took him inside. We're ready."

"All teams—go!"

Two men scurried forward carrying a black battering ram. Once in position, they glanced back at their leader.

He gave a thumbs-up.

The door splintered with the force of the ram.

"Police! Drop your weapons!"

Upon hearing the noise from the front door, team members breached the rear door, weapons drawn.

Shouts of "Clear!" echoed through the building.

The leader spoke into his hands-free communications system. "Bring in the forensics team. Scour this place from top to bottom. Bulldog-One, meet me outside the house."

When everyone joined the team leader, he glanced into each face. "Seems our prey flew before we arrived. Don't know if this was planned, something tipped them off, or if we have a leak. We'll find out of that, I'm positive." He took a deep breath, coughing when he inhaled the lingering smell of bleach wafting through the open door. "They tried to sanitize the scene. Let's hope they weren't thorough. Head back to the command post and await further instructions." The team leader shook his head. "I hope Bulldog-Two is having better luck."

Bulldog-Two used an abandoned warehouse parking lot outside Centreville as its staging area. Breaking into five three-person teams, they took different routes to their destination. Three of the teams, dressed in civilian clothing and carrying their weapons in gym bags, headed toward the rear of the property, hopping over fences, and keeping as low a profile as possible. The remaining groups, wearing full body armor and law enforcement windbreakers, crouched, weapons at the ready, as they approached from the front.

The team lead whispered into his mic. "Everyone in position?"

Multiple clicks came through his earpiece.

"Roger. Commence mission."

A burly officer rushed forward carrying a twelve-gauge breaching gun, followed by two officers holding MP-5 weapons. They stopped three feet from the front door.

The officer with the shotgun aimed at the lock. His finger tightened on the trigger ....

Ka-Blam!

The door blew apart, followed by a bright flash.

Boom!

Wood splinters, nails, and ball bearings shredded the three officers, blowing pieces of their bodies across the lawn.

The team at the rear of the property rushed forward.

They prepared to breach the door when one of the officers shouted a warning. "Watch out! There's—"

Flames shot into the air as a second explosion occurred at the rear of the property with the same devasting results.

41

T errace Suite, Biltmore Hotel
Miami

AJ's golden skin glistened in the midday sun as she and Javier lounged on the balcony of their Biltmore Hotel suite.

This beats being stuck in an office any day. He turned and studied AJ's profile, unable to take his eyes off her. *This is the life—could do this all the time.* "Ready for more champagne?" He reached for the iced bottle.

AJ shook her head. "Are you trying to get me drunk?" She rolled her eyes.

"Would I do something like that?" He chuckled.

"If you could get away with it—"

Javier scooped up his warbling phone from the table and accepted the call. "This better be important."

TJ's deep voice came through the speaker. "Wild and I just arrived. We're gonna stay at a cheap hotel near the airport. What's the game plan?"

"Hey, TJ. Still waiting for word from two guys who are going to let us know when suspicious boats appear in their area."

"Where did you find these guys?"

"They're actually a couple of kids looking to make some money. They held us at gunpoint, but we turned the tables on them." Javier laughed. "They carried .22s but weren't any match for us. You'll meet them tomorrow."

TJ chuckled. "Okay, we'll have a night on the town and see you in the morning."

Javier dropped the phone on the table and turned to AJ. "Hear that?"

"Yeah. So, what should we do for the remainder of the day?" She grinned. "We might not have another chance to be alone for a while."

"Room service?" He reached over and took her hand. "Or do you have a better idea?"

"I can think of something—hope you're up to it."

He scooted closer, held her in his arms, and kissed her. "I'm always ready."

JAVIER DROVE their rental car toward Biscayne Bay, followed by Wild and TJ in another vehicle. He tapped a tune on the steering wheel as he whistled.

AJ sat next to Javier, reseating the magazine in her SIG Sauer. "You're happy this morning. Why the change?"

Javier laughed. "As if you don't know."

She raised a brow as she tucked her pistol into a holster on her belt. "Be nice, or your chances of a repeat performance could dwindle."

"Yes, ma'am."

They burst into laughter.

Twenty minutes later, Javier pulled off Isla Dorada Boulevard onto the grass. Donning Ray-Bans, Javier and AJ climbed out of the vehicle, grabbed their backpacks from the rear seat, and walked toward the other car.

He nodded at Wild and TJ as they approached. "Ready?"

"Always, boss." TJ glanced around. "Where are these fellas you mentioned?"

Javier pointed toward the thicket. "They said they'd meet us by the water. Follow me." He weaved through the trees until he reached a wide grassy area and waited for the others to join him.

"There." He gestured toward the water.

Two men sat in lawn chairs, casting fishing lines.

Javier put a finger to his lips. "Shh." He picked his way through the thick and tall grass, using slow and methodical steps until he was within three feet of the chairs. "Wake up!"

Vern and Robbie jumped to their feet, their eyes filled with fright. The rods flew into the air, and their rifles fell to the ground.

"Gosh dang it! What in tarnation are you doing sneaking up on fellas?" Robbie tried to wipe spilled soda from his clothes. "Y'all done owe me for a drink—I jest opened it."

"Relax, guys. I want to introduce you to two others of my team." Javier gestured toward TJ and Wild.

Both stepped forward, hand extended.

Vern craned his neck as he gazed up at TJ. "Is you a giant like the one in *Jack and the Beanstalk*?"

"Ha, ha." TJ's laugh seemed to originate from the bottom of his shoes. "Just plenty of home cookin'. Helped both of my parents were tall, too."

With the introductions and handshakes over, Javier turned to business. "Robbie, any suspicious boats since we last spoke?"

Robbie's head bobbed up and down like a jack-in-the-box. "Y-yeah—jest this mornin' while it was still dark. Couldn't see the boat, but I recognized that there engine."

"We'll sit with you for a bit. Holler if you spot it."

Robbie nodded as he pointed to a stack of folding camp chairs. "We done brought y'all somethin' to sit on. The ground can get downright soggy."

"There's plenty of beer and a few soft drinks if yer thirsty." Vern gestured to the red and white ice chest he had been sitting on when Javier and the others arrived.

"Thanks. Think I'll pass on a drink for now." Javier picked up two chairs. He opened them, handing one to AJ.

"Hey, Javier."

He turned at the sound of TJ's voice.

"Glance over my shoulder—in the tree line. I thought I spotted the sun reflecting off a lens."

"Got it. Didn't you forget something in the car?" Javier grinned. "Circle around and find out who it is. Wonder who's tailing us?"

"We'll find out." TJ turned sideways and spoke in a louder voice. "Left some of my gear in the car—be right back." He headed toward their cars and disappeared into the trees.

Javier and AJ lined their chairs up with Robbie and Vern.

AJ pointed to one of the poles, where a line stretched into the water. "Fish biting?"

"Don't reckon they is. Not matter—we jest usin' them poles as props. We is watching for that boat to come back."

Javier patted Robbie on the arm. "Good—" He pulled his phone from a shirt pocket, noted the caller, and clicked the green button. "Hey, Mitch. What's up?"

"Received a report this morning from the Coast Guard. One of their Defender-class boats spotted the *Childhood Dream* off the coast early this morning, headed toward Biscayne Bay."

"Roger. We're sitting on the banks of one of the tributaries now. If we spot it, what should we do?"

"Hang tight as long as possible. I'll organize a response. But Javier ... don't do anything rash."

"Who, me?" Javier laughed. "If the situation presents itself, we might corner them and wait for your arrival."

"Sounds good. Stay safe. If you can't, at least duck."

"Gotcha." Javier broke the connection. "Keep your eyes peeled. The Coast Guard says our objective is headed this way."

Robbie spat tobacco juice on the ground. "Jest remember, we dun get any re-ward." He dropped his fishing pole on the ground and stood.

"Where are you going?"

"If they is coming this way, we dun need a boat. Pappy said we can use his." He gestured along the waterway. "He parked it by a public launch site. I'll fetch it up here."

JESÚS TURNED the wheel and cut the engine, so they coasted into the inlet. He raised a hand over his eyes to shield them from the sun. "Don't see our contact."

"Relax, man." Phoenix glanced at his watch. "We're a bit early. They should be here soon."

"I know, but I don't like hanging around here in the daylight. We should have dumped the cargo overboard this morning when it was still dark."

"What about payment? Not like we have a bank account where they can send the money. It's always been an equal trade—cash for our stuff."

"You're right, Jefe. I'm just nervous. The sooner we're back in Bermuda, the better."

"We'll probably remain here a few days. The forecast indicates the tropical storm we beat might become a hurricane."

"You're always full of good news." Jesús laughed. "Let's do some cruising like we belong—at least until we spot the correct side channel to head toward the airport."

ROBBIE EASED BACK on the throttle of the Cary 50 Express and nudged it against the bank. He threw a rope to Wild. "Two metal stakes is jammed in the ground over yonder. Tie us up."

Wild caught the rope and did as Robbie asked. "Some boat. What's it called?"

"My pappy called it *The Winner* on account of that lottery money."

"Must be a lucky guy. I've never won more than ten dollars on the lottery."

"My pappy, he done played every week for years before he hit the big one. Spent twenty bucks each time."

"Some people have all the luck." Wild turned and spotted TJ returning. "Let's find out what he learned."

TJ dropped two black rifle bags on the ground and sat in his chair, shaking his head. "Didn't find anyone, but someone was watching us. Found boot prints, chewing gum wrappers, but nothing else. Sorry."

Javier nodded. "Can't be helped. At least you confirmed our suspicions. We'll be ready."

Vern adjusted the focus on his binoculars as he watched a boat approach. "There she is—turned left in the channel. Jest like before. I can make out the name—it's the one we done been waitin' fer—the *Childhood Dream*."

"Load up." Javier grabbed one of the rifle bags. "We won't follow yet—don't want to alert them. Once onboard, keep your weapons ready."

"What about Mitch's warning?" AJ raised a brow.

"Did you really think we'd sit back and do nothing?"

AJ laughed as she picked up her backpack. "That's why I love you so much—always ready to buck the system."

Everyone boarded except Vern.

He removed the rope from the stakes, gave the side of the boat a shove, and jumped aboard.

Javier handed him one of the .22s. "No shooting until I give the word." He turned to Robbie. "Let's move out—slow and easy."

The *Childhood Dream* continued along the waterway, alternating its speed as it passed side channels.

Javier stood next to Robbie, binoculars focused on their prey. "Match their speed, but don't gain on them. They seem to be looking for something."

"They done the same thing the last time we saw them."

A twenty-foot blue and white Picton Royale shot out from an inlet on the right and chased after the *Childhood Dream*.

Moments later, they heard several loud, roaring cracks from the boat ahead.

"Close the distance, Robbie." Javier turned to the others. "Someone on the boat between the *Childhood Dream* and us just opened fire. Be ready—we're heading in."

THE MAN on the Picton Royale gunned the throttle, closing on his quarry. He emptied the AK-47's magazine, spraying and praying he'd hit his target. He popped out the old one and jammed in a new one, activating the charging handle. He continued shooting. "Roland will owe me loads for this. Don't care if he's my brother."

He adjusted his speed and pulled alongside the *Childhood Dream* as she floundered. He spotted the pilot reaching for a pistol.

Rat-a-tat-tat!

The pilot's body jerked and fell to the side.

Leading with his AK-47, the attacker scanned the boat. *Where is he?* He spotted movement from his peripheral vision. *Another boat!*

The Winner stopped behind the Picton Royale.

"Drop it!" Javier aimed the M4 he had pulled from the rifle bag earlier.

The man turned toward the intruder. "Go to hell!" He raised his weapon.

Blam!

Javier aimed his M4 and fired several three-round bursts at the boat. A lucky shot pierced the man's shoulder.

"Shit! What the hell?" The man dropped the AK-47, clutched his shoulder, and moaned. He slumped to the deck.

As soon as *The Winner* nudged the other boat, Javier leaped aboard. He kept his M4 trained on his target.

The man sat against the side of the boat, a bloody hand clasped over his shoulder.

Wild, TJ, and AJ joined Javier.

"AJ, grab his weapon. If he moves a muscle, shoot him."

"Will do." AJ kept her SIG Sauer trained on the wounded man as she retrieved his weapon.

"Wild, TJ ... board the *Childhood Dream*. Check those men over— watch for anyone else on board."

TJ went to the pilot. "He's dead—took one through his head."

"This one's alive." Wild stood. "Hey, it's Phoenix! I recognize him from the photos."

"Do what you can for him. I'll call for backup." Javier pulled out his phone and thumbed through his contacts while keeping the M4 trained on the assailant. "Hey, Mitch. We have the *Childhood Dream*."

"What? I told you to hang back and wait for us."

"Shit happens. Anyway, there's one dead and two injured. One of the wounded men killed the pilot and injured Phoenix. Send paramedics."

"Will do. And listen this time—don't do anything else—at least until I arrive!"

T

he Brusch Agency
Old Town, Alexandria, Virginia
New Intel

PHIL YAWNED and popped the top of an ice-cold Mountain Dew. As he guzzled, the phone rang. He glanced at the caller ID: *Unknown.* He chuckled. *Of course—must be one of the twins.* When he accepted the call, loud rock music violated his domain. He held the instrument at arm's length to protect his hearing.

"Hey, Phil, it's MacKenzie!"

"Turn the music down, MacKenzie. Or better yet, turn it off." Phil raised his voice and shook his head. *Nothing's changed—AJ's away, and the twins will play.*

Someone killed the music. "Oh, sorry about that. Just having a bit of fun while we're hammering through our analysis."

"Understood. But, why not something enlightening, such as classical music?"

"Get real, Phil. Classical music at our age? We're still in our twenties. No thanks—we'll save that for a galaxy far, far away."

Must be watching more sci-fi. "Anything new to pass along, MacKenzie?"

"Oh, yeah. More info about Alberto. Not just from our technical analysis but from emails, too. Ready?"

Phil's hands hovered over the keyboard. "Fire away."

"He's been in touch with a guy named Ismail. Alberto's looking to flee the area and asked for Ismail's help."

"On his own or with company?"

"Himself and one other. Makayla's analysis suggests Ismail was using an IP address in Mexico. Haven't nailed it down further yet, but she's still working on it."

"Great stuff. Anything else?"

"Yeah. Ismail called someone named Farooq in Madrid—the same number Alberto called a few times. Ismail told Alberto he would meet him in Ciudad Juárez and help him skip to Cuba. There used to be an extradition treaty between Cuba and the U.S., but it's no longer valid."

Phil stopped typing. "Hmm. If Alberto reaches Cuba, we won't be able to touch him."

"Exactamundo. Can you let AJ know? I've been trying to contact her for an hour, but her phone isn't switched on."

"Sure—I'll call Javier and pass along the info. Anything you need back from AJ?"

"Yeah. I can contact the *Centro de Investigación y Seguridad Nacional* but need AJ's approval. She read me the riot act when I did it before without checking with her."

"Right. The Mexican National Intelligence Center can reach Captain Hernández. He helped Javier and the Snakes in the past."

"Hurry up, Phil. Time's a-wastin'."

"Roger."

∼

Mitch led Javier and the others into a conference room in the DEA Miami Division headquarters. A platter of donuts, another piled high with fruit, bottles of water, and carafes of coffee sat on a corner table. "Help yourselves. I want an explanation of why you disobeyed my orders to wait for my arrival."

Javier poured a cup and grabbed a jelly-filled donut before sitting next to Mitch. "I'm the one to blame."

Mitch stared at him as he bit into a Golden Delicious apple. "Oh, I know that." He gestured at the two young men. "But why take them? They're just kids."

"I didn't have a choice—it was their boat, or rather it belongs to Robbie's father. Besides, someone on a third boat opened fire on the *Childhood Dream* before directing fire toward us. We had to protect ourselves."

"Hmm." Mitched glanced at Robbie. "What's your story?"

Powdered sugar surrounded Robbie's mouth. "I made him take us —no way we was lettin' him steal our re-ward."

Mitch shook his head as he smothered a grin. "Yeah, about that reward." He gestured toward Javier and AJ. "Don't worry about them —they're working for me, so they can't receive any reward. How much do you think you deserve?"

Robbie glanced at Vern. "What ya think?"

"I dunno." Vern glanced at the ceiling. "Perhaps, a thousand each?"

Mitch laughed. "Since your efforts led to the removal of twenty bricks from the supply chain—"

"What bricks? I thought it was cocaine?" Robbie raised a brow.

"A brick equates to a kilo. The street value of what we recovered will range from two hundred forty thousand to seven hundred thousand dollars, depending upon where it hits the American market."

Robbie whistled. "Well, I'll be danged."

"If you heard about whistleblowers receiving millions in rewards, that's for the drug cartel leaders. You're more than likely to each receive about twelve thousand."

'Holy smokes! I can buy my neighbor's pickup and have some change."

"I dunno, Robbie. Didn't he want five hunnert for that beat-up thing?" Vern raised a brow.

"That's why I done said I'd have some change. I think the rest should go in an edumacation fund like you is doing."

"Robbie, Vern." Mitch grinned. "Let's see what happens after I put you in for the rewards. Who knows? You might receive more for your ... uh ... edumacation accounts."

"Dang! That'd be somethin'." Robbie nudged Vern.

"Fer sure!"

"Why don't you gentlemen head to the back of the room and through the door leading into an office. I want to discuss something with Javier and his team in private."

"Sure thing, Mister DEA." Robbie grabbed another jelly donut and disappeared through the doorway into the office.

Vern followed but scooped up two donuts, shoving one in a shirt pocket.

Mitch shook his head and turned to Javier. "The injured suspects are in a local hospital under armed guard. They'll live. Once their heads clear from the effects of their surgery, we'll interrogate them." He sighed. "Unless they have some slick lawyer on retainer, I suppose they'll request public defenders, who'll tell them to keep quiet."

I'd keep my mouth shut, too, if I were them." Javier glanced at AJ, Wild, and TJ. "Guess that wraps up our involvement in your case, right?"

"We'll need your statements for the file. Also, don't forget to submit all your expense receipts. After the bean counters examine them, you'll be reimbursed for the valid ones."

"Sounds—"

Javier's phone thumped. He turned to Mitch. "Phil's calling. Might be more about this case. Okay to take it?"

Mitch nodded.

Javier accepted the call and put it on speaker. "Hey, Phil. What's up?"

"Hi, boss. The twins have been trying to reach AJ. Alberto's going to flee the country—he's heading to Mexico. They want her permission to contact the Mexican authorities."

"I'll let her know. Thanks, Phil." Javier broke the connection.

AJ pulled her phone from a hip pocket, turned it on, and dialed. She activated the speaker. "MacKenzie, what do you need?"

"The daring duo, namely Makayla and myself, found intel showing Alberto and another guy are gonna flee the country and head to Mexico near our border. Since you almost bit my head off for contacting the Centro de Investigación y Seguridad Nacional last time, I want your permission to do so."

AJ chuckled. "Granted. And MacKenzie—thanks for the intel. Request they contact Captain Hernández since the location is in his area of responsibility."

"Will do, boss."

After terminating the call, she grinned at the others. "Sounds like a road trip."

"I don't need anything else from you right now, so I'll escort you out of the building." Mitch stood. "Keep me posted, and we'll do your interviews when you return."

When Javier and the others returned to the parking lot, he gathered them around. "Wild and TJ. Why don't you take a couple of days off and enjoy Miami? We'll organize things for ...." He glanced at AJ. "Our road trip."

TJ grinned. "Are we going to Mexico with you?"

Javier shook his head. "Not this time. When you get back to Virginia, you'll be in charge of The Brusch Agency until we return."

"Gotcha."

After TJ and Wild departed, Javier and AJ climbed into their rental. Javier glanced in the rearview mirror. "So, what do you want to do? You missed out on the firefight in Mexico last time—I assume you want to come along?"

AJ tilted her head as she stared at him. "Damn straight. But we'll need more than the two of us."

"That's for sure." Javier opened his phone and punched a number.

Someone answered, "The Brusch Agency—need a fire put out?"

Javier laughed. "Cute, ET. Connect me to Dougie."

"Right away, sir."

Moments later, Dougie came on the line. "How's Miami, Javier? Getting a suntan?"

"Been too busy to relax. Want to return to the field with me for another adventure? Got a job for you. The rest of the Snakes, too, if they can break away. Say about a week."

"Charlie and Sam are back safe and sound. Sam still has to take it easy—doctor's orders. But Charlie checked in with the others, and they're bored. No mission on the horizon for them, just training. I'm sure they'll be able to slither away. What do you have planned?"

Javier chuckled. "We're making arrangements now, but if the Snakes are up for it, we're going hunting."

"What kind of game?"

"Two-legged terrorists."

"My favorite sport."

43

D enny's Restaurant
Breezewood, Pennsylvania

AT LAST—I'M tired and hungry. Alberto rubbed his eyes as he waited for the traffic light. The light turned green, and he steered to the right, heading toward a row of restaurants, gasoline stations, inexpensive hotels and motels.

He pulled into Denny's and sighed. *I don't know how these decadent Americans can drive for hours—it's like an obsession.*

Alberto climbed out of the vehicle and entered the restaurant. Spotting Walter, he joined him in a booth.

Walter shoved a pancake-laden fork into his mouth. "Want something to eat?"

How can he eat cake smothered in syrup? Alberto shook his head. "What happened to your hands?"

"Too much bleach—turned them red and puffy." Walter shrugged. "I told you we should have hired someone to clean up after us."

"And let more people know about our business? No, we did the right thing. Did you dispose of everything as I instructed?"

Walter scooped scrambled eggs into his mouth. "Yeah. Don't worry—you're just like my mother—always nagging. I did leave a few clothes in the closet, so they'll think someone is returning. Before you ask, I washed them first and handled them afterward with gloves, so there shouldn't be any DNA."

"Good thinking. I did the same, too." Alberto's stomach rumbled, and he stopped a passing waitress. *Better eat something.* "Would you bring me two fried eggs with runny yokes, white bread toasted, and tea?"

"Yes, sir."

After the waitress departed, Alberto glanced around. *No one close enough to overhear our conversation.* "I suggest we check into one of the hotels for the night. Tomorrow, we'll dump one of the cars here and drive to Altoona Airport. It's a small one, but we can get a flight to Pittsburgh. From there, we'll take another one to Texas."

Walter nodded. "I thought you wanted to drive to Texas."

"Would take too long. I always planned to fly."

Walter dropped his fork on the empty plate. "Why didn't we fly from one of the Washington airports?"

"I wanted to make things more difficult for any authorities trying to find us. If Hamza and the others gave up our names, it would be too easy to check the local airports to see if we boarded a flight." Alberto stirred his runny eggs.

"Good point." He looked around for a waitress. "I'll pay the bill while you finish eating."

"Go to the hotel next door. Get a room with two beds. No reason to give the infidels more of our money."

Twenty minutes later, Alberto and Walter entered their room, dragging carry-on luggage with them. A musty odor assaulted their senses.

Walter waved a hand to clear the air. "Don't think this room's been used for a few days. Musty, but clean enough for one night."

"Prop the door open for a few minutes to curb the smell." Alberto strolled to the small table and opened his laptop. "I want to give Ismail an update."

To: Ismail
  From: Abdul

MAY Allah find you in good health. Maheer and I have evaded the authorities thus far. We shall head in your direction tomorrow and likely cross the border in the evening.
  Look forward to seeing you again. Inshallah.

FINISHED WITH HIS EMAIL, Alberto closed his laptop and went into the small bathroom. After a hot shower, he dressed and stepped back into the room.

Light snores came from one of the beds. Walter snorted, rolled on his side, and curled into a ball.

Alberto pulled the covers down on the other bed. He picked up the pillow and glanced at Walter. *Would be so easy to end his life as I have done so many times to others.* He shook his head. *He is still of use to Allah's cause, but one day ....* Alberto climbed into bed and drifted off.

THE NEXT MORNING, Alberto and Walter entered the hotel's foyer and joined other guests sampling the continental breakfast. They shuffled through the line, gazing at the choices available.

"Ugh! How can anyone eat this swill?" Alberto dipped the serving spoon into the congealed eggs. "This isn't fit for humans." He glanced along the counter and bypassed several people waiting to use toasters. He picked up a banana and an apple and headed to an empty table.

Moments later, Walter joined him. He opened a small box of

cereal into a plastic bowl, added milk from a Styrofoam cup, and began to eat.

"Can you imagine? Not even real tea." Alberto peeled the banana. "Civilized people drink proper tea, not those herbal ones which smell better than they taste."

Walter pushed away his bowl and burped. "At least it's free."

"It would be an insult to make people pay for this slop. No wonder so many people in this accursed country are overweight." Alberto pushed back his chair, rubbed his stomach, and stood. "Time to go."

"Just a moment." Walter rushed over to the counter, grabbed two bananas, and met Alberto at the exit. "In case we're hungry later."

They checked out of the hotel and walked to their vehicles.

"We'll take your car. Mine can stay here." Alberto grinned. "Before anyone informs the police about an abandoned vehicle, we'll be in Mexico."

Thirty minutes later, they approached the jetway for their flight, tickets in hand.

An unsmiling armed security guard approached them. "May I see your tickets and identification?"

"Is there a problem?" Alberto glanced at Walter.

The guard held up their IDs, one at a time, as he compared the photos with the men standing in front of him.

"Where's your luggage?"

Walter pointed to a small pile of suitcases. "Over there. It was too big to take into the cabin, so they're storing it in the hold."

"Uh-huh." The guard took a final look at their identification, glanced at the tickets, and handed everything back to Alberto and Walter. "Sorry to inconvenience you. Enjoy your flight." The guard turned away.

A flight attendant waved an arm at Alberto and Walter. "Please board now, gentlemen. We're ready to depart."

Without a word, they boarded their first flight. A small aircraft, it bounced and swayed in the light turbulence. After they landed in Pittsburgh, they entered the terminal from the jetway.

Alberto turned to Walter. "Find a departure board and locate the Southwest Airlines gate for El Paso." He gestured toward a row of empty seats. "I'll wait here."

Walter nodded and weaved his way through passengers heading toward their gates or proceeding to the exit. He spotted what he was looking for and headed back to Alberto. "We're in the right concourse —gate ten." He pointed to the right. "Not far away. We better hurry— the flight's boarding."

"Excellent."

～

"GOT YOU!" Makayla turned to MacKenzie. "Hey, Sis. Alberto sent another email to Ismail last night. He's heading to the border today, along with a guy named Maheer."

"Fantastic!" MacKenzie high-fived her sister.

"Let's see if they're stupid enough to use their real names for their tickets." Makayla's fingers flew over the keyboard.

"Well?"

Makayla laughed. "Patience. You're getting more like AJ every day."

"What name are you using?"

"We know Alberto also goes by Abdul Rahman, so I'm searching on that. If we find his name, then I'll look for someone named Maheer on the same flight."

"Gotcha."

MacKenzie twiddled her fingers as she stared at her computer. "C'mon, c'mon."

At last, two manifests popped up on the screen as she glanced at the clock. "Yes! Abdul Rahman flew from Altoona to Pittsburgh. He's booked on a flight to El Paso."

"What about Maheer?"

"Let me check." Moments later, MacKenzie received her confirmation. "There's only one Maheer on both flights. Maheer Qabil."

"Fantastic! Better pass the information to AJ."

THE SOUTHWEST AIRLINES flight landed on time. After collecting their luggage, Alberto and Walter wormed their way to the door. As soon as it opened, they rushed up the jetway and headed toward ground transportation. Outside, they boarded an Enterprise courtesy bus.

After they found their rental car, Walter drove to Paso del Norte, where he joined a line of vehicles waiting to pass into Mexico.

They inched forward until a government official stopped them.

He glanced at the car and held out his hand. "Passports."

Walter handed over their documents. Despite the air conditioning, he wiped a sweaty palm on the bottom of his shirt. *I'll be glad to leave this accursed country.*

"Is there a problem?"

"It's a rental." Walter slapped the dash. "The AC worked fine when I picked it up, but it's not doing so good right now."

"Sitting still with the window down talking to me won't help either." The official examined their passports, paying close attention to the photographs. "How long will you be in Mexico?"

Alberto leaned over. "About a week, sir. We're going to a friend's wedding."

The man nodded and returned the passports. "Enjoy yourselves." He waved them on.

WHEN ALBERTO and Walter were out of sight, the customs and border protection official picked up a phone. "I let them enter Mexico as instructed. I sure hope the guys requesting this know what they're doing."

"Don't worry—they do."

AFTER ENTERING CIUDAD JUÁREZ, Walter weaved through the streets following Alberto's directions. "I thought they would detain us. How could you remain so calm?"

"It was Allah's will we should be allowed to cross. Nothing we could do if they refused to let us through, so no point worrying." *I'll feel safer when we're on the plane to Cuba.*

"I guess." Walter stopped near a seedy cantina. He glanced at the once white pockmarked walls and the rusty sign above the door—La Bandito. "Are you sure this is the place?"

"Yes. I first met Ismail here many years ago." Alberto pulled his phone from a shirt pocket and dialed.

"Alo."

"Alo. I'm parked outside the place where we first met. One person with me."

"Wait there. Someone will join you."

Moments later, a short, overweight man with a large mustache approached the vehicle. "Abdul?"

Alberto nodded.

"I'm to take you to Ismail. He couldn't make it."

"Get in."

The man climbed into the rear of the rental car and gave directions.

After a short ride, they pulled into a walled hacienda and stopped.

"Ismail is waiting for you inside. Give me your keys, and I'll hide your vehicle."

The house door opened as Alberto and Walter approached.

A wiry man bent with age and wearing a black eye patch greeted them. "Welcome to my home." He gripped each of their hands in turn. "Please, come inside. There is much to discuss and not much time."

Ismail led them into the dining room and gestured. "Take a seat. You'll be thirsty and hungry after your long journey. Someone will bring refreshments soon. In the meantime, we must—"

Bam! Bam!

Loud thumps came from the front of the house as the door splintered, hanging on one hinge.

Everyone jumped to their feet.

Alberto and Walter's contact rushed inside. "Ismail! Quick. We've been betrayed!"

44

W arehouse Near
Ismail's Hacienda
Ciudad Juárez, Mexico

JAVIER, AJ, and the Snakes jumped out of their black Denali SUVs inside a warehouse commandeered by Lieutenant Benito de Santa Anna. Used to store a variety of grains, including corn, wheat, sorghum, and rice, the building stood empty, waiting for the next harvesting season.

Javier approached de Santa Anna. "Good to see you again, Lieutenant."

"Likewise, Colonel." They shook hands.

"Please, call me Javier—I'm retired."

"Yes, sir—I mean Javier. I'm honored Captain Hernández chose me to work with you again. He sends his greetings."

"Thanks." He gestured toward AJ. "Have you met my partner? This is AJ Bruce—she works for the CIA."

"I have not had the pleasure." de Santa Anna extended a hand to her. "Welcome to Mexico, señora."

"Thank you. I wish it was under better circumstances."

He shrugged. "If we remove more terrorists, it will be worth it." De Santa Anna turned to Javier. "We launched a drone earlier." He led them to a nearby table. He pointed to the photos of the hacienda and the surrounding grounds located near the outskirts of the city. "This is our objective, according to an informant."

Javier studied the two-story building, surrounded by high concrete walls. A curved driveway, protected by black, wrought-iron gates, seemed to be the only entrance. Two armed guards stood inside the gates. "Good thing you spotted your guy at the cantina, or we'd be waiting for confirmation from Washington regarding Abdul and Maheer's location."

"Sí. He's helped us for years. We allow him some petty smuggling, and in return, he provides occasional intel about drug and human smugglers. When he found out about Ismail, he offered the information free of charge."

"Did he say why?"

"He might be a criminal, but he's a proud Mexican and detests what foreigners are doing to our country."

Javier nodded. "Because of his input, we should capture Abdul and Maheer." *I hope.*

"One of my teams is approaching the hacienda now to probe their defenses."

He should have waited. "Let's hope they catch them unawares."

BLAM! Rat-a-tat-tat! Bam! Rat-a-tat-tat! Bam!

"Fall back!" Lieutenant Benito de Santa Anna whispered into the comms unit to his soldiers encroaching on Ismail's property. He turned to Javier. "I am so sorry, Coronel. My men are young and inexperienced. The thought of capturing an international terrorist made them forget their training."

"Can't be helped." Javier shrugged.

Javier nodded as he gazed at the property through his night-vision goggles. "They're alert now. We'll wait a few hours and hit them while it's still dark. Keep a loose perimeter check on the property and have the rest of your men stand down." He turned to the man next to him. "Whaddya think, Adder?"

"Agreed. I'll pass the word to the rest of the Snakes." Adder disappeared into the night.

AJ placed a hand on Javier's arm. "What about me, Cobra?"

"Hang tight, Taipan. In a little while, you and I are going to be a lovesick couple stumbling past the hacienda. We'll check for any observation posts."

AJ smiled. "Sounds like fun. Can I improvise?"

"Of course." Javier wrapped an arm around AJ. "Improvision is part of the art of warfare. You've heard the expression by van Moltke, 'No plan survives first contact with the enemy.'" He glanced again at the hacienda before leading AJ away.

Ismail stared at the mustachioed man before pointing toward the kitchen. "Go out the side door and keep an eye on the men you spotted. I must know if they are a threat or if this is a coincidence."

"Do you believe in coincidences, Ismail?" Abdul glanced at Maheer.

Ismail turned to a sideboard, opened the top drawer, and extracted three loaded AK-47s and half a dozen magazines. "No, I don't. But there are many times innocent people have wandered past. My men are armed and always ready in case someone intends to attack." He handed a weapon and two magazines each to Abdul and Maheer.

Abdul released the magazine, checked over the weapon, and reseated the ammunition.

Maheer mimicked Abdul's actions, slinging his AK-47 over his shoulder when he was finished. "Where do you want us?"

"You and Abdul remain here." Ismail disappeared, returning

moments later with a heavy duffle bag. He reached inside, grabbed several items, and handed them to his guests. "Grenades."

JAVIER AND AJ meandered along the street. They enjoyed the evening calm as they occasionally paused for a quick kiss. When they approached Ismail's hacienda, they stopped in front of the gates. Javier wrapped his arms around her. He whispered, "Look over my shoulder."

She did before snuggling her head into his neck. "Elevated platform in the corner under the trees. Two guards—assume both are armed. One is careless—he's smoking a cigarette. Although he's cupped it in one hand, I spotted the glow. Might be enough to destroy their night vision." She laughed. "Twirl me as if we're dancing. I'll check the other corner."

Javier spun her in a circle, stopping so she had a clear line of sight over his shoulder.

She cradled his head and kissed him. "Another platform. No one smoking."

"Okay, we'll assume there are platforms at the rear of the property. We better continue our charade and head along the street. Don't want anyone approaching us."

They crossed at the end of the street and continued to their staging area.

Javier motioned toward the others. "Gather round."

He studied each person's face. "We're evenly matched. With Ismail, two dozen guards, Abdul and Maheer, they have a few more men and a defensive position, but we have something even better—years of precision training and combat experience." He turned to de Santa Anna. "Did you receive any rules of engagement from Captain Hernández?"

He nodded. "Just one—follow your lead."

Javier clenched his jaw as the cords in his neck became rigid. "Anyone in the compound holding a weapon is fair game. I'm not interested in justice—revenge will work just fine as these guys want to kill us. If they don't surrender, take them out."

He pointed to photos from the drone. "Lieutenant, split your men into three teams. You'll approach from the left, the right, and cover the rear. Snakes, two groups—take out the OPs at the corners."

"What about the front, Cobra?" Adder pursed his lips as he studied the photos.

Javier nudged AJ. "Why, Taipan and I are going to waltz through the front gate as if we own the place." He uncovered his watch and checked the time. "It's 0300. Let's do this."

JAVIER ADJUSTED HIS THROAT MIC. He whispered, "Everyone in position?"

A series of clicks from each of the teams confirmed they were ready.

"Lieutenant, please start the show."

Pfft! Pfft! Pfft! Pfft!

The muffled sounds of the silenced weapons were almost imperceptible in the early morning breeze.

"Rear positions cleared, Coronel. Moving forward to our next objective."

Javier clicked once to confirm de Santa Anna's report. He whispered again into his mic. "You're up, Snakes."

Pfft! Pfft! Pfft! Pfft!

"Cobra this is Adder. Coast clear. Entering compound."

After acknowledging Adder's report, Javier turned to AJ as he positioned his M4 over a shoulder. "Ready for a repeat performance?"

She examined her SIG Sauer before tucking it into a convenient spot in her belt. "Ready."

Javier and AJ sauntered along the street, stopping for another kiss in front of the hacienda's gates.

"Clear." AJ squeezed Javier's arm.

He walked up to the gates and attached a small block of C4 before returning to AJ's side. They scurried away, stopping in a sheltered location.

Javier whispered into his mic, "Fire in the hole." He flipped a cover on the detonator and keyed a switch.

Ka-Blam!

The gates hung from their hinges.

Windows shattered as gunshots erupted from inside the hacienda.

Javier shouted, "Fire at will!" He knelt and fired three-round bursts into the house.

A short, overweight man with a large mustache ran around the side of the house, arms in the air. "Don't shoot! I'm not armed!" Chest heaving, he flopped to the ground.

"Taipan, get him—that's de Santa Anna's snitch."

"Roger." AJ fired several shots at the hacienda as she crabbed toward the man.

A man holding an AK-47 jumped out from behind tall shrubs. He aimed at AJ as she approached the building.

"AJ, duck!"

Javier fired a three-round burst at the man, hitting him in the head and upper chest.

The man flew backward, hitting the ground with a thud. His head moved once, and he remained still.

"Hurry, AJ! Grab de Santa Anna's snitch and run!"

She sped through helped him to his feet, and they dashed toward safety.

Bam! Craack!

Lieutenant de Santa Anna's men used a battering ram to force open the rear door of the hacienda. His shouts burst through the radio. "*Degüello!* Take them down—no mercy!"

Screams filled the air as the soldiers dispatched four men in the kitchen.

Shots continued to ring out as the Snakes forced the front door. Adder and Rattler went high and low to the left, followed by Viper and Mamba to the right.

The four men laid down withering fire, their rounds shattering the bodies of those opposing them.

Gunfire tapered off. The silence became overwhelming as the stench of weapons fire and blood filled the air.

"Coming in!" Javier dashed up the steps into the property.

The walls and interior furnishings had been reduced to kindling by the assault. Bullet-ridden bodies dotted the floor.

Adder knelt next to Rattler and Mamba while Viper remained alert, his M4 trained away from his friends.

"Everyone okay?" Cobra scanned the room before glancing at a doorway. He tensed, aiming his M4, before relaxing when he recognized Lieutenant de Santa Ana. "Your men okay, Lieutenant?"

"Sí." He jerked a thumb over his shoulder. "A few flesh wounds, but nothing serious, and we eliminated the opposition."

"Excellent." Cobra turned to Adder, who was applying bandages to the arms of Rattler and Mamba. "How are they?"

"Through and through, but missed anything vital." Adder grinned. "Of course, they'll make their injuries out to be something more back at the unit."

"Just like fishermen who talk about the one that got away. When you finish wrapping them up, get some photos of the dead and meet us back at the staging area. Don't forget to take their fingerprints, too."

"What about DNA samples?" Adder held up his Ka-Bar knife. "They won't miss a finger or two."

Cobra nodded. "Do what you think is necessary." He glanced around. "Where's AJ?"

Adder gestured outside. "Last I saw, she was dragging someone to safety. I'm sure she's okay."

"I hope so."

～

An hour later, they reassembled at the warehouse. Everyone grabbed bottles of water and power bars as they relaxed.

"Great job, everyone." Javier gave a thumbs up. "Appears no one got away. We were lucky—a few flesh wounds, but nothing life-threatening. The photos and fingerprints will be forwarded to Washington so they can be run through the databases. Same with the DNA samples. Hopefully, we'll get confirmation of who we eliminated."

Echoes of "hear, hear" filled the warehouse.

"Snakes, go ahead and head back to CONUS. We'll meet in a couple of days at The Brusch Agency for a wrap-up." He turned to de Santa Anna. "Many thanks to you and your men—couldn't have done this without your help. Please thank Captain Hernández." He held out a hand.

Lieutenant de Santa Anna grinned as he grasped Javier's hand. "Always a pleasure working with you to cleanse Mexico of scum. Please call upon me—anytime."

Javier nodded. "Will do. Adios." He turned to AJ and extended an arm. "Well, my fair lady, shall we head home?"

She glanced at Javier's dirty appearance as she linked arms. "A grand idea, my not-so-clean but still handsome gentleman."

T he Brusch Agency
Old Town, Alexandria, Virginia

JAVIER WHISTLED as he walked into the packed conference room two days after returning to the United States. He sipped fresh coffee from a red, white, and blue Brusch Agency mug as he surveyed the team members and a guest occupying eleven of the twelve brown leather chairs surrounding the rectangular oak table. An additional row of seats lined each wall.

"Attention!" Dougie jumped to his feet, followed by the other Snakes.

"Sit down, guys—you're a laugh a minute." Javier took his own seat at the head of the table, with AJ on his right. He raised a hand to quiet the group. "First things first." He glanced at Sam, still wearing a red sling. "Glad you're back on your feet."

Sam smiled. "Many thanks, boss."

Javier scanned the room and grinned. "We've done it—made The

Brusch Agency a reality. Couldn't have achieved this without each and every one of you."

"Does that mean we're getting bonuses?" Dougie stared at the ceiling and whistled.

"What do you want a bonus for?" Javier chortled. "I heard you just sat in my chair drinking coffee and eating donuts."

Dougie glanced around the table. "Alright. Who told?"

Everyone burst into laughter.

Javier waved his hands for quiet. "Just as soon as more money comes in, bonuses will be paid. In the meantime, you'll have to do with the beer, champagne, and snacks which will follow this meeting."

Dougie shrugged, a grin creeping across his face. "Worth a shot."

"Keep trying—one day, you might be lucky. Of course, it might be easier to win the lottery. But you know the saying, 'You can't win if you don't play.'" Javier turned to his left. "Mitch, you wanna go first?"

"Sure. First of all, great job, everyone. Although this is just one piece of the never-ending battle against the influx of illegal drugs into the country, any effort to thwart the smugglers' efforts is worthwhile."

Mitch pulled an envelope from an inside pocket of his sports coat. "This contains a paid invoice to The Brusch Agency for services rendered—plus your expenses. The money should be in your account later today. The amount is far less than what the team deserves, but then—I work for the government, and we never pay top dollar." He handed the envelope to Javier. "Hopefully, this will be the first of many."

Javier took the offering and placed it on the table. "Greatly appreciate you and the DEA taking a chance on us. Any update?"

"Yes. I spoke with Cedric last night. He confirmed the guy you dispatched as Blake Russell. He's the younger brother of a Londoner named Roland Russell, AKA Daddy, a player in the Bermuda drug scene. Cedric said they've lost track of him. Interpol issued an alert, so we'll wait to see if this helps locate Roland."

Javier nodded. "Good to know."

"Also, Phoenix Vanidestine, AKA Maverick, is singing away. Turns out he's wanted for questioning by the Met Police in London for the murder of a young woman. He's spilling everything he knows about Roland in the hopes of avoiding extradition." Mitch shook his head. "Won't make a difference. The only thing to be decided is whether he's shipped to Bermuda or London."

"What about Maverick's girlfriend?"

"Zaine Greenly? She's disappeared, too." Mitch pulled back the sleeve of his coat and glanced at his watch. "That's all I have right now. I gotta run—a meeting with the bean counters."

"Enjoy—better you than me." Javier stood and shook Mitch's hand. "Keep us in mind for any future projects."

"No worries—you'll be the first to find out." Mitch worked his way toward the exit. He stopped, hand on the door, and turned back to the others. "By the way, Robbie and Vern fooled all of you. They're both DEA agents with degrees from Wake Forest, and their English is better than mine. What you witnessed was their undercover roles, which can sometimes be overdone to the point of being insulting. However, you'd be amazed at the number of drug smugglers taken in by their act."

"Wait—what about their father winning the lottery and buying a house on the water and the boat?" TJ glanced around the room.

"All true, except their father is a retired DEA agent with a PhD in criminology."

Laughter erupted as Mitch departed.

"Guess more training is needed for all of us, so we don't let guys like Robbie and Vern get the better of us in the future." Javier returned to his seat. "Remind me never to play poker with Mitch and those guys." He chuckled. "I also want to stress my thanks and support for those involved with terminating Alberto Cabrera's efforts to eradicate us." He gestured toward Makayla, MacKenzie, and Phil seated against the wall behind AJ. "Thanks to their painstaking analysis, they confirmed he was also known as Abdul Rahman, an Argentinian member of Islamic State."

AJ turned to the twins and Phil. She smiled. "Well done, gang."

The three nodded.

A slight grin creased Makayla and MacKenzie's faces.

"For those who might be unaware, Alberto escaped from the warehouse we attacked with the Mexican Army last year outside Monclova. No one knew where he was. If he'd not attempted to exact vengeance on us for killing a friend of his named Michael, he'd probably still be causing mayhem."

"What about the other two guys who were with him in Ciudad Juárez?"

Javier tilted his head. "Ismail has been wanted for years for organizing Islamic State's attacks against soft targets in Europe. Maheer Qabil was one of their bomb makers. With the demise of these terrorists, hopefully, we've put a dent in future attacks—at least for now."

A round of applause filled the room.

"Unfortunately, there's some very sad news as well. According to Captain Brian Zorkin, a friend of mine with the Virginia State Police, when law enforcement units raided houses being used by Alberto and Maheer, everything didn't go as planned. As they breached Maheer's home, explosions ripped apart the building, killing four police officers and wounding nine others. The doors were booby-trapped with C4." He turned to Cesar. "Two of the injured were your FBI friends, Ivan and Robert."

"Yes. I saw them at the hospital yesterday. Their injuries aren't life-threatening, but they'll remain in the hospital for a few more days."

Javier closed his eyes. "Please join me for a moment of silence to honor the fallen."

The announcement sucked the air from the room. Everyone bowed their heads.

Javier glanced up and raised a hand. "I think that about covers everything."

AJ shook her head. "Not quite. Yesterday, I was grilled and reprimanded for participating in an unsanctioned operation. My boss wasn't too pleased."

Dougie pursed his lips. "Did you explain the situation to him? Besides, weren't you on your own time?"

"Yes, to both questions. However, you know he's a straitlaced guy who does everything by the rules and can't think outside the box. He said if I stepped out of line again, I'd be demoted."

Javier smirked, a chuckle escaping. "How did that work out for him?"

AJ grinned. "I told him to drop dead but in more colorful words. I unclipped my badge and threw it at him, cleared out my desk, and walked out of the building. Hope I can still find a job here."

"Of course. There are a few spots open. Dishwasher? Cleaner? Receptionist?" Javier gave her a playful wink.

Laughter and whistles filled the room.

"Seriously, I'm sorry you gave up your CIA job, but I understand. You haven't enjoyed being stuck behind a desk. You gave it almost a year—about twice as long as I thought you'd last." Javier reached over and squeezed her hand. "Welcome to The Brusch Agency."

"Yeah, well, I think some changes might be in order."

"Such as?"

"I'm going to reorganize your office. Can't see all that real estate going to waste. So, I'm moving in."

Javier grinned. "As you wish. Any—"

He picked up the ringing phone. "The Brusch Agency." He listened to the caller. "I see. We're in a meeting now, but I'll pass along the message. 'Bye." He hung up. "Hey, ET. Phone home."

A chant broke out. "ET, phone home. ET, phone home."

Javier raised his voice over the cacophony. "I couldn't resist." He struggled to maintain proper decorum as he gestured to calm the room. "Any other business to discuss?"

"Yes." Charlie glanced around the table. "I put in my transfer request to the reserves."

Javier smiled.

"We did, too," the Walker brothers chimed.

"Excellent. Once you're available, you'll become our quick reaction force, along with Dougie, who will be the team leader. Anything else?"

Everyone shook their head.

"Well, there's one last item to cover before we pop the corks." Javier stood and knelt beside AJ. "I know this is corny, but it's only gonna happen once in my lifetime." He reached into his pocket and retrieved a small black box. "It's not much, but it was my great-grandmother's ring. Since I'm the last of the line, it's yours if you'll have me." He handed it to her. "I can't picture anyone else I'd rather share my life with."

AJ took the box and opened it. She gasped before using a pinkie finger to remove the contents. She held it up to catch the light.

The ring sparkled. A large emerald took center stage on a platinum band. Nestled around the emerald was a cluster of diamonds and smaller emeralds.

"On your feet and face the music, future husband. That's a yes, in the event you didn't get it." AJ's eyes glistened as Javier removed it from her pinkie and slid it on her ringer finger. "Yes, you big softie. I was beginning to wonder if I'd have to ask you."

The team broke into cheers and applause.

Dougie walked forward, grasping Javier and AJ by their shoulders. "About time!"

Cheers and whistles echoed throughout the room as everyone stood and applauded.

Rosemont Manor
    Shenandoah Valley, Berryville, Virginia

JAVIER PUSHED ASIDE the plate with the remains of his early morning breakfast. He opened the local newspaper, sipping an orange juice as he scanned the headlines.

"You're up early. Dollar for your thoughts?"

He lowered the paper and studied AJ's face. "A dollar? I thought it was, 'A penny for your thoughts.'"

She shrugged. "Used to be, until inflation kicked in." AJ sat across from him. "Getting cold feet?"

"No way!" He grinned. "Why, are you?"

"Hell no!" She intertwined her fingers in his. "What a fantastic place you picked. How'd you manage it?"

"I can't take all the credit—in fact, none. I had Sindee scouring the area for weeks looking for a suitable place in case you said yes. Of course, I assumed I'd eventually find the courage to ask you. It was tougher than going on covert missions."

"Well, you and Sindee couldn't have picked a better location." She glanced at her engagement ring as the inner corners of her eyebrows angled upward. "Too bad neither of us have any family to invite."

"No control over that, but at least some of our closest friends will be here."

"How did you convince Phil to give me away? You know how he avoids any limelight."

Javier laughed. "Easy. When he hemmed and hawed about doing it, I threatened to turn him over to the authorities for computer hacking—took him about two seconds to agree."

"Remind me never to let you back me into a corner." She chuckled. "Not sure what the outcome would be."

"Want to go for a stroll through the grounds and check everything is as planned?"

"Sure. There's still time before we need to get ready."

They stood and walked arm-in-arm through the manor house and toward the expansive park-like setting.

As Javier stepped through the doors, he bumped someone's shoulder. "Sorry. Didn't see you."

A man glared at him as he massaged his shoulder. "Oaf." He twisted his gold pinkie ring. "Watch where you're going." He brushed past and entered the building.

"Don't worry about him, Javier." AJ smiled as she tugged his arm. "Let's go."

They stepped outside, pausing between gray colonnades to view the grounds. A vast planted section contained trees from around the world, including Hinoki cypress, katsura, khanzan cherry, European hornbeam, and Lebanon cedar, along with beeches, maples, and oaks. A red brick path lined with white folding chairs led to an arched pergola adorned with red, yellow, and white roses.

"Whaddya think?"

A radiant smile etched across AJ's face. "Perfect—as long as I don't trip on the stairs."

Javier laughed. "I'm sure Phil will provide a guiding hand."

AJ, dressed in an off-the-shoulder white crepe taffeta bow gown, clasped Phil's arm. She glanced at the twins, who wore the same style of dress, but in light green. "I think this is the first time I've seen you two in something other than jeans."

"Better take a picture—won't happen again any time soon," the twins chimed.

Phil tapped AJ's arm. "Ready to get to the altar?"

AJ took a deep breath. "As soon as the music starts. But you're leading the way, Makayla."

Piano music, playing Wagner's "Wedding March" filtered through an array of hidden speakers.

"Time to go." Phil gestured toward the pergola. "Javier's waiting."

Makayla took each of the five steps in a graceful manner, timed to the music, with MacKenzie following.

"Ready, boss?"

"As ready as I'll ever be, Phil. Thank you for doing this."

"Are you kidding? I'll be the first one to kiss you."

They both chuckled as they followed the twins.

The guests stood as AJ and Phil approached.

As promised, Phil gave AJ a peck on the cheek before turning her over to Javier, who was dressed in a black tuxedo. "Good luck, you two."

Arm-in-arm, Javier and AJ turned to the minister, with the twins serving as maids of honor and Brian acting as the best man.

"We are gathered here in the presence of friends and colleagues to share your special …."

AFTER THE MINISTER told Javier he could kiss his bride, he grabbed AJ in his arms to the accompaniment of cheers, clapping, and whistling. They turned toward their guests and grinned.

Two of the Snakes stood on either side of the walkway, dressed in their U.S. Army dress uniforms, complete with swords.

"Present .... Arms!" Four swords flashed in the sunlight at Dougie's command.

Javier and AJ laughed as they stepped under the crossed swords. They stopped as their guests rushed forward and surrounded them.

"Plenty of time, folks." Javier hugged AJ and pointed toward a covered area. "Food and drink are available. Don't know about you, but I'm hungry." He guided AJ toward the wedding table, where the manor staff waited to seat them.

After they had a quick bite, Javier escorted AJ to the first table.

Her face beamed. "Thank you for coming today and making it such a memorable occasion. An excellent venue, Sindee."

"I'm so glad you like it. I was really nervous when Javier asked me to find a place."

"With your attention to detail, it's no wonder he selected you as his logistics expert." AJ smiled as Javier led her to the next table.

They continued working their way among the eight round tables before turning toward the manor house.

"Hey, where are you guys going? It's still early, and the party's just getting started." Dougie held a glass in the air and grinned. "Hurry back."

JAVIER AND AJ returned to the Roosevelt Suite, where the wedding party had prepared for the ceremony. They changed into casual clothes.

"It's been a fantastic day." AJ turned to Javier. "So, where are we going on our honeymoon?" She smiled. "You've kept this well-hidden."

"We'll spend tonight in the Byrd's Nest Honeymoon Cottage. Tomorrow we'll fly to Europe. You mentioned before you'd like to spend more time there. We'll be going on a couple of river cruises. Just you, me—some wine and—"

AJ leaned forward and smothered him with a kiss. "I might just keep you around."

HIGH ABOVE THE wedding celebration and hidden within the thick trees, a man gazed through the scope of a rifle. He adjusted the sight, focusing on Javier. "Soon. Very soon, you will be mine."

He backed away and secured the weapon in a rifle bag. Taking a final look, he twisted his pinkie ring before curling his right hand. With his index finger, he motioned for his target to come toward him.

"Come to Daddy."

~ The End ~

THANK YOU!

Dear Reader,

Thank you! I hope you've enjoyed reading this story as much as I did in creating it. If you did, I'd greatly appreciate it if you could take a minute or two to write a brief review on Amazon. It doesn't need to be long, but your feedback helps other readers and me.

Reviews are so important to all authors. For me, I don't have the benefit of being supported by one of the major New York publishers, nor can I afford to take out ads in the newspapers and on television. Your review helps to get the word out, not just on Amazon, but also through various social media outlets as I use these to create posts on Facebook, Twitter, and LinkedIn. Many thanks for your support!
Randall

ALSO BY RANDALL KRZAK

If you enjoyed *Colombian Betrayal*, you might also enjoy reading my award-winning novels:

The Kurdish Connection

A semi-finalist in the 2018 Chanticleer International Book Awards (CIBAs) in the global thrillers category.

In their daily struggle for survival, Iraqi Kurdish scavengers uncover a cache of chemical weapons. They offer the weapons to fellow Kurdish rebels in Turkey and Syria to assist in their quest to free an imprisoned leader and create a unified homeland. After receiving a tip from an unlikely source, the newly formed Special Operations Bedlam team is called to arms!

Travel with Craig Cameron and his international team on their covert operation as they weave their way through war-torn regions seeking to locate and recover the weapons before they can be used to cause irreparable harm and instigate a world crisis.

The odds are stacked against them. Can they manage to keep their operation hidden and prevent further clashes before it's too late?

Universal link - books2read.com/u/bovxOZ

Chanticleer Editorial Review - https://bit.ly/3zInlLm

DANGEROUS ALLIANCE

One of seven First in Category Winners in the 2018 CIBAs, global thrillers category.

United Nations' sanctions are crippling North Korea. China has turned her back on her malevolent partner. The North Korean military machine is crumbling, unable to function. Oil reserves are minimal, and the government seeks new alliances.

Cargo and tourist ships are disappearing along the Somali and Kenyan coastline at an alarming rate. Speeches abound, but inaction emboldens Al-Shabaab to seek their next prize: Kenya. The terror organization controls land but requires weapons.

Bedlam Bravo team leader Colonel (Ret.) Trevor Franklin leads the small international team into East Africa. Tempers flare as the team is embroiled in a political quagmire. The axis must be stopped to avert an international crisis but at what cost?

Universal link - books2read.com/u/bzoxRj

Chanticleer Editorial Review - https://bit.ly/3AvQBpR

CARNAGE IN SINGAPORE

One of seven First in Category Winners in the 2019 CIBAs, global thrillers category.

Terrorist groups such as Abu Sayyaf and Jemaah Islamiyah have flourished in recent years with new recruits joining them and ISIS-affiliates at an alarming rate. Blended operations by various Asian countries have forced the groups to work together to identify a new operational base.

They seek an island nation to call home, one where they can plot against countries who oppose their ideals. They found a target, a small nation-state, perfect for their needs: The Republic of Singapore.

Before anyone can respond, the ambassadors of the United States, Great Britain, and Australia are kidnapped from their residences in Singapore. Right index fingers of each victim are sent as a warning. Any attempt to recover the ambassadors will result in the removal of additional body parts.

Bedlam Charlie team leader, Evelyn Evinrude, leads the group to rescue the ambassadors and capture the local leaders of Abu Sayyaf and Jemaah Islamiyah. Can Bedlam succeed or will events escalate, resulting in more deaths?

Universal link - books2read.com/u/3LD2vw

Chanticleer Editorial Review - https://bit.ly/3tZtJwB

COLOMBIAN BETRAYAL

One of seven First in Category Winners in the 2020 CIBAs, global thrillers category.

Colombian drug lord watched her profits diminish over the years. Unable to increase market share because of a shrinking consumer base and a new international competitor, she formed an unholy alliance.

Olivia Moreno, head of the Barranquilla Cartel, struck a deal with a regional leader within the Revolutionary Armed Forces of Colombia. Little did she know but she initiated her own death warrant. FARC had an unknown support group who wanted a foothold in South America – Islamic State.

Forced to flee, Moreno is captured by a small CIA team. Fearing for her life, she spins a tale about using her money and manpower to destroy ISIS. Laws and rules of engagement mean nothing to her, only her life and family matter.

Will team leader AJ Bruce strike a deal to turn the tables on ISIS and stop them from launching a concentrated attack on the United States? Or will they be too late? If successful, will Moreno's reward be total control of Afghanistan's poppy fields, or will she be doubled-crossed?

Universal link - books2read.com/u/4Azojo

MISSION: ANGOLA

A finalist in the 2021 Page Turner Book Awards (as of September 2021)

Joao and Caterina Regaleria's twentieth wedding anniversary celebration was fast approaching when a contact from the past reaches out for his assistance.

Colonel Theodore Mwelewe, a former enemy commander during the Angolan war and now an important politician, requests Joao's help. The colonel's adult son, Peter, was kidnapped while working as a doctor for the Christian Aid Mission in the Democratic Republic of Congo.

Reluctant to get involved, Joao contacts Xavier Sear, a former CIA operative. They became friends when Joao served as a member of the United Nations Peace-Keeping Forces in Angola and Sear was an observer.

After Caterina's persuasive intervention, Joao and Sear head to the DRC to rescue Peter. Treachery abounds at each step of the way. Will they be successful, or will the situation deteriorate even further?

Universal link - books2read.com/u/3LRV71

Dangerous Alliance, Carnage in Singapore, Colombian Betrayal, and Mission: Angola are also available for free if you're a member of Kindle Unlimited.

"BLACK OPS IN FICTION"

Randall's first non-fiction article, "Black Ops in Fiction," was featured in the March 2021 edition of the web daily, *Mystery and Suspense.*

https://bit.ly/3tZX3Ty

ABOUT THE AUTHOR

Randall Krzak is a U.S. Army veteran and retired senior civil servant, spending thirty years in Europe, Africa, Central America, and the Middle East. His residency abroad qualifies him to build rich worlds in his action-adventure novels and short stories. Familiar with customs, laws, and social norms, he promotes these to create authentic characters and scenery.

His first novel, *The Kurdish Connection*, was released by Moonshine Cove Publishing in 2017. It competed in the 2018 Chanticleer International Book Awards (CIBAs) in their Global Thrillers category and finished as a semi-finalist.

His second and third novels, *Dangerous Alliance* and *Carnage in Singapore*, were released in 2018 and 2019 by Solstice Publishing. They all competed in the 2018 and 2019 CIBAs, with both being selected as First in Category winners.

In 2020, Randall self-published his fourth novel, *Colombian Betrayal*, the first in a six-to-ten volume series. It was a First in Category CIBAs winner in 2020.

His fifth novel, *Mission: Angola (Xavier Sear Thriller Book 1)* was released by Solstice Publishing in January 2021. As of September 2021, it was a finalist in the 2021 Page Turner Book Awards.

He also authored a non-fiction article featured on the web daily, *Mystery & Suspense Magazine*, entitled, "Black Ops in Fiction", which was released in March 2021. Randall's currently working on *Ultimate*, the fourth in his Bedlam series.

He holds a Bachelor of Science degree from the University of Maryland and a general Master in Business Administration (MBA) and a MBA with an emphasis in Strategic Focus, both from Heriot-Watt University, Edinburgh, Scotland. He currently resides with his wife, Sylvia, and four cats in Dunfermline, Scotland. He's originally from Michigan, while Sylvia is a proud Scot. In addition to writing, he enjoys hiking, reading, candle making, pyrography, and sightseeing.

Keep in touch with Randall on Facebook, Twitter, LinkedIn, or his website: http://www.randallkrzak